T0197294

THE CORRUPTION OF BLOOD

Drastic moments, Dark memories collide, as one mans' journey

Jermayne J. Davis

Order this book online at www.trafford.com
or email orders@trafford.com

Most Trafford titles are also available at major online book retailers.

Printed in the United States of America.

ISBN: 978-1-4669-3404-7 (sc)
ISBN: 978-1-4669-3403-0 (e)

Trafford rev. 07/13/2012

 www.trafford.com

North America & international
toll-free: 1 888 232 4444 (USA & Canada)
phone: 250 383 6864 ♦ fax: 812 355 4082

FAMILIA

Paul   Larry
        James

THE WILLIAMS BROTHERS
THE DAVIS FAMILY

Billy Green

Little Harvey Bell &

Raheem Muhammid

Staring in

The Corruption of Blood

ACKNOWLEDGEMENTS

"I dedicate this book"

To: My son *Jermayne Yakeem Davis*

To: My beloved cousins *"Dawn & Tamika Hicks"*
Two beautiful women who has passed on to a better place. Rest in peace. I will always love and miss you two.

To: My Mother and Father *"Connie and John Davis"* for their love, understanding and support herein the story.

To: *My Brothers,* For being the men that they are

To: *Walter Royster* for inspiring me to write.

To: *Robin Walker* for believing in my dreams

To: *Terrel Carter* for his Friendship

Title: **"THE CORRUPTION OF BLOOD"**

Special dedications: To everyone who has experienced wise crime and clever double cross.

. . . PLEASE ENJOY . . .

WRITTEN BY: *Jermayne J. Davis*

CONTENTS

INTRODUCTION

This is the story of my life. Due to confidentiality some minor adjustments of the actual characters names' has been changed. Some events herein this story has been altered and some use of language is used as jargon, or considered to be harsh, vulgar and/or profound.

From my own up close and personal experiences' in life, this book contains truth and would help you to understand some forms of corruption. In many ways we have all faced the evil aspects of some kind of clever double-cross, or corruption. It's indeed without a saying that they come in all shapes, forms and sizes. Many may come as your closest friend's, lovers, or even as a family member.

Living most of my days as a ghetto youth, I was overwhelmed with the fascination of loyalty, love, honor and materialistic items. I am now face to face with its evil. Evil that has been of an uncomprehending state. Methodically, it has been placed upon me and upon those of whom I love; in which this story is based.

This story simply describes itself. I was totally unprepared for what was expected; furthermore, I needed a plan, or a strategy of some kind. I never thought the scent of betrayal would ever come in my direction; so bold and in such as invisible form. I tried to travel the path to understand my position in life; unfortunately, I was brought back to reality with the realism of intellect. An intelligent style that has been so close yet placed so far. Through it all, time captured my attention, and in this strange process it made me realize that the journey I was on to survive, was simply my destiny to become a better man.

FROM THE STREETS, I GIVE YOU. "**THE CORRUPTION OF BLOOD**"

. . . BASED ON TRUE EVENTS . . .

PROLOGUE

THE CORRUPTION OF BLOOD

March 12, 1998, 2:34 a.m.

. . . Knife now in hand. I started walking towards him. The tears started to roll with every inch of a step I took. Every breath of oxygen that flowed into my shivering lungs, and heart shattering soul was a step of me being closer to a man who cleverly smuggled himself into my time challenging world. He's a man of observed honor, loyalty and good dignity.

Greasy sweat ran down my face endlessly. I felt the warm dampness of the sweat as it makes its way down my forehead and into my eyes. I couldn't wipe its flow away. It blurred my vision with the sensation of a slight burn. My neck and chest area was filled with the aroma of nervous aggression. My hand clutched the handle of the knife tightly. The thrives of electricity flowed around my palms with extreme animosity.

He looked comfortable at peace; just laying there in silence, sleeping away helplessly. He has not one evil thought. Not one ounce of fear. He was overwhelmingly relaxed as he dreamed on. It was the perfect opportunity to seize this imposter. My heart rhythmically rumbled with loud thunders against my quivering chest, "pound after pound, after pound, after pound." A good man's life was in my hands to face his moment of judgment. I looked down over top of him murderously. It was a vision I hated, but a vision I must oversee. I was now in position. Quickly, I grabbed him roughly around the throat area. His eyes opened with shocking and bone-chilling fear. He observed the sparkling tears flowing down my face. He turned and fought wildly to get me up off of him; unfortunately, my aggressiveness and force made it impossible for him to succeed at releasing my grip. My deep dark eyes connected with his. I read the emotions that sat so openly in his eyes. They asked me why. He fought and struggled no longer, he knew that death has shouted check mate . . .

CHAPTER ONE

August 8, 1994. Paul Williams has been on the run for several weeks now. Finally he decided to lay things to rest. Realization from streets rumors has sat in that the police were looking for him for several counts of aggravated assault, and two first degree murder charges.

Knowing his days of running from the law was over; at 3112 S. 31st, in the Philadelphia area is where the conclusion of his journey began. It was the ending of his street legacy. The ending of a legend that was characterized as one of the smoothest criminal minded kids from a small community called *Tasker*. This was his day of disappointment, indeed this was a day in which the city will never forget.

His heart hammered his chest with an unforgettable thump of weakness. He was tired, fight-less and finally finished. He was willing to except whatever punishment came in his direction. Never in a thousand years was he prepared for the destiny of penitentiary. A place where the mind is sometimes forced to see what the eyes can't and where emotions are locked up along your body. Prison has its own zip code of solid soldiers, and true worriers. They say the strong survive and it's true. This was the beginning of how a young man slightly experienced his metamorphosis from a young man to adulthood. But before everything came crashing down, this man wanted to explain everything to his girlfriend Connie. One again he has failed her.

Just days after the murders of the two Philadelphia Police Officers, Paul had nowhere to go; therefore he wanted everything painful in his heart to end. He thought of all his troubles, as they individually killed him mentally. On top of it all, his girlfriend has just turned eight months. The ending of her pregnancy was near. He realized his stupidity more and more as he walked back and forth of the small block of her home. His lifestyle has leaded him to a dead end. Its and old saying, "you either get murdered by some street punk, or spend the rest of your natural life in jail". Finally he arrived at her home. He hesitated before knocking. Building himself up, he lifted up his right hand, and knocked almost silently on the screen-door. But no one answered. He rang the new door bell that has recently been repaired. As he continued to ring the door bell, he didn't realize that it was three a.m. in the morning. He took a short step back off the steps to call for her at her window. He shouted her name in a loud whisper.

"C! Hey C!" C was a nick name he called Connie.

Suddenly a voice appeared that wasn't C's.

"Why don't you shut your mouth out there child, people are trying to get some rest here". The voice was from an old neighborly woman named Ms. Mandellah Fintain. People in the community called her the wicked witch of South Philly.

"For God sakes, its three something in the damn morning", she stated through an old dirty window screen.

"Why don't you take your old ass back to sleep, and mind your own business lady", Paul responded. He was never one to disrespect his elders, but now was not the time to be pushing any of his buttons.

"Oh my! How disrespectful. I am now going to call the authorities on you. How you like that?" The old woman stated. Her face quickly disappeared from the window.

"You do as you fuckin' please, if that's what it will take to shut your old ass up!" Paul said sharply. He started shouting again for Connie.

"C! Hey C!" Before he could finish.

"Paul. What're you doing out there, and why are you talking to Ms. Mandellah that way?" Connie asked in an aggressive tone, cutting him off from shouting her name again. She continues.

"Wait right there, I am on my way down to open the door." Paul stood there waiting patiently. The old woman has returned back to her window. She couldn't help herself from saying something.

"Well it's about time," she said roughly. "Now perhaps I could get some rest." Paul raised his right hand and flagged the old woman off. The old woman just looked on with her eyes squinting at the slim thug saying nothing else, and allowing him to move on. The door has now opened.

"Boy if you don't get your behind in here, and leave that crazy old woman alone, I am going to hurt you." Connie stated. Connie was very demanding and normally she would have her way in the relationship. She was twenty three, with a beautiful high yellow skin tone. Her body was sensuously slim. Her hair was cut short with a sexy bark brownish, burgundy type color. Paul on the other hand was a real handsome brother. He stood about five feet nine inches, with a small fragile body frame; however, he was well respected by many in his community growing up. He never went for anyone's bull, and was indeed a gentleman to his girlfriend. She believed he was the love of her life.

"Hey baby," he said softly. The two kissed, and Paul then made his way through the door.

"Paul it's late. Where have you been? I have been looking all over for you. You didn't answer your pager and your mother hasn't heard from you either. We were worried sick about you." Paul humbled himself before speaking.

"Something came up. I was going to call you, but I never got around doing so." Connie looked on and felt somewhat uncomfortable when she noticed his change in body language. She quickly spoke.

"Paul you're shaking, and why aren't you looking at me?" Connie knew him like the back of her hand. She could tell when he has done something wrong. Lifting up his head, she looked into his face to make eye contact. He spoke softly.

"Well baby girl, I am going to give it to you clean. I will not hold anything back." He stood before the woman he thought would be sharing in the rest of his life. He gazed sadly down into her beautiful eyes and said. "C, I have done some wrong things."

"Wrong things like what. Is what I am hearing about you in the streets true?" She asked speaking very fast, thinking he might have cheated on her with another woman. "Well what did you do so wrong that would have you this way? Baby whatever it is we can work it out." Her voice was now expressing major concern, but before he could answer.

"Connie . . . who is that at my door and why are they coming to my home three something in the morning?" Spoke the voice of Connie's mother. Paul always wanted C, to come live with him but her mother was suffering from cancer and had not very long to live; therefore, she held the need to be close with her during her dyeing days. Her mother continued to shout.

"Connie! Child, I know you hear me talking to you!"

"Yes mom, I hear you." Connie said back. Connie, holding her hands over Paul's mouth, so that he could be quiet while she talked with her mother. Paul pushed her hands away several times.

"Well answer me when I am talking to you child."

Paul quickly spoke.

"It's just me Ms. Perkins! He shouted out. Connie was now sitting on the sofa looking at Paul, her eyes in worry. She notices the huge cut on his forehead. She really realized something was seriously wrong.

"Oh hello Paul," Ms. Perking said from the top of the steps.

"Hello to you as well," he responded. He stood there looking down at Connie, holding her hand tightly.

"Paul is everything okay honey?"

"Yes mam, everything is fine," he said, hoping that she would go lay back down so that they could attend to their conversation. Connie father, Mr. Jermayne J. Perkins, was killed long ago in the army. It was said that he was considered to be a wise hero. Supposedly, he has rescued five United States soldiers from a Soviet Union Kidnapping squad in the early 1970's. After his death, Ms. Perkins was rewarded several medals honoring her husband, with a large check for an unknown amount.

"Okay then, you may return to your business!" She said.

"Good night Mam," Paul hollered out.

"Good night baby," she responded as he headed back toward her bedroom.

Paul looked at C, once again and said.

"As I was saying, I got myself into this rough situation. But it's also a situation I am going to need your undivided help and support". Paul got down on one knee, while holding her hand. The moisture that has now appeared on his forehead started to glisten, causing the wide wound to slightly burn.

"Anything for you Paul." Connie has gained some weight from the pregnancy, therefore, her belly stuck out right into Paul's face. As she now looked down at Paul, the small tears started falling down her soft checks. Before he could do or say anything else, Connie asked.

"Paul Williams. What did you do?"

"Well, I don't know what you been hearing but, I have been on the run from the police for several days now." Before he could finish.

"WHAT! ON THE FUCKIN' RUN!" She shouted. Her tired, heavy body lifted up off the sofa. Instantly she was very angry. She looked into his face. He knew she was a very special woman. A woman he may have lost forever because of his foolish mishaps.

"Baby, I've been on the run because of a rumor that I killed a man". He stated as his eyes hit the floor.

"What do you mean it's a rumor? Either you did it, or you didn't. Either way you had something to do with it, right!" She stated, voice now becoming a bit louder. Her tears flowed heavier. She smacked his face. She was so disappointed from the news she just received. Paul just stood their motionless.

"Please Connie don't be this way with me."

"Baby please! Don't be this way! Fuck you!" She said after marking his statement.

"Paul how could you pull this now? Why would you even be involved in anything like this again"? She continues. "We had a deal, and you promised me. I am now eight months pregnant, because of the deal you made me and you come here to me with the shit. How could you do this to me . . . to us?" She asked over and over as she pounded on his chest. Paul stood dumbfounded. Connie sat back down to cry her small heart out. Paul had more news, but instead he figured it wasn't the right time to tell her. Connie inhaled deeply, and humbly said.

"Paul, I really don't understand you sometimes. I don't know what I am going to do without you, but I'm guessing I'll manage." Paul was lost as to what she was saying. She continued. "For you to go and get yourself involved into these wrong things has shown me that your love for me has faded and that you've got no respect for me or your unborn child. I honestly cannot say what I am going to do with you, nor without you." Paul just listened on. He knew she had all the right in the world to say what she felt. She held her hands over her mouth, and cried some more. Then she spoke again. "Paul I am about to give birth to your child. Your only child next month, and now you probably won't be around to see me through that. What give you the fucking right to come in here with this news? How could you be so careless? Boy I loved you with all my heart and soul, but I don't think I can love you anymore". Paul eyes became watery, as he listened on. I am so sick of your unthinkable actions. By the grace of God, I'll do my best in remaining as strong as I can for the baby. Now, I must ask you to leave." She took another deep breath, closed her eyes and pointed towards the door.

"C, I'll deal with this. Someway, I'll deal with this I promise. I promise you that we'll get through this together. Right now, I need for you to be strong with me. C, I need you more now then ever before. More then I've ever needed anyone". Paul said, as tears started to flow down his boyish face. He reached out for her hand, and she smacked it away. She looked up at him with hatred in her eyes and said directly.

"Save that shit for another bitch. What you lost was a good woman. Now, you get the hell out of this house. Just leave me alone, because I don't ever want to see your tired ass again." Shouting these words, her teeth tightened together, showing nothing but frustration upon her face. Paul stood still; he turned and reached for the door. Before exiting the house he said,

"C, please don't do this. Plea . . ."

"GET OUT! GET THE FUCK OUT! GET OUT! OUT! OUT! She shouted over and over before hearing anymore of his words.

Suddenly, "Connie! Connie! What's wrong? What's going on child?" It was her mother asking loudly as she stormed down the steps to her daughters rescue. She looked at Paul who stood in the doorway about to leave and said.

"What did you do to my daughter?

Paul just shook his head and said. "I've done nothing Ms. Perkins," he said looking at Connie. His heart was now crushed; however, he knew it was nothing more he could do there. So slowly he walked out. He turned his head back one last time, and Connie and her mother stood there hugged up tightly. Connie cried louder in her mother's arms shouting.

"Mom! Oh mom, I love him so much. Why would he do something like this to me?" Paul just put his head down and walked away.

"It's going to be okay baby. Everything is going to be okay," Ms. Perkins said, while holding onto her oldest child. She was hoping Connie would calm down so she could find out what was troubling her, but for that moment she just had to comfort her. As Paul walked away, he looked up and noticed the old woman in her window, and before he could do or say anything.

"Huh! I always knew you weren't shit," the old woman stated, looking down on him. Paul continued to walk away without saying a word in return. He just shook his head to what has just happened, but the old woman continued to verbally abuse him.

"Yeah, that right, I said you weren't shit. I called the police also. I heard that girl crying. I know you were down there smacking her around. How you like that Mr. Smart ass? Why you go and do that to that nice young lady?" Her words dragged from her voice as if she was up all that night drinking booze. She continued on to assassinate the character of Mr. Williams. He was now almost a half block away, and slowly her words faded. As he walked he focused in on getting as far away as possible. However, while walking down the long street, he arrived at the old Stinger Square Recreational Center. He gently leaned on an old tree to collect his thoughts. His body slowly glided down as his face expressed deep humiliation towards himself. He felt as if he had nothing left. As he thought of all the things that have just gone wrong, he began shouting them out loudly.

"First them double crossing Bell's pull that shit on me, then them god-damn police officers come around harassing me, and now C, with this!" He looked down at the chrome twenty five automatic hand gun, and continued to shout once again. "I don't need her anymore! I don't need anyone! The hell with them all (Little Harvey Bell, The Police, and Connie). Paul looked around as if he was loosing his mind. Everything appeared to be moving simultaneously. To him if felt like everybody and everything was looking directly at him. He was becoming paranoid, looking down at the hand gun once more. He realized the small weapon in his possession was indeed a murder weapon.

"I must get ride of this," he stated as he slowly lift his depressed, weak body up off the brittle tree. He started walking towards a nearby bridge on thirty eighth and Grace Ferry. As he arrived there, he stood quietly. He looked down into the cold and dirty water sadly. He lifts up his right arm, while holding the gun with a tight grip in his palm; while during so, the small chrome pistol reflected off the headlights of an on coming automobile. However, it happened so fast Paul didn't even notice it. He slung the little gun as far as he could have possibly thrown it. He shouted with laughter, and rage. "YEAH, YOU GO ALONG WITH EVERYBODY ELSE! I DON'T NEED YOU EITHER!" So much stress has traveled away with the dirty weapon. Only two places he was welcomed, and that's his long term friend and partner Billy Green or his Mother's home. He didn't know what happened to Billy after the cop shooting, and it really started to bother him. Paul couldn't go to his own place because of the police. His brothers' Larry and James were away on business, and didn't hear of the latest news. Although he held a spare key to both their homes, he decided that he just wanted to go somewhere safe. He decided to go back home to mom, for some warm laughs and some hot tea. He understood that her place may be highly under surveillance, but it mattered to him none. Soon as he turned to walk away, a loud voice appeared.

"Hey! Hey you! I know you can hear me calling you," a short chubby man stated as he called out to Paul.

"Are you talking to me?" Paul asked, while looking back at the man. Paul's face expressed evil, as if he was about to kill the innocent gentlemen.

"You damn right, I am talking to you," the man responded, dressed up in a security uniform. "Do you know who I am?" He asked.

"No, but I a pretty sure your going to tell me," Paul responded.

"Well let me help you to know that I am the security officer who's patrolling this here bridge." Paul just looked on, now in complete surprise. He wondered if the man just witnessed him throwing the weapon in the water.

"Now, I need for you to tell me what exactly you're doing out here this late, and what was that you just threw into the water?" The fat guard moved his flashlight around as if he was a real detective; furthermore, he places his hand onto his hip like a woman would. Paul found that to be somewhat amusing.

"Oh that. That was nothing but some rocks," he responded softly.

"Just some rocks you say",

"Yeah, some muthafuckin' hard, crusty, rocks." The man looked at Paul and if Paul was trying to deceive him. Paul became agitated. He suddenly realized at that moment that man has saw nothing, therefore, he could put the fake cop in his place.

"Well okay then young fellah. I apologize. I just wanted to make sure you weren't trying to dispose of a body, weapon or even try and murder yourself. You can understand that it's just a job. I didn't mean to burst your balls pal." Paul felt much better, and didn't feel the need to check the man. Paul just turned and walked away, and so did the guard. Paul just smiled and realized that the guard was just board with nothing else to do, and fucking with him has made his night. Paul walked down a long narrow bridge. Now wanting his mother's comfort even more, he walked and roamed around on the streets for several more hours. He sat down on the side of an old abandon building to come to his senses, so that his mother would only see him in good spirits. Most importantly, he needed to think of Connie. He sat there thinking of the very first time they encountered each other at the Philadelphia International Airport.

. . . .

June 24, 1990,

"Pardon me Ms.," Paul said, grinning uncontrollably.

"Yes, may I help you?" The young female asked. "Can't you see that I am having a real difficult time here," she said angrily. She stood slim, firm and very fragile. Her back was facing Paul's direction. Still grinning, Paul spoke again.

"Yes, I can see that. However, I really would like to know why you're trying your hardest to pull the handle off my luggage."

"Excuse you!" The woman responded in a nonchalant manner. She swung her lean body around swiftly to become face to face with her accuser. "I believe that this here is my luggage, thank you very much," she said, rolling her eyes at Paul in a stubborn way. Paul reached out for the handle to the luggage. It was still heavy, just like he remembered. She stood there looking into Paul's face as he just reached by her like she never was there. Her eyes lit-up in disbelief, as she couldn't believe how bold he was. She quickly calmed down and her face begun to glow brighter with the sensation of passion. Paul was slim and stood immaculately handsome in his off white, shinny silk-like expensive clothing. He looked back at the woman smiling, showing off his white teeth. The woman folded her arms and patted her feet like a child wanting to play rope, but instead she awaited the outcome of the luggage. Paul laid the luggage onto a small counter top, and pulled out a folded piece of paper that read off six numbers. The numbers he held matched number by number to the luggage.

"See this here Ms. Lady, this here is my luggage," Paul said as the two made deep eye contact. The female stood in silence. She realized that she has made a terrible mistake.

"Oh my God. I am so sorry. You must forgive me for acting so foolish," the beautiful young woman stated. Paul just smiled at the woman.

"No need for apologies, things like this happen all the time. Come lets get together to look for your luggage." The two smiled at one another in a flirtatious manner. Strong vibes of attraction shot through the body of the slender woman. She has now observed him closer. She has been watching Paul's every move. His male sexuality captivated her. Paul couldn't believe the sensuousness this young lady exhibited. Her eyes were a sparking greenish gray color. Her skin tone was a light caramel brown that looked smoothly soft; that went perfectly with her round face. Her lips glittered red lipstick when she would speak.

"Did you find my luggage yet?" she asked in a soft voice tone."

"Nope, not yet. I am still looking". Paul said. Paul looked up at her and continued to speak. "By the way, my name is Paul Williams, and you are?"

"Connie, Connie Perkin's, from Philadelphia", she said while moving aside a few more baggage. Paul looked at the feisty woman with excitement in his eyes. He wanted to know more about her. Looking at her from head to toe, he noticed that she had on some very nice threads of her own. She wore heavy padded, ladies crocodile free lace shoes that matched perfectly with her crocodile hand bag. Paul thought that her dress style shown elegance in her way of design and clothing. Paul inhaled the smell of her perfume and smiled beneath his breath.

"Philadelphia, you say?" he asked. "Well now, I am also from Philly. I've just returned back from a long stressful trip in the Big Apple. I had to meet up with my brothers' on business. I am so tired, I can barely stand. I cannot wait until I can relax.

"I know exactly what you mean", Connie responded. "Yes! Yes! Here's my luggage," she said. She expressed relief in finding her luggage. Her luggage was almost impossible of knowing hers from his. Connie looked at her number tag, and the numbers' matched. She realizes she should've done that from the beginning; fortunately, Paul, was someone she really needed to meet.

"So, what part of Philadelphia are you from?" he asked just to make small talk. "Just maybe we are headed into the same direction," he stated.

"Truly, I am uncertain," she said. Paul's face expressed more curiosity. "I'm sorry; allow me to restate what I've just said. I must call my mother for further directions," she continued. "When I was away at school for one year, my mother moved to another state. The neighborhood is in, umm, I believe it's South Philadelphia". Paul laughed in disbelief. "Well, what's so funny? Is there something wrong with that neighborhood?" She asked.

"No, it's nothing like that. You must forgive me," Paul responded, still having a smile on his face. "Either you're a match made in heaven, or it's just one strange coincidence that you and I met".

"What are you saying," asked Connie.

"I am also from that neighborhood," he stated. "What's your mother's name? Do you have any brother's? Perhaps I know them," Paul said. "Being as though we're from the same community, I think it would be best for us both, if we were to become a little more acquainted as friends".

"I don't think so," Connie said, as she headed towards the telephone. "I thought if you were going my way, perhaps, I could like give you a lift," Paul said.

"Give me a lift," Connie responded. "Boy, I don't even know you. Why should I think of getting into a vehicle with a stranger? How do I know you're not some deranged lunatic or something," Connie applied. Paul just looked at her and smiled. Once again expressing his pure whites, and thinking to himself; knowing that she couldn't be serious. He rubbed his head a questionable way. His clean soft hand and manicured fingernails glistening of the large lighting that surrounded the airport station. Connie, she recognized his cleanness, and begun to blush.

"Do something weird or strange you say." Paul responded wickedly. They both laughed loudly, at the crazy thought. Connie began to dial her mother's new telephone number.

"How are you going to get home then?" Paul asked. Connie put up her index finger, suggesting Paul to wait a moment as someone picked up the receiver on the other end. Paul stood silently.

"Yes it's me, where's mom? Connie looked at Paul and blushed once more. "Yes mom, it's me. I am calling from the Philadelphia International Airport, and I need more directions." Paul looked down at his watch, realizing that he needed to go. "Tell the cab driver what? Oh . . . okay. You say 31st and Tasker Street." Paul's eyes jumped in surprise. Connie was heading straight in his home area, but he knew she was going to show some stubbornness, before she would comply with his suggestions.

"Okay then, I'll see you soon." Before she could hang up the telephone, Paul grabbed her arm.

"What's your mother's name?" He asked with a small smile on his face.

"Boy, what are you doing?" Connie asked.

"What's her name," Paul asked once again, and again.

"Okay! All right! Dammit! I'll tell you gosh." Her name is Mrs. Dawn Perkins," she said with her face looking agitated.

"Not my good friend Mrs. Perkins'," Paul said almost in an over-sealed way.

"Don't tell me you know my mother," Connie wondered.

"Yes, a matter of fact, I do know your mother. Allow me to say hello." She handed Paul the telephone, hoping he wasn't playing any psychological games or something.

"Hello Mrs. Perkins' . . . Hi, it's me Paul . . . yes, that Paul. I have just arrived in from New York City, and I ran into your beautiful little girl. She and I had a little mix-up with her luggage . . . no, no mam, everything is fine now." Connie stood there smiling away, shocked that he really did know her mother. "Would you please allow your stubborn daughter to know that she'll arrive home in all pieces . . . no, yes Mrs. Perkins . . . okay, you too." Paul handed Connie the telephone. Connie rolled her eyes delightfully. Placing the receiver back up to her ear, she spoke again to her mother. "Yes mother . . . okay mother . . . okay, okay, okay. I love you more." Paul headed towards the exit. Connie, never trusted anyone before; but today she was feeling overwhelmed in this stranger's company. She felt as if she lost her aggressive side. Paul walked towards a man in an all red working suit. He handed him a brownish color ticket, and the man walked away. Moments later, the same man returned driving a baby blue jeep grand Cherokee. Paul placed the two bags of luggage in the back seats. He then gave the large gentleman a crispy ten. Connie got in the passenger side. Paul looked over from the driver's seat and smiled at her slight attitude. The two drove away smoothly. Paul then made conversation.

"You know, your mother is a very wonderful, and sweet woman." "Umm, humm," Connie muttered, not really wanting to talk, as if she was trying to hold on to her fake attitude. Paul felt her mild uncomfortable-ness, and said nothing else. After about another ten minutes or so has past, Connie relaxed. She began to smile into Paul's direction. Then she started asking questions about his personal life. Paul, being the smooth person that he was, didn't care about the questions one bit. "So, what do you do for a living?" Connie asked. "I am a business man."

"What kind of business man. I know you're not talking about drug dealing." She said. Her bright eyes widened. "No, not drugs," Paul quickly said. "I do business deals, something you wouldn't understand."

"Yeah, whatever. I bet it does have something to do with drugs or something illegal."

"Okay, enough about what it is I do," cutting her off completely. "What are some of the things you like to do, or plan on doing for a living?" Paul asked while shifting lanes to get in front of a slow moving truck. "Well, if you must know. I am presently going to modeling school. I would like to become a professional model," Connie took her eyes off Paul, while she spoke, to imagine herself as a successful model.

"Oh yeah! Okay, that's great. You definitely got what it takes to be a professional." "You think so?" Connie asked. "Babygirl, I know so," as Paul complimented her. "I really wish you the best of luck." "Thank you, Connie responded.

"Would you like to see my modeling portfolio?" Connie shouted excitedly, now completely relaxed in Paul's presence. "Yeah, sure, let's see it." The portfolio captured Paul's attention instantaneously. "Wow," Paul said. "You are so beautiful," he said, while looking at the road and the large pictures as well. In the photo's she wore her sexy tight bikini swim suits. "Thank you," she said shyly.

After several more minutes of communication the two has finally reached South Philly. Pulling off the 76 expressway, five minutes later they arrived at Connie's new home. Paul beeped the horn several times, but before anyone answered the door, Paul spoke to Connie once again. "So, tell me something; do you feel safe with me now?" The two looked at one another as if they never wanted to separate. "Yes, I feel completely safe Mr. Williams, the business man." Connie stepped out of the jeep, and headed towards the doorsteps of her new home. Her little brother Kevin, who was just turning seven years old, came running out of the house calling her name over and over.

"Hey Connie's home! Connie's home! Connie is home! Connie! Connie! Connie!" The child shouted. "I missed you so very much, big sister," he stated as he jumped into her arms. The two embraced each others' companionship.

"Hey big guy, I missed you too," Connie responded. Paul just sat back and observed the charming joy of happy faces.

"Well Connie, looks like I'll be on my way now!" Paul shouted. "Paul, wait just a minute!" Connie shouted.

"Will I see you again?" Connie asked, breathing heavily from the brief jog back to Paul's jeep. She dazed into Paul's eyes attractively. "Well, how about tonight? Say around eight o'clock. We can have a friendly chat, and get a small bite to eat," Paul suggested. "Sounds good to me," Connie said as she smiled openly. "So, I guess I'll see you tonight same place," Paul whispered casually. "You bet, it's a date," Connie stated as she slowly jogged backed towards her little brother, to tightly pick him back up. At that moment, Connie's mother walked out into the doorway. Paul was driving away; but before he was completely gone, he spoke to Connie's mother.

"Hello Mrs. Perkins!" he said.

"Hello handsome!" she responded. "Thank you for bringing my daughter home safe and sound! She shouted.

"You're welcome!" Paul shouted back. "It was no problem at all!" Paul said as he drove down the street heading towards his own mother's house. Connie little brother Kevin, continued to laugh and tease Connie about her new male companion.

"Connie have a boyfriend . . . Connie have a boyfriend!" Connie just laughed and squeezed him even tighter. They all headed into their home. After the night of their first date, Connie and Paul have never been separated from one another again.

. . . .

CHAPTER TWO

THE ARREST

August 9, 1994, I've been sighted by Mrs. Mandella Fontain, the neighborhood watcher. No soon as I arrived at my mother's front door, the telephone rung. Its 5:20 a.m., I wondered who it could be calling this house so late in the hour. Answering the telephone, I was not at all pleased with whom ever it was. I was tired, and unable to focus clearly.

"Hello," I answered. I slouched down on my mother's sofa. It was a long term friend of the family, Mike Wilkins, but we always called him Black. I guess it was because of his dark skin tone. Mike, he knew the danger I've placed myself in with the law, and realized that they were hot on my trail. He called out my name loudly.

"Paul! Is that you?" he asked. I responded.

"Yes, it's me", I said in a low voice tone.

"Good, I am glad I caught you. Have you been listening to your police scanner within the last forty-five minutes or so?" he questioned.

"No, I haven't", I said.

"Well, I have all night, and to make a long story short, you better exit the neighborhood as quickly, and as quietly as you possibly can." I became angry. I shouted.

"Black! What's your reason for calling this house at this hour, telling me I better exit the neighborhood?"

"Because your family is like my own family; besides, I know all about your situation with the police. You know news travels fast around here", he said while continuing. "So when I heard you were sighted in the neighborhood, I decided to call your mother's home in good faith."

"Good faith!" I shouted. "Good faith how?" I asked.

"Good faith, because the police are on their way to your mother's house as we speak." Quickly, I slammed down the telephone receiver and started walking back and forth nervously. My body suddenly froze. Never-the-less, I was in a deep predicament. I knew that if I was to stay at my mother's home, I was definitely going to jail. I also knew that my body and mind probably wouldn't be able to handle much more of the running pressure. I started to think more and more of Connie. I needed her and wanted to call her very badly; unfortunately, I knew she was a bit upset with me. I sat down again on the sofa. I placed my hands onto my head and whispered to myself. "What am I going to do?" Seconds turned into minutes and I realized that it would be best to give myself up; besides, running would only make me look guiltier. "No one was around to pin point me doing anything, so why continue to run," I figured.

I must now awake my mother, to give her the disappointing news. Her baby son was on his way to jail. However, I needed a small conversation with her before our departure, and/or before the police arrived. My mother, her name is Mrs. Paulette Williams; she's a very pleasant, warmhearted person to many. She's well known in my neighborhood as one of the kindest or sweetest adults in our area. She's beautiful and she is someone who doesn't deserve cruelty or should she ever be hurt. The most pain for her always, somehow comes from her own children. It's not our fault. Society has provided my mother to survive her best in the ghetto. We as men, my brothers and I, never asked for the inner animal to come raging out. But if you back anyone of God's smallest creatures up in a corner, it will somehow find a way to defend itself. The hunger for money brought out the best in us, so, if we wanted happiness, we were to expect pain.

I called out for my mother. She answered, voice still cracked up from a long restful night.

"Paul, is that you? Is everything alright?" she questioned.

"Yes mother it's me," I responded. She came down the steps. Eyes full of questions, curiosity, nervousness, and happiness. I hugged her in my arms. I grabbed her hand, and we sat down. I told her about my current situation. I looked into her warm face to explain detail by detail. I wanted to prepare her for the police arrival. I told her that they were on their way as we spoke. She looked so sad, but it was best she heard the news from me then anyone else. She started stuttering over her words like she had never done before. She asked. "What's wrong baby?" I couldn't answer. I realized my stupidity once more. "Why must I continue to hurt the ones I love," I asked myself. I spoke to my mother. "Oh, it's nothing," I said. "I don't want you to worry your precious self. I just wanted you to know what was about to happen, that way, we could prepare for their entrance, and when they do arrive I'll straighten everything out." I felt very bad. Her face was soft and cunning. I continued. "Once again, I am more than sure it's nothing."

"Well, okay baby, if you say it's nothing, then it must be nothing," she said. "I'll just go into the kitchen and make you some warm tea." Just like I'd remembered, my mother would always keep her baby boy warm. We now departed. I headed up the steps towards my old room and she headed towards the kitchen. I looked around my old room nervously. I knew that me telling my mother the situation was nothing, it wasn't totally accurate. I knew it was much more serious. Going up the steps, I peeped over at her. She was just walking comfortably in silence. I shook my head and apologized to her beneath my breath. In my old room, I sat down on the edge of the bed. I looked around for the remote to the stereo, but I never found it. I reached out thoroughly, to press the on button and to turn the large volume knob by hand. I sat there thinking of Billy, wondering where he was, or why hasn't he contacted my mother to see if I was alright or not. Unfortunately, three minutes into my thoughts, I heard cars driving up to the house. It was the police. It sounded as if they were building/setting up, a small perimeter. I started blasting my stereo louder. My adrenaline flow was flowing heavier than it has ever flowed. The cowardly thought of running, has once again crossed my mind. Truthfully, I was mentally done. The tiredness has taken its toll. The prolonging of this chase must end.

The thought of torturing my mind again has become unimaginable. I was suffering from the thought of invisibility. Whereas, reality has proven that every criminal has its day to face justice. My roughness towards others' has finally been concluded. This was the ending of my ability to slip through the fingertips of our so called system.

"Paul!" my mother called.

"Yes!" I responded.

"The policemen are here, and they would like to ask you some questions. Hearing her words, I just smiled to myself. I knew that asking me some questions was nothing but bull-shit. I took in a huge chunk of oxygen, turned off my music and headed slowly down the stairs. I recognized the three officers who stood in my mother's living room. My body quivered slightly. I felt my world coming to an end from each and every step I took towards the detectives. I smiled when they placed the handcuffs on me. Clear strips of emotions flowed down the cheeks of my mother. Another one of her boys is on his way to jail. Soon as the police opened the doors, my vision was blinded by many different lights. My world jumped in a shocking surprise. Standing outside of the house, was what looked like the whole "Philadelphia Police District." I moved passively step by step. The officers' held my arms tightly under the armpit. I can only imagine what would of happened if I would've resisted arrest. (Good thing I didn't run or I would've just made a fool out of myself). We headed towards the police automobile, without a word said from either side. Spectators' hung around; they looked at me with faces of unawareness. Many knew of my corrupted behaviors, while others had not a clue. The swat team followed my every movement, with small fully-automatic guns aimed at my head. They looked at me as a cop killer and a drug dealer; A young black male whom either had to kill or be killed. However, I knew they feared that in me. Once again, I smiled at the bastards who looked at me with anger in their hearts. The ones who stood there waiting for me to act out so they could end my young life. Before I entered the detective's car, I turned to catch another glimpse at my mother. I froze briefly; her face expressed the image of melting gold. I blew a kiss to my beloved one. I shouted, "Don't worry, everything will be okay!"

I was then taken away. I was being characterized as low life and it wasn't anything anyone could do, nor say about it. The police station was located at twenty fourth and wolf, in South Philadelphia. Before reaching the station, I momentarily thought of Billy, James, Larry, Little Harvey and Connie. These people were my friends. My soul survivors' in the ghetto. Arriving at the police station gave me the willies. My body started experiencing a case of the shakes. I had two cop killings' and other things many men only dream of doing. Even though we were smart individuals, I may have missed something; however, it could also be an assumption by them as well.

A detective walked passed me and stated, "Well, well, we finally caught up with the notorious Paul Williams." He looked at me smiling. The pig smiled at me as if he knew of my solid conviction. I turned to look at his partner. I asked. "What's this all about officer?" He placed his folder down, looked at me as if I was nothing, and turned his head away. His partner's face turned a dark bluish-red. I guess he was a bit upset at my question. The calmest officer spoke. "Mr. Williams, you're arrested for several separate counts of first degree aggravated assault, and two additional counts of first degree murder on Philadelphia police officer's. He continued, as I sat silently. "Many people made positive identification on you, stating they saw, or heard you say you shot and or killed someone." I sat and thought to myself. "What!" They must think I am a fool to believe this crap." Quickly, I spoke. "Sorry, but I am lost. This must be a case of that mistaken identity thing." However, my face must have showed some concern. My acting skills were on point. I continued, "Several counts of aggravated assaults and two counts of murder. What are you people trying to do to me? These accusations are impossible!" I shouted. "Impossible!" The angrier detective of the two shouted. "Listen here you little shit! Paul! Gangster or whatever the hell they call you punks out there. We've been following you and your brothers for sometime now; furthermore, we know all about your misunderstanding with the Bells' family. So before you say something is impossible, you better reflect back on the actions you once made." I sat there with the face expression of nothing. His partner walked over and whispered something into his ear. He stood and walked away. When he returned, the more aggressive questions were asked. Some held some truth, while others had no merit. Whatever the case may be, I wasn't about to fold, or fall victim to their games. I wasn't about to hang myself by saying the wrong things, but I needed to say something, so I spoke again. "Look sir," I humbly said. "I don't know anything. If you people are going to continue on with this meaningless interrogation process, then I am asking for a lawyer to be present. Furthermore, if this interview is no longer of a major priority, and I am not under arrest, then politely, I am asking to be released." I understood the police ways of doing business. They don't always have the evidence they say they have. They used a strong technique, a wise strategy that's performed in their daily duty as reverse psychology. The officer looked on and smiled. He spoke. "Okay, well then, seems as if we have nothing here, but before you get booked, just make sure you tell all that to the judge just before he sentence you to death, or life in prison with no chance of parole," he stated sarcastically, with a small smile. I felt a sharp pain in my stomach after he spoke those words. I felt real shitty. I knew that I was guilty of murder. It also sounded as if they had me by the balls with some solid evidence. I was really starting to worry about what was going to happen.

August 10, 1994, I was awaken by the sound of some jingling keys. They were ready to take me to eighth and race; located in the down town section of Philadelphia. I was on my way to the booking processing unit. After the fifteen minute drive to this place, arriving there was no surprise. I've been there before on a petty cocaine charge. However, that charge was thrown out for the lack of evidence.

Therefore, the view and smell wasn't a main concern. In fact, my surroundings were the last thing flowing through my head. After I was fingerprinted and photographed, I was placed in a holding cell. I couldn't calculate the exact amount of criminals that was in their; but it was around thirty to forty men awaiting their chance to see the honorable judge. This place was small, stinky and completely unsanitary. After scanning the area over and over, I asked myself, "What have you gotten yourself into?" Even after the room was full, they continued to bring in more men. It was now really crowded and I had no where to sit. The day was being dragged out slowly. At that moment, it was no telling how long I was going to be there. It was no telling if it was night or day. Many hours had gone by; but just when I felt like snapping, my name was finally called. I stood in front of the Honorable Judge Carlton W. Patterson. My heart started racing like a mice caught wickedly in a trap. I was afraid of what was going to happen; but this was my reality, and I was going to face it. My chin was high and my shoulders were straight. I was prepared for a battle.

"Mr. Williams, you have before me some very serious charges," the judge said while looking over my rap sheet. He continued. "The charges that sit before this court are all first degree offenses. They are very serious with deadly weapons. I've already read over the evidence, and I must place this case in the hands of trial; therefore, I have no other choice but to place you in custody at a county correctional facility unit further notice." His words flowed, and my mind stood unresponsive. I started to understand my deep ditch. I was in a big hole and the hole was getting deeper. The judge spoke again. "Mr. Williams, you will be held without bail for the safety of the community. Do you understand?

"Yes," I responded.

"Sheriff, please take this man out of my courtroom," the judge stated. I looked around upset. I was salty, and my face expressed it. It expressed hatred towards the judge. Again, I felt the coldness of the handcuffs. I was placed into a small room with six other men. This was it; I was on my way to the Detention Center.

"GOOD BROTHER"

The sound of the music went mellow as Billy turned into the Graceferry gas station. Billy suddenly squeezed the breaks. He observed two young boys walking in the center of the street, holding their hands out, and what seemed as if they were asking strangers for change. Billy shook his head in an unbelievable way.

"What the hell are they doing out there?" Billy questioned himself. "Are they crazy?" Another car drove up behind him, pressing his horn for Billy to move on. "Okay ass-hole, hold your horses!" Billy shouted through his rearview mirror. Billy pulled up into the gas station, parking his car next to the number twelve pump. He opened his car door and stepped out, removing his gold and platinum fashion Gucci sun glasses that sat perfectly on his face. Billy took the bottom of his polo sports shirt and wiped the dust off the high quality, cinnamon colored lens. While doing so, he continued to look in the direction of the children. Now approaching the gas stations window, he placed his order; not before saying,

"Damn, they must be around nine or ten years old." Billy couldn't help himself but to worry about the life threatening maneuvers they were practicing just for a quarter or fifty cents.

"May I help you sir?" Asked the gas station attendant. Billy just stood their looking at the boys in a slight daze. He turned to answer her question, despite the disappointment he felt for the kid's family.

"Yes you can," Billy said. "I'll have twenty dollars on the number twelve." Looking through the six inch thick, bullet-proof glass window. In order for him to make his order, he had to shout into seven small holes. At the bottom of the thick window, was a metal flip-slot compartment to protect the clerk. They could either give or receive money and items without the risk of dangering themselves.

Billy mumbled beneath, smiling and now flirting with the clerk. She was a skinny woman with long brown hair and very thick eyebrows. Her hands were very small, and her nails were perfectly manicured with pink and white fingernail polish that matched her small top shirt. The shirt showed off her cute belly button briefly.

"Damn, I would like to have some of that," Billy stated to himself over and over, while giving her a crispy fifty dollar bill. The woman noticed the thick knot of money before she spoke.

"Will there be anything else sir?"

"Ummm, yes! I'll have two packs of big red gum, and two snicker bars. Oh, I almost forgot the most important thing here. I would like to have you as soon as you get off work." The woman stood flattered in the moment of Billy's dazzling display. She gathered the items together and gave it to him through the compartment, along with his remaining change.

"Maybe you didn't hear what I just stated," Billy said.

"I heard every word you said, and to make maters real simple, I am completely overwhelmed with the offer; but baby I am married. I have a good husband at home maybe you haven't noticed the ring, (holding it up high enough so Billy could see the large diamond engagement and wedding rings). Another thing, I have two adorable children by this man, so thanks, but no thanks," the clerk applied smilingly. Billy smiled back at the sexy woman. He had only wished he could be represented the way this woman was representing her man, so strong and so stern.

"Oh well," Billy said, while pocketing his change. He turned and walked towards his car; opened the door, and placed the big red gum inside the cup holder beside the ashtray. He stood back up, looking around for the two boys. He noticed them both. He began to beep his horn for the kids to come over. He beeped three more times before they looked up, quickly ran over, not even looking out for on coming traffic. Billy couldn't believe what he was seeing. He started remembering when he was just a child and had things hard. He knew that he wasn't foolish enough to stand out in the center of the street, asking strange people for money. The two small simple-minded boys walked up and stood directly in front of Billy's car. The one who looked the oldest had his hands in his pockets. His pants were dirty and at the knees were two large holes. Their hair wasn't combed in what looked like days. Their faces had dry marks of dirt from the lack of a bath. Billy sat on his soft, white leather seats, and leaned forward to press his hands onto the steering wheel and just looked at the boys. The other boy, the younger looking one of the two, had on run down sneakers and dirty pants. His shirt looked like somebody has cleaned their ass with it. Billy closed his eyes to feel some compassion for the two children. He stepped out of the car and walked over to them both.

"What are you doing standing out there in them streets for? Are you two kids crazy or something?" Billy asked. One of the boys snickered a little at Billy's comment. The other boy stood close to the other one and looked at Billy with sadness and fear in his little eyes, as his body expressed hidden nervousness. Billy knew very well what they were doing; however, he needed them to admit that it was unsafe for them to stand out there.

"Wee . . . wee was asking for some money, sooo, so we can get something to eat." The one who looked older of the two said. Billy felt an instant sharp pain in his lower abdomen. He wanted to comfort the boys, as a father; but he understood that society has done wrong too many, even the ones who didn't deserve it. That was one of the reasons why Billy turned to the life of corruption and crime. He had no love, no family, and no way of surviving, if it wasn't for the help of his street intelligence.

"Where are your parents?" Billy asked. The two boys shrugged their shoulders simultaneously.

"We don't know," The little of the two said.

"Okay, let's make a deal," Billy inquired. "If I give you guys some money, will y'all promise me that y'all will stay out of them streets?" Billy asked.

"Yes sir," the boys replied.

"Well, you know you guys need to work for what y'all want in this rough world today. Therefore, I need for one of you to pump the gas for me, while the other one can wipe down the windows." They both took off running in different directions. Billy thought to himself. "It's better for them to be doing this then standing out there in them crazy streets." The two boys were moving swiftly and finished the job before Billy could decide what new tape to play in the cassette player. Billy gave the boys ten dollars each, along with a snickers bar. Billy wondered what they were going to do with the money. "Make sure you two buy something good to eat from that Roy Randy's restaurant down the street. No cookies and chips okay," Billy said. The two boys shook their heads, agreeing to what Billy asked them to do. "Maybe the feel of good, hard earned money, can motivate them in working for what they need in life instead of begging," Billy thought. "Nothing is free," Billy said. "Nothing is free." Billy sat back down in his car, closing the door to his BMW. He started the soundless engine. Look at the boys once more, concerned about their safety. "What's y'all name and age?" Billy asked before driving away.

"My name is David, and I am ten," the one said who looked the oldest.

"Me, I'm John-John, and I just turned twelve three days ago." The little one was older then the big one.

"Okay Dav and John, my name is Billy Green, and I am a friend. Here's my pager number; if you two need anything or help with something, you can give me a call at anytime okay. But remember that we had a deal. Stay out of them streets."

"Yes sir, Mr. Billy," the boys said. The taller boy ripped open his candy bar as if he hasn't eaten in days. They started walking away, looking at the gas station attendant, and she shook her head, letting Billy know that he was a good man. Billy smiled back, winking his eye at the woman. Put his car in drive and pulled off into the streets of traffic. He drove past David and John-John, beeping his horn, and waved goodbye. They waved back. Billy continued to look in the rearview mirror until he couldn't see the tiny bodies anymore.

CHAPTER THREE

Going to Jail wasn't that upsetting. Paul has everything a person need to do time. There was love and support behind him regardless of the outcome. No matter what, his friends and brothers were going to be there through thick and thin. The one person Paul was really concerned about was Connie. Even though she's a little upset with him right now, he knew deep in his heart, that if he needed her she'll be there for him regardless of his situation. Honestly, she was all Paul needed to make it, and them words of her being there, was all he needed to remember.

In Paul's corner was his number one friend, Billy Green. In their community Billy was known by the name of Geeze. He was the real smooth lookin' type all the ladies loved to be around. He stood around 5'9" with a dark brown skin tone. He had the methods, the built body and the brains of an over seas assassin. Geeze is twenty-seven and is very well respected. Paul figured with his help and support, whoever came to court against him had some major explaining to do. Paul knew Billy wasn't about any dumb shit; furthermore, he knew Billy wasn't going to just sit around and allow some unknown snitch to testify against him. Billy name and what he stands for will always mean legendary in their neighborhood. At that point of thinking, Paul knew it was only a matter of time upon his release. In their neighborhood, Paul's family had their place. They were known to handle any kind of trouble that came down their way. Not only did Paul have the support of Billy, but he even had the support of his two brothers Larry and James Williams. These two men were considered to be real deal. Some true believers in the game called fuck society. Paul had nothing but unconditional love and support for his older brothers. Paul was the youngest of the bunch. He knew that they were not just going to sit around either. Boy, Paul have it all figured out.

After many more hours has gone by, I was on my way to the Detention Center, Arriving there on **August 11, 1994**, the officers at this place was real frightening looking. All of them looked as if they had nothing better to with their lives but to fuck with a nigga like me. Paul just continued to walk on smiling. Even though their faces looked as crazy as they could possible get them, they all maintained their job responsibilities, and did the job they was ordered to do. I was once again placed in another holding cell, better known as the *Big Boy Bubble*. Because I've never been in this kind of position before, I was a little afraid. I looked around concerned like. Sitting on the floor was an elderly looking gentlemen. This fella was taking up most of the floor space. Paul assumed that the man was homeless because of his actions and the bad smell that aroused from his body. "Damn he needs a bath," Paul mumbled to himself. "No wonder he has most of the floor space," Paul continued to look towards the man. He laughed wickedly to himself. All of the other men was your regular looking criminals, you know, some cracks heads, petty thief cats, and some killers. The killers were easily recognizable. They looked on in silence and expressed faces of worry. I just sat there and looked around over and over at least eleven times at each individual's appearance and attitude. I was starting to realize that I was now encountered with men who might be just as smooth as me. At least seventy-five percent of these men were very amusing; however, the other twenty-five percent was cold hearted. I was in this place and was only twenty-one years old, but the age thing meant nothing. I figured that I've probably done wilder shit in my young years than many could possibly accomplish in their entire lives. I only weighed in about 145lbs; moreover, I was a young man of everlasting street knowledge. I've also run and roamed the wild with true lions. Furthermore, I wasn't about to show any weakness to anyone. I've prepared myself more roughly for the psychopathic, the manipulators and the normal. I guess it was all about the treatment of prison.

After about another three to four hours has gone by, my armband number was called. I was being moved farther into the system. Preparing myself carefully, I took a real deep breath and walked out of the holding cell. As I made a small turn towards my right and another towards the left, I walked into what seemed like the practice of hell. Everything in my view suddenly slowed down, or froze as if I've just entered another galaxy. I wondered about that particular moment in my life. Either everything or everybody around me got quiet or I was so much in shock that my vision became blurry, and my ears shut out all responses. There I was, standing there looking at people in some unthinkable positions. I noticed everyone's mouths moving but I was unable to hear the words they expressed. At that point the pounding of my heart was the only thing I could hear. I continued to walk forward. The things in my view had me feeling as if I was experiencing and suffering from a toxic shock syndrome. This place was definitely dramatic, demeaning and degrading to everything I've saw and/or thought about seeing men do. It was about twenty to thirty adult men up against walls. Many of then unfortunately were completely naked. Some were naked and others were showering to get checked in. I was told aggressively to get against the wall and to take off all me clothing. I had no problem with this order, but I realize I must go through this profound experience for the next month or two was highly depressing. I was giving orders to hold up my testicles with my right hand, with my left hand in the air. To drop both my hands, turn around, grip each of my ass cheeks and spread them apart while I bent over. I couldn't believe what I was ordered to do. The part that was very hurtful was the way it had to be done. Every father and son, grandfather and grandson was literally standing there watching me grip my ass cheeks, spread them apart and act as if I am okay with it. I felt completely disrespected because of the many different types of homosexuals and perverts amongst men in prison, whom also just seen first hand my goods. I have never felt so helpless in my entire life. I was completely speechless, but everyone else had to do it therefore, I done it without incident. I knew nothing about being incarcerated so like a new born tiger in the wild, I had to adjust to my new habitat. I had to roll with the punches.

At this time my clothing were taken away and I was given some county blues I had now been checked into the county prison system. It was around ten to fifteen of us who were given the same housing unit. None of the men I knew. H-Block, the housing unit where I was housed. As the doors opened slowly, I saw just what I'd expected, the sight of untamed animals as audacious as they could possibly come motherfuckers' were running around like children with their heads cut off. For me, I started to understand. I understood that I was placed on this block better described as a battle zone. Why was I placed on this particular block was unexplained, maybe it was my many cases. However, I started thinking of all kinds of crazy things to do for protection of myself. Hell, I wasn't about to lay down my manly ways for anyone, moreover, majority of these men looked like some wild brothers. I figured if I had to live there and fight to show some aggressive behavior, and if fighting is what they want, then fighting is what they'll receive. So I held my head up high, stuck my chest out proudly and walked forwards towards the field of distrustfulness.

CHAPTER FOUR

STRATEGIC PLANNING

I continued to walk forward. I had to find my place on H-Block. In order to get to my destination, I had to travel pass six brothers. These men looked somewhat okay. about five of them where paying me no serious attention, but it was this one particular individual I just couldn't avoid. His face was extremely vogue looking and he was watching me with the eyes of death. He acknowledges me out of the clear blue sky. To know more about me, he questioned me,

"Yo, my man!" He shouted. I turned around to see who he was talking too. "Yeah you", he said directing the other five guys attention in my direction. I turned, and started walking back towards him. What he wanted me for was unknown. I figured it wasn't anything too serious. As I approached him, he spoke again. "Do I know you from somewhere?"

"Naw, I don't think so," I said. He looked deep into my eyes and asked,

"What part of the city you from?" I was somewhat lost as to why where I lived mattered, but if he was trying to make small conversation, then it was all good.

"I'm from South Philly," I said, a little more confident in the way I spoke to him. As the words flowed from my mouth, his face balled up like a germen bull dog. He double looked and asked again.

"What part did you say?"

"I said South Philly." His face started getting real sad looking. I spoke. "So do you know me or not?" I asked, still completely confident. He just looked at me deep, as if I just killed his family. Audaciously, he said.

"**No Negro, I don't know you or the type of men you've been around, but around this mutherfucker, men come through this camp with respect.**" I stood silently, listening to him talk, wondering what just happened to cause him to change so quickly. He continued. "**I will say this once, because I don't repeat myself. That little attitude you just walked on the block with, I suggest you change it as fast as you can, and if you don't change that attitude, then I'll be more than overwhelmed to accommodate your stay here. Now, I want you to roll away unless you feel the need for some special attention.**" I was like,

"Damn! What +crawled up this dudes ass and died?" As I turned to walk away, I looked back over my shoulders slightly. That chump had his eyes set on me like a hulk. I was now beginning to get paranoid. I knew right then and there that this character was going to be a major pain in my doing time. Later on that same day, I found out that he was from the North Philadelphia area, and was very geographical towards brothers that lived in other neighborhoods. He was also known on the block to always keep dumb things going. I started to understand my situation. I understood that if I wanted some respect then I had to earn it, and he was the one I had to earn it from. From that point on I knew in my heart that I had to squash and eliminate this lost soul like an extinct species. Every since that day of meeting him, I've been receiving and feeling dirty vibes of unexplained tension. I knew that I had to take care of this situation soon. I wasn't going to stand for that kind of disrespect too much longer. I was starting to second guess the way things were to be performed. This brother had plenty of backup and I was in no position to take on the responsibility of going after all them. I just had to do something soon; besides, he was the telephone monitor. He was the person that would issue out the phone time to whoever wanted to call their families. Unfortunately, he and his so call gang had other plans. They had everybody in line for only five minutes per call. That was for the whole day. As for all the rest of the telephone time; he and his group of misfits would split it evenly having about a half hour each. I knew I wasn't going to use the telephone until I handled my business. As badly and impatient I was to call Connie, I must show some discipline. Connie was eight months pregnant with my only child. Honestly, I'd been worrying myself sick about her every since I've entered into this institution. Connie was becoming a major priority in my thoughts. I really needed to talk to her. However, I wasn't about to belittle myself in assassinating my own character by standing in some line for a five minute telephone call. That brother from North Philadelphia had his special friends that held special privileges. More then that, as a true warrior on this planet, I wanted some special privileges as well, therefore, I started looking around to see if I could recognize any familiar faces. I saw this one brother that I knew from my neighborhood. I thought maybe we could get together to go after these chumps; but suddenly I realized he was just another crack-head in my community. So I didn't say anything to him; besides, he was in line to sign up for the five minutes. Honestly, I didn't know what to do. So, I started preparing myself carefully for a mission. The man, who was once considered the hunter on the block for an everyday meal, is now being stalked and prayed on as the hunted. If I was going to move on him, I knew that the job had to be done with one hundred and fifty percent accuracy. If I wanted to gain some proper respect, then this was the only open opportunity available. It was a glorifying opportunity to show everybody who was somebody on that block what the brother Paul was made of, or about. After I've decided to take matters into my own hands, I spent all nights thinking and replaying my moves. It was now *August 13*, and I have still come to no solid conclusion. I still haven't called my family and it was deeply beginning to agitate me. For about another two days, all I could do is watch him closely. Prey on him like a true predator. I watch all his ways of sleeping, relaxing, and being comfortable in an insensible state. I was really trying my hardest to figure out how my performance had to be done exactly. I was going to handle this problem, but I had no direct date issued for the completion of that quest. Indeed I needed a weapon of some kind. I just knew that someone in the unit other then myself was feeling the same way I was feeling at that particular moment. I began asking around, but it was no one strong enough to work with me. It seemed like I was the only one on the block looking and seeking some kind of justice. Again I started thinking to myself and again, I came up with nothing. Looking around for some help, I noticed a thick piece of metal hanging off a gate that separated the two units where we slept. I carefully broke off the metal, and smuggled it into the bathroom where I examined it. It was okay. Everyday during my shower time I would begin to sharpen the tip of the metal as pointy as I could. I wanted the point to be like an ice pick. That way when I started stabbing him, the knife will not break, and the point will go in and out at its smoothest ability. I knew I wanted this man to feel pain. I wanted this man to call out for God. I wanted that ass-hole to understand that life is too short to be taking anyone's life for granted. I wanted him to call out for all of his so called friends. I wanted and needed some telephone time and honestly, I wanted that shit yesterday. I started thinking if I don't call home soon, my family will probably start wondering if something bad has happened to me. I was so frustrated and angry about my current situation; it tired me. I just placed my head down gently on my pillow and fell slightly asleep.

August 17, I was awakened by a loud crash against my bed frame. Looking up, I saw two men fighting roughly with one another. I didn't know where the police were, but from the looks of things they were fighting for some time. I sat myself up on the bed and looked on like everybody else. Jumping down off my bunk to see more of the action, in my view was the man that I loved to hate. He was shouting at the fighters, encouraging the fight to continue. I mean, all do respect to a cat with some heart, but this one individual had some major balls hanging from his body. I started looking around. I notice people looking at him instead of the fight. I knew they wanted to say something, but I guess they were too afraid.

As for myself, like I said before, if I wanted to gain some respect I had to take it. I slipped my skippies on quietly, grabbing my jail house knife in the process by the handle from under my pillow. I was ready for attack. No sooner as another space opened up between my victim and I, like a raging bull, I charged. Running towards him, everybody moved out of my way. Everyone looked on as if I was going crazy. I was not at all going crazy, I was on a mission to get and gain all I could at that moment. My reactions were impressively done. My mind had no time to think twice. My victim looked at me in a surprise manner. A surprise as if I was coming after the wrong person. Little did he understand, he was the main course of the day. I couldn't believe what I was seeing when Mr. Big man himself, started running from little, no respect me. Seeing him take flight was a bit humoristic to many. He wasn't anything but a pusillanimous of a man. Anyhow, that shit encouraged me to be more aggressive. In my head I was like, *"No you don't . . .*

I'll be good and God-damned if you're getting' away from this here." Chasing after him, I reached my left arm out, grabbing him roughly and tightly by the top of his county jumpsuit.

He struggled and pulled, trying to get himself freed. My grip, however, was extremely tight. I yanked him back towards me. Holding him with my left hand; I had my weapon up in the air in my right hand. I slammed in down directly into his chest. Other men ran away as the stabbing begun. His lips puckered and his eyes closed tightly. His face showed an unforgettable emotion. I continued to stab him over and over, placing multiple stab wounds to his abdomen, back, shoulders, arms and face. What a sight, all of his so called friends just looked on in shock. My mind was at total darkness. All I could think about was how disrespectful that sorry bastard has been towards everybody on the block. The remaining people looked on as he fell face first towards the ground. He was in a fetus position. Seeing him fall to the ground, I thought I've killed him. I even heard somebody behind me say that he was dead. He wasn't moving; on top of that, he was bleeding and shaking all over the place. The moment stood in silence. I stood there in an unfinished aggression. Looking down over top of him, I couldn't believe what I've done. Was he dead or not, was the question flowing through my head. Fortunately, his hand moved. He tried to get up off the floor, but his body weight pulled him back down. I continued to stand over top of him, wanting to kick him in the face. He rolled over, the wideness of his mouth shown some blood. His brain was unable to receive the proper oxygen needed to survive.

"Goddamn brother, you killed him! Somebody go and get some help before the slaughter of Tony continues!!" Tony. After all this time, I never knew the cowards name. The name suited him swell, *Tough-Tony*. However, Double T has now been eliminated. In the moment of my success, I quickly returned back to reality. A jail house homicide was something I never wanted, nor needed. I understood that if he dies, I was going up the river, with no life boat or life jacket; man my ass was out. Unfortunately, my feelings felt strange. I didn't feel bad at all. I felt relief in more ways then one. I figured finally, I've gotten that bastard.

After about another one or two minutes went pass, I was attacked and rushed roughly to the ground. I was placed on the floor by some correctional officers. Knife still in hand. While lying there, I turned my head towards the left slowly. I relaxed there silently. They put the cold handcuffs on me. My eyes opened widely. In my visions was Tony. He was just laying there beside me without a smart word said, without any dirty looks and was definitely without a friend in sight. Simultaneously, we were both taken off the block. Me, I was in handcuffs going straight to solitary confinement, better describe as the hole. As for Tony, he was laying on a stretcher going towards the left; straight to the infirmary. Before leaving the block, I looked around the small unit. That moment I suddenly realized that I've just became the new idolized one on the block. I was taken away, and charged with another aggravated assault. That's if he doesn't die, or it would be upgraded to murder one. If it goes to court and I am convicted, I could get up to three years in prison. I must now hope and pray that the chump doesn't die, or in the same token testify against me. Once again, I have placed myself into a shitty position. On top of it all, I still haven't used the telephone. I've just placed myself into a deeper hole. I knew once I arrived in court for the first assault, the D.A. (*District Attorney*) would be more then overwhelmed to bring up this new charge as well. Just to show and prove to the Commonwealth Courts that I was and is still an aggressive individual. And that I could in fact commit the crimes that I am charged with. Sadly to say, I have no regrets.

One day later, I was given a jail house court hearing to see if he was dead, and to see for how long I was going to be in solitary confinement. Like I wished for, Tony was alive, and doing very well. However, I was found guilty and was waiting to see if any farther charges were to be filed from Tony. I was to spend thirty days in confinement. As soon as I got to the hole, I was once again surprised. The scene was completely dirty looking. I was even worried about where they were taken me. Crazy thoughts came upon me. I was thinking that maybe they were taken me somewhere to jack me up like they do in the movies. Good thing I lucked out. That wasn't the case at all. It was just another part of the institution, and the inmates there were as harden criminals as the ones before. The hole was nothing like I expected. The brother already there was what you could consider to be cool, or easy to get along with. Soon as I got there, I was asked if I wanted to use the telephone. I made that call, and boy was I happy to talk to Connie. After that ordeal I just went through, I didn't even have the decency to call my own mother. I didn't know what it was about Connie, but she really has done a magnificent job in satisfying me. Everyday that I am away from her was a day that I thought of her. I wasn't even digging that I was caught up. I figured I was no chump, but at that moment in my life, she was like the only thing, or person I could think about. I have never experienced falling in love before. That's why I am refusing to believe it now. It was my duty to maintain this situation, to tell myself over and over that I was not in love. I just wanted to hear her voice plain and simple. Anyhow, the hole was manageable. It was nothing like people talked about. We were on locked down twenty two and two, meaning, out of twenty four hours in a day, we were locked down in our cells twenty two of them. The other two hours are for recreation. Majority of that free time I stood in my cell contemplation. I only came out to use the telephone, then I would go right back in. I never talked to James, Larry or Billy throughout them thirty days. I thought, thought and thought, but never did I come to a conclusion of figuring out who was coming to court against me for the aggravated assaults. The main thing crossed my mind is that I was also charged with the two murders'. After I've gotten comfortable in the hole, and truly meeting some solid soldiers, it was that time for me to move on back into population. September 13th, a few days early, I was released from confinement. After all that has taken place on H-Block, would you believe that these stupid ass guards had the audacity to return me back to the same housing unit? At first I was surprised, but what the hell, at the same time I said fuck it. I was refusing to allow anyone to see me sweat. Walking on the block with my property was of a shocking experience to all that has witnessed what I've done one month ago. Everything froze. At that point I knew from the way I was feeling, I just had to come in contact with some more bad luck. Honestly, it was no way out; therefore, I needed to maintain my nervousness. Either I was going to get the hell off the block, or in the same, get another victim. Violence is what I lived for, so I had to move silently with the facial expression of emptiness. I looked around the block, my heart pumped with plenty of fear. I looked over my shoulders over and over as if I was being prayed on. Stalked or chased by lions I felt like a man that couldn't handle his own doing. My nerves were unstable, shaking wildly on the inside, but still I never once in my entire life been afraid to die, and I quickly understood that perhaps that moment has arrived. I just knew that his friends were going to try and retaliate on me. As his friends, this would be the appropriate thing to do. I was expecting the worse, besides, I had no weapon. I had no way of protecting myself from any attacks. I was completely naked in a place where I was most hated. I've had some scary moments in my life time of growing up, but at this point, I believed that this was one of the scariest moments I've ever faced. I knew if I was going to die that day, as a warrior, I just had to go out with some dignity.

Looking around I saw these two brothers talking, and pointing in my direction. As soon as I saw this I became hype. I thought oh well, here we go again. The two gentlemen calmly started walking into my direction. I stood up off my bed. I will be crazy if I was going to let them move on me while sitting down. My heart pumped like a new born thoroughbred race horse. I shouted, hoping that some would hear my cry for help, and rescue me from the upcoming brutal beating.

"Yeah, bring it right on mutherfuckers'. If you bastards want me then come and get me!" I didn't know what to do really. Was I supposed to run, or just stand there to face the consequences? So with some dignity, I stood my ground. Out of complete shock to me, one of the men spoke.

"Hold on family, this isn't that kind of party. I just wanted you to know that I am the telephone monitor on the block, and because you just came from the hole you're entitled to a fifteen minute call." The brother had a real country approach behind him, moreover, man did I feel stupid, but at the same time I felt large. I felt as if these men were now trying to become friends with me. On the inside I was laughing like crazy, but on the outside, my face was showing the honor of a true king. I am now being feared by men who just a month ago placed an enormous amount of fear in my heart. I figured being as though I was now feared why not have some fun with it.

My telephone time is now unlimited. Sometimes I am on the phone for forty-five minutes to an hour without anything said. I felt kind of bad for some of the other brothers. I figured if they wanted some special privileges they better get theirs like I got mine. Through it all, I never stopped to realize that I've became Tough Tony, in my own weird way.

"BIRTH OF MY SON"

September 17, 1994, I got on the telephone to once again call my dearest Connie. After three tries of her not answering, I was starting to worry because she's always home whenever I called. Her whereabouts was starting to concern me. I waited and waited, and then I tried again. Still nothing. I was beginning to have bad thoughts. I called Billy's house and he wasn't at home either. I called my mother's home to find out what was going on out there. *Would you believe it, Connie was in the hospital giving birth to our son.*

I have never experienced so much enjoyment in my entire life. My heart was totally overwhelmed with happiness. I was entering a more serious responsibility called fatherhood. Finally, I have someone whom I can call my very own. I have someone who will love me regardless of my mistakes, and whom I'll love with undivided attention. I was so happy, I started feeling somewhat depress. I felt this way because this was my first child, and I was unable to see him come into this world. Furthermore, I was not able to stand by Connie's side throughout this special ordeal. I felt as if I was less of a man. In more ways then one I've told Connie that I would be there for her regardless of my positions, and/or situation. Once again, I have failed her. My happiness has overpowered my depressive state. I quickly over talked my mother, cutting her off briefly. I asked for the telephone number to Connie's room. At that point, I wanted every number available to her. I really couldn't believe that I was going to be a father. I dialed her room number, and it rung around three to four times before she answered it. Her voice was soft and sweet. She sounded as if they took the last bit of everything she held in her small sensuous body. Her voice touched my heart instantaneously. My soul rapidly responded to her warmness. I called out her name gently.

"Connie?"

"Yes Paul, I am here," she responded softly.

"How are you doing baby-girl? I asked as my voice expressed slight anxiety.

"I am all right Paul," she said.

"Connie, please forgive me. I am so sorry that I was unable to stand by your side when you needed me the most. I wanted to stand firmly and watch my child come into this rough world. Yes, I have let you down; and as a man I realize that I have just made one of the biggest mistakes in my life. Please understand that you are my pride and joy. You just gave birth to my only child, and it's the most exceptional and glorifying gift a man could ever receive from his future wife," I said as she listened silently. My hands clutched the telephone receiver tightly, as I expressed my open emotions.

"Paul, please listen to me now. Everything is okay. My mother is here with me, besides, I really do understand now. I know things that happen in life are unpredictable, and it has difficult ways of expressing true love. Paul, I know you love me, and GOD, knows I love you,

I know that if you could have been here to see me through this situation you would've. Now, I ask for your forgiveness for getting upset with you before finding out what was really going on. So, Paul, do you forgive me?" She asked.

"Yes, I forgive you always." I sharply responded.

"So, how's everything coming along in there?" She asked. After that moment, we talked and talked. Honestly, I have never felt what I felt at that particular moment. My emotions have gone wild. I mean, I had no control over being humbly happy, and expressing myself openly through the telephone. I really wanted to brake down and cry, or maybe just express a glorious outburst. Unfortunately, I was still surrounded by criminals. My surrounds made that thought highly impossible to do. Hell, I have just got things in place where I was somewhat comfortable. I just didn't feel like losing my position because I needed to show some weakness for a hot minute. I was now feeling much better. I was satisfied that my baby was mature enough to understand my lifestyle. She was able to open her eyes to see the larger picture. She ignored my stupidity and stood firmly by her man. We now had to focus on our new responsibilities. Connie was the only woman I've ever felt comfortable around. I felt safe around her. I felt as if she would never in a million years go against what I stood for (Honor, Loyalty, Love and Power). I considered myself to be a true soldier; furthermore, as a soldier I needed a good strong woman and Connie was the one. Hopefully she feels the same for me. She's my strength to do this time.

My son was born at Jefferson's University Hospital of Pennsylvania. He was born on Wednesday, September 17, 1994. He weighed in at six pounds three ounces. His name is Paul Yakeem Williams. My son is my life. I was now a father, and very proud to be one. What more can a man ask for.

CHAPTER FIVE

PRELIMINARY COURT

October 17, 1994, I've now been incarcerated for over two months. I was seriously starting to worry about my situation more often. Later on in that same day, I received a letter from the Courts of Common Plea. I was told that a preliminary hearing was scheduled for me on October 20th. As that day came up slowly, I was finally going to find out who it was that was coming to court against me.

October 20, 1994, The day of court. It was a breezy morning and butterflies were rumbling around strongly in my stomach. It was a day of judgment. I wasn't hungry that particular morning. All I wanted was eye contact with the snake or snakes who dear to slash my name in the hands of the devils. Soon we all will find out who they are.

Arriving at the courthouse was everything like I thought it would be; the television news cameras, the highly protected police security. I guess they feared that someone would try and get revenge on my life for being the accused killer of two fellow officers. However, that was the least of my worries. I worried more about being found guilty as a cop killer, then someone trying to seek vengeance. As I entered the court room, I recognized no one. I stood in front of the Honorable Judge, Melvin R. Davis. He was a black man that was really old looking. I felt as if I have already lost the case. His face expressed an old man with serious issues against young blacks. I thought to myself that this day was not at all going good. However, I will come face to face with the individuals who are trying to end my life. My name was finally called after the court house has settled down. As I sat there listening to my charges being read off, my legs started shaking. I realized that I was truly facing some drama. I felt impatient. I felt like making an outburst. I needed to find out who my enemies was. My representation counselor was a clean cut Italian attorney from a very professional law firm. His name was Donnie W. Denovicci. Personally, I feel as if he wanted too much money for a case with no serious evidence; but what the hell $40,000.00 in payments was enough for my freedom, besides, I felt really comfortable with his professional clientele. The District Attorney was this crazy mutherfucker every criminal hated. He's a true enemy to the underground world. Throughout his career he has eliminated some of the biggest and strongest cartels in Pennsylvania's history. His name is Roger "House Nigga" Jones. A black man who hated is own people. Plus this cat can do his work very well. He would always make a complete fool out of the individuals he was prosecuting. I mean this man was good. He has a 96% conviction rate. I figured that my lawyer was excellent enough to handle him. So let get to fighting, I thought to myself. Let's rumble and brawl.

The Judge spoke softly. His voice was extremely to the point. He asked. "Mr. Rogers are there any witnesses against the accused." I sort of smiled at that question. I knew I never left a witness behind. I knew after the hearing I was going to be discharged; that's until I heard.

"Yes, we do your honor!"

My heart stopped for a split second. I was like who the fuck could that be. My lawyer jumped up quickly and exchanged words with the district attorney. Then Mr. Nigga, stated.

"We have two witnesses that could place Mr. Williams on the scene of the double police shootings."

I started thinking rationally. Only one was with me was Billy, and he would've never broken the bond of trust. Unlike the mafia, we're not going down that road.

"The commonwealth also have one witness who could positively identify the defendant as the alleged gunmen in one of the aggravated assaults charges."

As the distract attorney continued, I wondered to myself. Only person I remember trying to put bullet slugs into me was Mr. Harvey Bells, and his son Little Harvey Bells. However, these particular individuals were no snitches. The were considered to be stand up people. Therefore, the courts had nothing. I was surer now, then ever before that I was going to walk. I started moving around in my chair as if I already won, but nothing is guaranteed, besides, there were some shaky feelings.

The DA—"We have two additional witnesses to say that the accuser shot them."
At that point I was getting more and more agitated as this ass-hole kept on talking

The DA—"Unfortunately, your honor, do to Mr. Williams, cowardly acts in our society, one of the witnesses are afraid to corroborate because they fear for the safety of their lives. It seems to me that the reputation of the defendant's aggressive behavior has frightened them completely, moreover, far as the heartless acts of the defendant and the loss of two fine fellow police officers. The witnesses against this man will only come forward during trial; furthermore, we have a sworn and signed affidavit to confirm their identity, and the statement in which I just made. This affidavit will state that indeed the defendant was at the scene of the crime during the time of the police killings."

The Judge—"Very well then. I'll allow it to be held over for trail."

The Judge continued—It's to my knowledge that you do have a witness present here today that is going to testify on one of the aggravated assaults charges?"

The DA—"Yes we do."
I had nothing else on my mind. I needed to find out who these people were. I couldn't wait to look them in the face, just to let them know that their asses were over.

The Judge—"Well according to the law Mr. Rogers' and because this man is charged with two counts of murder and several counts of aggravated assault, I looked closely at the unsupported details of the complaining witnesses, therefore, I have no other choice but to discharge Mr. Williams of two of the aggravated assaults charges."
The district attorney stood in silence. He spoke.

"Very well your honor!"

I felt somewhat relieved, but I knew it was a long ride before it was over.

The Judge—"Bailiff, bring in the witness."

As the door opened slowly, everybody in the court room looked towards the back door. I notice one man sitting in a wheel chair. My heart dropped like a tone of bricks. I felt like I was about to get the death penalty. Everybody oozed as the man rolled in the court room. The witness was this low life, double crossing chump, name *Mr. Harvey Bell*. So take a ride with me as I brief you on the story of this cat.—

(Years back. The situation with his family was simple. Mr. Harvey Bells gave birth to three healthy boys who grew up to be will respected in our neighborhood. The oldest of the three was Little Harvey Bells. This brother always stayed on top of his P's and Q's. He was definitely not going for any stupid behavior from anybody. He maintained all his females respectfully, as well as his money situations. He was the respected and dominate one in their family. Then you had Terrell Bells. This brother was young, wild and full of unwanted energy. For some reason when trouble walked down his alley, it never made it out the other side. He was given the nick name "Funny Fingers" because his last two fingers would start shaking whenever he got angry. He was a real die hard and stand up dude in the game of hard knocks. Unfortunately, Terrell's young life was taken away in the blink of an eye. It was a big drug deal that had gone sour. It appeared that he and his father was having some difficult understanding, so Mr. Bells kicked him into the streets. Terell had no other choice but to survive the best was he could. He was only sixteen years old. Now, you had the youngest of the bunch, Aaron Bells. Aaron was now nineteen years old. He was your ordinary dude. You know, definitely about getting over on anyone who was less educated then he was. He was given the nick name "Lucky Lesson" because of the way he always somehow slipped through the cracks of getting' his ass murdered. Everyone knew what he was into; everyone knew that it would be only a matter of time before he ran across that special bullet with his name on it. But because of Little Harvey's reputation, Aaron was able to walk the streets unharmed. I personally never liked the little snake. Because of Terell, and Little Harvey's friendship, I had no other choice but to respect the man. If anyone wanted to put Aaron in the dirt, it was definitely my brother James. Like they say, "every dog has their day," and Aaron day was creeping up slowly.

At one time or another, our families was a close as any family could ever have been, moreover, after the death of "Funny Fingers" Aaron and Little Harvey, was excepted into my life as well as my families lives. We were well known in the neighborhood to hold things together. These people were my family. Furthermore, I was extremely close to "Fingers". He was there for me when ever I needed someone to chit chat with. That was my main man. (RIP HOMIE) Sadly things changed. Our two families had a major fallin' out over some cocaine, money and plenty of weaponry. I was the only one in my family to do business with the Bells family. But after I was doubled crossed on some cocaine by this family, the business was closed down. Furthermore, I declared war with the Bells. Now as I sit and think about it, shit is starting to make sense. I mean, me being locked up for one of the aggravated assaults was becoming more and more ironic. I can now understand why I never knew who this bastard was, but it still doesn't explain how he made it to court. I just thought of our situation as a strange coincidence. I was told that Mr. Harvey Bells was shot twice on the left side of his lower body part, as a warning behind something his boys done over some much more money and drugs. This incident took place on *August 7*th *1994,* the same time that our families were declared enemies. Damn! I was arrested on *August 9*th *1994,* and the whole time I was on the streets, them no good sons of bitches has given me up to the police. They always said drugs will destroy a happy family. I guess I am living proof of that theory (So close and in such an invisible form). Besides I was never in a million years prepared for the testimony giving in that court room that day. To hear a member of the Bells family identify me as the person who put the slugs into his body was heart crushing. To be a slimy nigga was one thing, but to sit and look me in the eyes, to testify against me was down right fucked up. I always knew my days was numbered, I mean, if you were in the game by dealing drugs and not giving me what I wanted, then yes, we did have some bad complications. In fact, that was the circumstances with them and I. They had plenty of that green currency, and my currency was starting to look funny. Don't get the wrong idea. I will never knock a man for getting that money, but out off all the people to get over on, these cats got over on me. I found out that every time we needed to re-up on our supply, Little Harvey, would somehow smuggle in an extra three in one half kilos for him and his family without my knowledge. A long time ago this base head name Joe Jones, nick name "BUGGIE" turned himself around and started getting plenty of money. Even though he was a real low life, he was the one to do business with. You had other cats like "Big Charlie" but Charlie never dealt with niggas who wasn't purchasing ten bricks and up. Charlie was too expensive for our thin blood. So we stuck with Buggy. Now, when it was time to do business with Buggy I was never present. I was told by Little Harvey that the coward was afraid of me. I figured that was cool, besides, he just let me know that my name had meaning. From what I understand he was suppose to purchase only five kilos, that's all we were working with. Five bricks was only 180 ounces of uncut, pure cocaine. Thinking of Little Harvey as a true partner I felt the deals were being done without any problems. However, Buggie on the other hand and because of who we were, would give us an extra three in one half bricks as a front, in which we had to return the money later. We paid the same price he paid for it. (17,000.00) We sold them on the streets for (22,000.00). But Little

Harvey never tells me about the front; knowing or hoping that Buggie and I will never be in the same place at the same time. He and his family started another small business on the side which led to his father being shot. As a young man coming up in the rough world of the hood, a front of three and one half kilos was something major, not only to me, but to our business. Finding out this cruel evidence that a so called friend has done to me has left me dumbfounded. A friend that I've accepted into my heart as a brother. My mind went on tilt. I was losing out easy on thousands. It was nothing he could tell me to justify his actions. So, everything that was ours on the streets, I collected and I kept . . . It's funny how it all played out. One morning while cruising about, I stopped at a nearby fast food joint for an early morning breakfast meal. Soon as I walked through the doors I notice Buggy, standing at the counter. No soon as he saw me, he grabbed his meal and stormed towards the nearest exit. Cutting him off, I spoke.

"Buggy, hey playa. How ya doing?" His eyes showed fear. "I just know you wasn't about to leave. I have been meaning to talk to you."

"I'm sorry Paul, but now is a real bad time. I was just on my way to pick up my daughter from school . . . she's sick."

"Common man, this will only take a minute" I looked deep into his eyes just to frighten him just a little more.

"Okay, I need for you to make it quick though."

"Well it's about my financial status. I mean, my money is okay, but it could be better. I know with your help Harvey and I could look forward to bigger and better things."

"So what are you trying to say?

"What I'm trying to say is with your help, our money could increase tremendously. I need for you to look out for us a little more. You know, bring some more powder to the table so we can really eat." His eyes lit up in disappointment.

"A little more powder!" He shouted. "What do you mean a little more powder? I already give you and your man three in one half bricks as a front. For GOD sakes, y'all only buy five at a time. Tell me something Paul, how much more help do you want from me? I give it to him on every business deal." My words were stuck in time. I already understood that he was afraid of me, so I figured why would this chump lie to me. I had to change the ball game.

"Owl, Buggie man, I was just fucking around. Look at you getting all upset and shit." His face stood cold at my sudden change. "You go right ahead and pick up your little girl. I apologize. I just wanted to say thank you for everything you do for us. You a good dude Buggie. I hope we can do this again sometime."

"Likewise," he said, while hurrying to get as far away from me as possible. As for the way I was feeling, words will never describe it in detail. I was so upset, I never ordered my food.

As soon as I arrived at my spot, I realized it was time to call an urgent meeting. After I called everyone, I sat on my steps and waited for their arrival.

The news I just received ached my heart with strange thoughts. I wondered why he would do something like this to me. I always knew, or felt something fishy, but couldn't exactly pinpoint the betrayal. "I would have never shown disrespect to either of them. I wonder who else is in on this ordeal." Paul wondered. Paul waited patiently; but angrily he thought of Little Harvey, James, Billy, and Larry. They needed to return his emergency pager call; he left the code of 612. It was for them to return as soon as it was received. Paul held the mobile phone in his right hand, he never thought of placing it down. In his other hand, he held an orange soda. Unfortunately, his stomach was filled with rumbles of disappointment, giving him the incompetent need for the soda. Therefore, he placed the soda down and just sat on the porch. Turning the corner was a clean white 1993 sports addition BMW, with deep dish momo rims. The soft musical sound of Shirley Murdocks song, *As We Lay*. Paul's eyebrows rose in relief. He knew he had to maintain his self-composure. A small cracked smile appeared across Paul's face. He inhaled and exhaled a deep breath of air. Billy parked the car, halfway in the street, and halfway on the curb. Paul stood to acknowledge the two men. Billy held out his hand to Paul, for a well respected greeting, and so did James.

"Hey little brother?" James said, trying to relax the moment. He still expressed curiosity in his voice. "Yeah, we both received your pager at the same time," Billy stated. Paul looked up at them and said nothing. James continued.

"So, is everything alright?" he asked in a worry like tone.

"No, everything is all bad", Paul responded, looking down at the ground and shaking his head. Billy frowned his face in wanting to know the news. "I've just found out some unexplained information about Little Harvey, and the business we do together." James sat down next to Paul. Billy continued to stand firmly with his arms folded.

"What kind of information did you find out? Would you care to elaborate a little more," Billy said acidly.

"No!" Paul shouted to Billy. "Not yet. I want everyone to be here. Then I'll explain everything to everybody." Billy sat down on the opposite side of James to await Larry, and Little Harvey. At that moment of thought, silence and terrible images traveled throughout the curious minds of the three men. Moments later, Music of *Cool G. Rap, "Got A Brother On The Run"* ricocheted off the walls of Paul's home. A black Pathfinder drove to park in front of Paul's house. Each man had on different songs. Larry in the luxury cream coated car, and Little Harvey, in the big boy Path. The music went silent, as they turned off their cars. Larry took off his glasses, as he walked up towards the three quiet men on the steps. Harvey got out and placed something into the trunk. Very nonchalantly, he turned and looked at everyone, and continued to do as he pleased. As Harvey was holding the men up; Billy became a little impatient.

"Damn, can you show us a little more respect!" Knowing the problem was about him, James looked on with the eyes of mild hatred."

Hold on a moment, I'll be right there!" Harvey shouted back, as if things were unimportant. Larry was a bit shocked at the not so good, hidden attitudes expressed in the men. Even though the news was about Harvey, he still had the balls to make matters worst.

All the men were now together. Paul turned to look at Harvey with the eyes of an unbelieved and extremely hurt man. He spoke softly.

"Harvey," he said looking down at his feet, and back up into his eyes to be face to face. "I've just been talking to your close friend Buggy, in a fast food joint, and he informed me of some unfortunate news." He continued. "News of a friend who cleverly corrupted another friend out of his money." Harvey eyes opened with sudden worry to get the full understanding of Paul's message. Everyone else, stood with silent mouths, but opened ears. Paul continued. "He stated things to me that dumbfounded me completely. I approached him to put more pressure on him for another two kilos or so and he informed me that he gives you three and a half extra ones on every pick up delivery."

"ALL SHIT!" Billy shouted, interrupting the bondage of complete silence. "You mean to tell me that you've been a sneaky sidewinder; keeping almost four kilos from Paul's knowledge," Billy's words expressed deep emotions.

"Look here, I don't need to justify any of my actions. "Yes, he have been producing extra weight to me, but-

"But! But nothing'," James said cutting him off of his words. "You know good and goddamn well what respect and disrespect mean. You and Paul have been doing business together for some time now. You were the only one who could do the negotiating, with that Buggy." Paul stood back as James expressed his feelings in the matter. Billy stood next to an old photo of them all together. He looked at Larry, and Larry turned away. Billy looked back to Harvey with disappointment. James was just about finish. "That means, that you were keeping plenty of money from Paul, and was never going to tell him about it, until he found out himself, like he did today."

"What is everybody trying to accuse me of?" Harvey shouted with aggression. "I did what I did and can't any of you change that. I told Larry about it like-

"What did you just say?" Paul interrupted. "You told Larry?"

"Yeah, I told Larry! What part of it you don't understand.

"Larry, you knew of this bull-shit even when you knew of my financial backups. You still wouldn't say anything."

"Look here little bro, I-

"Fuck that little bro shit, Larry!" Paul said cutting Larry off. I was down on my ass with bills, and you two was fucking me over like an enemy would." He continued. "How and why would y'all do something like this to me?" Billy sat down, with a surprising look on his face. He knew Paul was in the right. He was willing to stand behind Paul on whatever Paul decided to do. It was a very sad moment for them all. But betrayal was something they never seen before. It has hit home, by men most closets to Paul.

"I had nothing to do with the money!" Larry shouted. Larry felt the need to explain, before he looked completely guilty. "Harvey stated to me that he was receiving extra powder from that bastard, Buggy. I was under the assumption that Paul knew of the extra powder. I had nothing to do with what was done with the extra powder." James stood in a corner clenching and unclenching his jaw muscles. He was very angry with Harvey. Larry finished. "Paul, I really thought you knew of this ordeal. You are my brother, and I love you. When you and Harvey decided to do business on the side, I figured good. The side dealings were definitely between you two." Everyone stood and watched Larry express his words of sorrow. "Furthermore little brother, I feel as if it's still between you guys. Now I must say that you two better settle this bull-shit, and keep my mutherfuckin' name out of this non-sense." Larry walked off the porch towards his car. Got in, turned on the engine; turned his head back to look at the four remaining men, and shook his head in disappointment. He turned the steering wheel and sped away.

Billy looked at James and whispered silently.

"Now what James."

"I don't quite know. We must leave everything else up to Paul and Harvey."

"But what Harvey has done was real dirty. It was well against the bond of our trusting ways," Billy stated very seriously.

"Well Harvey, it appears to me that you owe me a few thousand dollars," Paul said.

"Like hell I do!" Harvey shouted back huskily.

"Harvey, you know that Buggy is afraid of Paul, and Paul could have easily taken everything he wanted from Buggy, but he didn't for the respect of yawls friendship. So, he dealt with the high prices, and everything else that went along." Billy continued. "You know that Larry, James, and I do our own thing, but what you've done to Paul was wrong. We believe that you could at least reimburse him with something."

"Man, I am not going to give him a damn dime," Harvey responded, with a mild smirk. Harvey got into his jeep, and also sped off. He never turned back to look at either of the men.

"He is a self-centered bastard," Billy said.

"What are you going to do Paul?" James asked.

"Well first of all, Larry was right, the problem is between us. I'll deal with it on my time" Paul responded.

"How much did he burn you out of?" Billy asked.

"About forty grand, depending on how long it's been going on," Paul said, hurting on the inside.

"Well, I am done here as well. Paul I want you to give me a call, to let me know what you are going to do." James continued. "I am going home, so, Paul I need your car keys. My car is in the shop getting cleaned. I'll bring it back later on tonight." Paul dug into his pants pocket and pulled out a small row of keys. Took two keys off and tossed James the rest. The keys to Paul's red Acura Legend was designed funny. James paid them no mind. James walked away; arrived to the car, got in, and drove away. He beeped the horn as he drove away to say his goodbyes.

"What are you going to do?" Billy asked Paul. "What would you do, if you were in my position?" Paul responded, and finished. "I am going to declare war on Harvey, and all of those he's involved with.

"What about your brothers' Larry and James?" Billy asked.

"No, the question is what about you?" Paul counter asked.

"Me!" Billy responded shocked.

"Yes you." Paul looked deep into Billy's eyes. He felt the taste of a loyal man. Billy spoke. "Hell Paul, I can't believe you would ask me something like that. You my man and I'll be there for you until death do us part," Billy said, and then continued. "I never really liked that mutherfucka anyway." Billy said, smiling at the thought of ending Harvey's life. Paul smiled back at Billy.

"Don't worry about James and Larry; I'll handle them. The two men sat on the sofa quietly for a brief moment. Billy rose to his feet.

"I'll call you later family, meantime think wisely, and remember that I love you like a brother."

"Thank you Billy," Paul said. "You're a good friend."

"The best," Billy said. Paul smiled and watched Billy depart from their tight handshake. Billy drove away, and Paul walked into the house. The meeting was over, and the moment of truth has begun. The war against Harvey and his associates, has taken its first steps . . . .

CHAPTER SIX

THE DEATH OF A FRIEND

Meanwhile, later that same night, Billy continued to have thoughts of John-John and David. He realized that he needed to drive out 31st and Tasker to check up on the younger brothers who looked up to him and Paul. After knowing if they were alright or not, he had to make another stop at a close friend house named, Yolanda Davis. He was going by for old times, and have a romantic night with the woman he thought of settling down with. After not talking to Paul, Billy was really starting to miss him deeply. Paul and James were the ones he really trusted. He knew that Larry and Little Harvey became good friends. Billy stood empty-minded behind Larry's audacious actions towards his own brother. "Maybe Larry has his reasons," Billy thought. Even though, they were not as close as they were years ago and he would've been there for Larry, if needed. Little Harvey was the one Billy never trusted totally. Little Harvey knew the rules and decided to disrespect and use bad tactics towards Paul, while doing business. Once hearing of Harvey's father going to court on Paul, Billy was devastated. Everyone knew Paul never played any games when it came down to his money situations. "And neither did I," Billy said as he pulled up on the corner of Tasker street. The streets were happening; it was around 11:30pm, and people hung out like it was twelve noon. The corner bar threw a celebration party for their new opening night. The Chinese Store on the other side of the bar remained opened until 2:00am. Billy put the BMW in park, opened the door, and stepped out like a glamorous superstar. He changed his clothing for a special night with Yolanda. His off-white size 8.5 crocodile, mid rippled sole boots, went perfectly with his thin cotton black Giorgio Armani slacks. His boots had three buckles that hung loose, with two holes for a small shoe string lace, to tie at the top. The buckles was making every step of his laid back walk jiggle, as if he had spears like a cowboy would. His crispy slacks hung just above the last buckle to cover the laced up shoe laces. His matching crocodile belt clipped together with smoothness that captured his nine millimeter Ruger, comfortably. His long silk black and white dress shirt blew helplessly in the calm wind, as he walked from his car to one of the little brothers whom he was looking for. Other eyes around looked on in complete jealousy and envy. Billy felt the hard stares, but it mattered none. The blue stainless steel nine millimeter, hidden under his silk shirt, was ready for any dumbness. Billy talked, and his hands moved swiftly, symbolizing every word. Billy wore his hair low with waves. He never liked jewelry; he considered it to be a waste of good cash.

The little brother he walked up to was nothing more than a thug, waiting for his set of county blues, or browns in the penitentiary. He wore a black baggy hooded top, a baggy pair of Levi jeans, and a pair of dark brown timberland boots with real loose shoe laces. The young brother walked around with a snub nose 38 special with six shots. Paul and Billy always tried talkin' knowledge to him, but it was no good. So, they just allow him to be, as he pleased.

"How's everything around here Bobby?" Billy asked, while looking around the area.

"Everything around here is so-so. You know, a little bit of this, and a little bit of that," The young sixteen year old kid stated, while holding his crouch. Bobby always talked about going to war, or dying for Billy or Paul. But they both knew that he was only blowing out hot words; so, they paid him no serious attention.

"Well, I am about to go around to Paul's mother house, to drop off some cash for Paul. I guess I'll be seeing you around little buddy," Billy said as he turned to walk away. Getting closer to his car, the young boy shouted.

"Okay, Alright, Billy . . . I'll be seeing you around! He continued. "Make sure you tell Paul that I am holding things down for him until he gets home!" Bobby smirked at the future-less kid. He got into the BMW, and started the soft engine. Placed it in reverse, and looked through the rearview mirror to go backwards. He noticed Connie crossing the street.

"What the fuck," Billy said aggressively in the car. "Here she is, out on the streets after twelve with no respect for Paul," Billy said. He wanted to ask her what was she doing, but her bull-shit was something he hadn't had time for. Billy figured that maybe she was just buying something to eat, or maybe she was creeping from some niggas home. Billy, having the car in reverse, stepped on the gas peddle mildly, to see who she was with, or what direction she was coming from. Backing up, his eyes widened acidly. She was coming from the area where Little Harvey, Larry, and plenty of other females and brothers stood. He thought no more of Connie's sneaky ass. His new aggression was focused on that sonuvabitch, Little Harvey.

"That fucking rat and his family need to die," Billy said out loud in the car. His windows were slightly tinted and halfway down. Billy slammed the gear back in park. Turning the ignition off, he opened the door and stepped out. Bobby eyes sparked with fear, as he saw Billy's face. Bobby reached for his 38 special, pulling it out down by his side. He figured Billy was in some trouble. Billy's mind was fully in a predatory state. Little Harvey looked up and noticed Billy's face. The heat from his face turned his eyes a dark red. Billy's face expression was frowned up like he had stomach cramps. Larry stood surprise to see Billy without Paul being home. Billy, spoke.

"Harvey, may I have a word with you?" Billy asked politely, so that they could come to a positive understanding. Billy wanted to know why his family was going to court on Paul.

"Not right now, I'm busy," Harvey said sarcastically. "What the fuck you mean, you busy mutherfucker!" Billy shouted. Larry eyes sprouted in major concern.

"Wait, wait, wait, wait," Larry said. "We are not going to have this here." Bobby realized who Billy was angry at; even though he feared them all, he stood by Billy's side and asked,

"Billy what's going on? Do you need a piece?" Billy just ignored Bobby's request. Bobby looked at the back of Billy's shirt and noticed the hug lump. He then smiled, realizing that Billy was on top of his game like always.

"Okay tough guy, if you want to see me, let's put everything aside and step into the streets to handle this like men, and old friends," Billy suggested. Larry and Harvey both knew that Billy fought like a professional boxer. Harvey wasn't stupid.

"I'm not doing any fighting Billy," Harvey stated, revealing his chrome glock nine millimeter that sat comfortably on his waist line. Larry knew things were a little too hot to control, so he moved to the side when he saw Harvey's foolish gesture to Billy. Billy's body now covered in steam. His eyes turned a darker red.

"So you want gun play, is that what you want!" Billy shouted in anger. Everybody stepped back, away from Billy and Harvey, when they started noticing Billy reaching for his Ruger. Simultaneously, so did Harvey.

Almost in an instant, the streets roared with thunder. Billy went for the draw first. He pointed the nine, and fired shots accurately in Harvey's direction. The bullets flowed smoothly in the air, one by one, two by two, and three by three. Little Harvey was no slouch though. He moved out the way before Billy could hit him. Being in the same game as Billy, Harvey knew exactly what to expect. Harvey got in position to fire off a couple of shots, when he heard, and then felt two bullets strike his chest. It stumbled him backwards, almost placing him on the ground. Lucky for him, his car was parked behind him; it captured his fall. The bullets struck his bulletproof vest like a twenty pound sludge hammer. Harvey maintained his balance and fired back at Billy. Six fast squeezes of the trigger at Billy, ripping small diameter holes into Billy's dress shirt and abdomen area. Holding his chest to breathe, Harvey felt the wooziness for the lack of oxygen. It felt like his chest cavity was cracked from Billy's bullet blows. Harvey staggered to his car, firing three more times at Billy, who was now barely holding himself up from collapsing. The three extra bullets Harvey spit out, hit Billy again in the chest, and graze his head. Larry drew his pistol; but didn't fire at either man. The little kid Bobby took off running no sooner as the guns were pulled, and the loud shots rumbled through the neighborhood. Harvey, stumbling to his car, opened the door, sat in the driver's side, turned the ignition key, threw it in drive, and slammed on the gas peddle with the force of panic and fear. He looked at Billy as he drove past. Billy was now down, eyes facing the sky. Hearing no sound, but his heart slowing down the thumps of life. Harvey was really zeal to get away, causing his car to swerve; missing Billy's BMW by inches. Harvey's passenger side window was shattered. Below it, in the door, was three bullet holes. Billy's car stood unmarked. Harvey was now gone. Billy, crawled, moaned, and swerved in the direction to make it to his car. Unfortunately, for him;

his muscles felt the easiness of relaxation. His body gave-way in the center of the streets. He was unable to move. However, his life was still maintaining its consciousness. Crowds of loud noised people came from nowhere, to watch the brutality of another human fight endlessly for their life off acts of senselessness. Billy continued to moan, and call out for Larry's help.

"Larry! Larry! Oh, God Larry! Larry please don't let me die out here on this corner." He continued, "Please, Larry! Where are you?" Larry stood in the ally way looking. He feared of what to do. He really wanted to help, but he didn't want his name coming up in another shooting, or homicide. He wanted to leave the scene as soon as possible, but the sight of Billy needing his help held him there like a fit tight glove. Larry couldn't stand it anymore, so he rushed over to Billy; but now it was too late. Billy was dead. He had bled to death. If in minutes, someone would've helped him and saved some of his blood, he would've survived. Arriving on the scene was the emergency rescue team. They worked on him in the streets because Billy was a close friend to one of the surgeons. They pumped, blew, fought, and shouted; but the life of Billy Green was gone for good. They continued to rush him in the ambulance, and getting him to the nearest hospital. Billy's family ran up after he was gone. They shouted and cried as they looked at the thick blood of their beloved one. It sat helplessly in the center of the street, right next to his untouched, clean BMW. As the crowd walked away, two voices appeared out of nowhere.

"Wasn't that the guy who gave us the big ten dollars today?" David asked John-John.

"Yeah man, I think so," John-John responded. "Come on David, lets go back into the house," John-John said. The two boys ran together. David and John-John were never caught asking people for money in the streets again . . . .

As for Mr. Harvey Bells, he would do some of the transactions for us as well. Everything was all starting to come together. This family had it in for me. It was only right to eliminate me as soon as they could, by the best ways that they could. Little Harvey and I have had some wild shoot outs at each others team. We went back and forth at each others property as if it was no tomorrow. Our war has taken place around the same time Mr. Harvey was shot. Now it was the eliminating process. Not only did they have huge testicles, but they knew how to utilize their brain in overcoming any problems in their way. Here I am sitting in the courtroom being fucked by some real so call killers. This entire scene has freaked me out.

Mr. Harvey came into the courtroom in a Goddamn wheelchair. Only thing I was able to do was to sit there and look on in complete silence. At that moment I started to really worry about my future. His acting skills were paying off that day. I figured, if he was acting that good at only the preliminary hearing; just imagine what he could do at trial. The things he spoke of touched the souls of everybody listening. Hell, he even had me feeling sorry for the old bastard.

I even thought for a split second that I was in fact guilty. As he finished up singing like the mob, he rolled from the testimony stand, getting himself closer to where I was sitting. I looked him straight in the eyes; the double crosser turned his head away; but before doing so, he let off a small smirk, directing it towards me. At that point, I knew I was going to kill him. As for my testimony, there wasn't any given. I was stripped of the opportunity to quote my version of what took place, where I was and how my rights were being violated of due process. The Judge looked at me as being guilty! After Mr. Harvey's testimony the honorable Judge stood me up and spoke. "Mr. Williams, based upon the evidence, and from what I've heard here today, gives me the understanding that I have more than enough evidence to prepare, schedule and provide this case with the safest constitutional proceeding available."

"Yeah, right," I thought.

The Judge continued.

"Therefore, you are now being once again held without bail, and we'll be prepared for trial to decide the appropriate outcome of your case . . . . Thank you . . . Please take this man away."

"This old grouchy, evil ass bastard," I thought to myself as I just sat there dumbfounded. At this point I had nothing to say anyway. I felt like nothing. I wasn't even giving the chance to defend myself, and my lawyer went along with everything as if he was playing a game of unskilled chess. There I was looking at a man once again who just testified against me and could do nothing about it. This man once told me that I was like another son to him.

Getting up to leave, I looked around sadly. I wanted to see my family, or show my beloved brothers who the betrayer was. My family was sitting in the back right hand corner. I saw everybody; however, neither James, Billy, or Larry showed up for my hearing. I expressed devastation.

After looking at my mother, Connie, and the new born baby (Little Paul), I felt as if I was never going to make it home again. The preliminary hearing for the police killings' has been scheduled for another day. A large breath of steamed air rushed throughout my lungs. I was looking for and needed desperately of some sympathy. I felt as if I've already lost both cases before trial has even started. I understood from that point on that I was going to be incarcerated for the next eight to twelve months awaiting, and preparing for trial. Unbelievable was my present state of emotion. I was about to go to trial against people who I once considered my own family. It felt much better knowing who was trying to get me prosecuted. For some reason, or reasons I still don't understand how he made it to court. Regardless of how close we once were as family, this so called getting justice shit is now much bigger then anything. Something just had to be done about this. I knew it was only the matter of time before someone seeks revenge for me.

Arriving back at the Detention Center, I was flaming with hatred. I wanted to call my brothers to find out why they haven't showed up for my hearing; unfortunately, I wasn't in that mood either. I wanted to let out some frustration. I have never experienced the feeling, or cruelty of betrayal. I was angry. My body was starting to weaken by the minute. I just needed some rest, or somebody to tell me what just happened.

I was starting to second guess myself, by being in a confused manner; thinking that I shouldn't have been dealing with them snake ass Bells in the first place. I understood that maybe this was my time to be the seeker of revenge. I have done plenty of bad and highly disrespectful things towards people; however, from my point of view, they were people who deserved every bit of my disrespectful behavior. Furthermore, my past actions don't justify what has happened today. In my younger days of growing up, I've never once thought about betraying the people I loved. I always believed in unconditional loyalty towards a friend. As a man, I had to understand what exactly I was up against or into. In time I started to realize my position in life, unfortunately, I was too much of a stand up guy for my own good. I was in a bad situation and was in too deep; therefore, I stayed in the game. I tried carefully to prepare myself for the extreme, or the unexpected, but now my luck has run out.

The cruel things that I've done towards an individual were simply because of my inner excitement; the thrill to be recognized, but mostly because they deserved it. Now I can believe in the old saying "That God does his best work in mysterious ways." I am now a true believer of his work. I have become face to face with my mysteriousness. There wasn't anything I could do about my current situation until trial. I couldn't believe the disrespect I was receiving from people who once looked me in my eyes to tell me they love me, and they were willing to die in order to prove that love. All I could think of was how I was going to give them all a painful experience of my revenge. Even though Mr. Bells was the only one to testify against me from that family, I was upset enough to make all of them pay the consequences for their father's actions. I must retaliate; it was now becoming my every thought. It was starting to dictate my emotions. It was going to be done, no sooner then I was released back into our community; but for now, I must prepare myself for court. I must not overlook the dangerousness of my situation. It was said from an older convict that a young man received five to ten years in an upstate prison for a fixed up aggravated assault charge. I realized it was now or never; besides, I still had to fight a double murder charge. However, I was not trying to do five years behind them double crossing bastards.

I spent days preparing and planning a successful court outcome. It was right after that upsetting court date that everything seemed to go haywire. ***October 22,*** of that year, a little more than a month after little Paul was conceived. I will never forget the day of this traumatizing episode. It was just an ordinary day of doing county time; same shit, but different day. It was around noon, and I've just returned on the block from the jails cafeteria. I have been trying to make contact with Billy/Geeze for a few days now so that I can have my witnesses ready for court, and in the same, for general conversation. Unfortunately, like the other four times I tried to call before I went to chow, there was no answer. Billy, he's something special to my heart. Knowing that we were some unwanted brothers in our own community, we still found the strength to maintain the whole neighborhood. I just sat on the bed smiling, continuing to think of Billy. Remembering the last time we communicated. We talked about him taking the rest of the remains of our money that was just collected down to my mother's house for safe keeping. This is the type of man Billy is, the kind that always take care of important business when needed. Besides, he stated that he was going back in the neighborhood because he wanted to check up on the younger brothers, just so they could be on the safe side of things. I was now doing time; therefore I was unable to check up on them. I told Billy, to be careful and to watch his ass. We both knew of our enemies in South Philly, moreover, we both understood that we both didn't give a flying fuck. Billy, he was mainly my oldest brothers' friend. His name is Al-min Williams a.k.a. Deeze. Around the time I was growing up, Billy and Al-min, had a lot of respect. They went down in our neighborhood history as "_Deeze & Geeze_"; the two nigga's who were some real outlaws. I really admired them both and wanted to be just like them. Unfortunately, all that came crashing down when Al-min was sentenced to life in prison for a first degree murder rap. Billy was devastated. My brother has been in prison for over seven years now and his chances of seeing the streets again were very slim. The two of them was as close as they could come; therefore, Billy, Harvey, James, and Larry, and I accepted as brothers. It's now twelve forty two, and I am undecided if I wanted to get back on the telephone to reach Billy. So I came to the conclusion to just lay back and think of my past times some more. I started thinking of this chick named Denise Jamerson; I called her "Shorty Smalls." She was a real supporting person as a friend, but I couldn't stop myself from thinking of her sexually. So, I thought of her and slowly slipped into a world of wild passion.

. . . .

"A DREAM OF PASSION"

Never have I dreamed of a woman such as this; nor, have I imagined, or experienced a woman of such beauteousness. This woman is my queen. She's my love, my soul-mate, my knowledge. Indeed, she's ***"My True Desire For Passion"*** . . . .

Her eyes, they sparkle like a diamond floating to the bottom of the ocean, reflecting off the properness of pure blue ocean water. Her lips, they are as soft as a feather of a new born bird. She's only five feet five inches tall, with the heart of exquisiteness. Her face brightens my daily days with energy like the sun, with the overwhelming sensation of love and joy like the moon. She has a unique body, a body that's design for pure lusciousness. She's the completed piece to my unfinished puzzle. She has concluded my craving for unconditional love. A love that has been unidentified for years . . . .

On our day of romance, I'll approach my love nervously; but indeed courageously. In my left hand, I shall hold the sentimental value of a beautiful white rose. With my right hand, I shall place it over my heart gently, to honor my heart in her name, and in the name of love. This woman of mine is indeed one of a kind. Furthermore, this will be our special night, a night that is coherent enough for many to understand. The introduction of our compassionate breath taking love, has slightly reached its destination. Therefore, I shall begin to prepare myself generously for the upcoming night ahead. She's my lady, and she's oh so beautiful. She makes me feel over-zealous with her everlasting persistence to comfort my heart with sympathy, and warmness in her own adorable way. My love; her name is (***DENISE,***) "D.E.N.I.S.E." . . . . She's the precious jewel in me, that sites in the darkness, deep in the center of my soul . . . .

"The ***"D"***, stands for her desirable ways to make love. The diligently way she expresses the desperation whenever she devote her womanhood to a man. The way she describes her travels to an un-dictated destiny, in search of true love. The ***"E"***, is for the way she has always embraced my emotions. The way she always knew how to enhance my emptiness. I am now ready to commit myself to her. I am now ready to enter into her warmness with an enormous erection. The ***"N"***, is for the nastiness that humbly sits deep within her naughty mind. In which, one will always admire and never neglect. The ***"I"***, is for her intelligence and self independence. The way she has always illustrated her impassioning intellectualism before me. Now, my love is incomparable. The ***"S"***, is for the sensitivity in her sensuous sexuality. My love is her love, and her love is mine. Her love is full of serious great-heartedness. The last ***"E"***, is for the enjoyment that we both share together as one. The enthusiasm she provide in my heart whenever I see her smile. The experiences we shared throughout good and bad ordeals. Our entire episode has been exceptionally overwhelming. Therefore, together we'll always be able to build our world on an empire of passionate love. One day I'll be with my love in reality; until that day comes, I'll satisfy myself with imaginary thoughts of her beauty. I will be hoping, wishing, praying, and wondering what it will feel like to close my eyes every night; just to be in her presence, loving her for eternity. To feel our hearts pounding and pumping together to one rhythm. The sound of our hearts pumping together will be classical music to my ears. She is the beloved one to my broken heart. I am now thinking of her as she touches me all over my body. Gently rubbing her long nails up and down my back, "her hands is oh, so soft, and warm." She's definitely my soul mate. She's, ***"My True Desire For Passion"*** . . . .

. . . .

CHAPTER SEVEN

MEMORIES

A voice appeared.

"Family, hey there family."

I became heated. My dream of passion has now been smashed to pieces. I opened my eyes slightly to see who they were talking to, and to find out why they were so loud around me, while I was resting. Opening my eyes; in my vision was this tall, skinny, light brown skinned brother, whose character showed humbleness as an individual; moreover, he wasn't very talkative to too many people. Standing close to where I was, I didn't know what to expect. Quickly, I jumped to my feet, shoeless and all. I really wondered if he smelt some trouble; furthermore, I wasn't about to give up any extra telephone time to someone who really didn't deserve it. Now on my feet, I figured if he wanted to prove his masculinity, then he should've done it while I was sleep.

"What's up," I said while wiping the restful stains from my eyes. I stared directly into his eyes. I detected his fear. I expressed myself as if I was a cold hearted person. My hands balled tightly together into a fist. I spoke again. "What is it that you want? And why are you babbling over top of me like you are fuckin' crazy?" Everyone felt the tension rise above normal. Again I observed the nervousness showing throughout his facial expression. Finally, the gentleman spoke.

"I apologize for awakening you," he said. "My name is **Earl Wilson**, and what I have to say is very important. I mean no disrespect, but I know who you are. Your name is Paul/Gangsta, and you're from 31st and Tasker down in South Philly." I stood silently to listen on. His voice trembled and his body language started expressing images of a scared man. I spoke my words.

"Yes, that is who I am," I said.

"You have a friend name Billy Green, but most people call him Geeze?" He said. I looked at him questionable and figured; here we go again with another dude trying to become friends with me. So what he knows me and Billy, that doesn't prove anything.

"Yeah I do know Billy, the one you're referring to; but, the question is why does his name speak from your mouth?" I asked sarcastically. Besides, I knew this character Earl wasn't in my league, furthermore, I was still sleepy and his conversation was starting to bore me.

"Well it's no need to get like that," Earl said. "I just wanted you to know that I have always recognized you from the moment you entered on this unit. I was really happy you took care of that low life Tony," he said looking as if I freed him from Tony's torture. At that point I spoke with aggression.

"I don't mean to cut you off from your fascination with how I handled or handle my business, but is this conversation going anywhere, because you're really starting to beat around the bush. What was your reason for waking me up in the first place?" I stated.

"Yes, yeah, your right let me get to my point," he responded. "I just got finished looking at the noon news, it flashed a recent killing out in your neighborhood just last night. I know that is no surprise to you, but the man who was killed, well they labeled him as a 30 year old male by the name of Billy Green, and . . . .

"What the fuck did you just say? What the fuck did you just say?" I shouted over and over cutting him off. I pushed Earl out of my way; turned around and ran off; stopped, turned back around and walked back towards him. I pointed my index finger into his face and shouted once more. "You better not be fuckin' around! I swear you better not be fuckin' with my head!" I rushed towards the telephone. It was my telephone time; therefore, no one was using it. My heart was racing. My nerves were shaking as if they were trying to attack my heart, to stop it from beating. I stood there after dialing the same number several times. I held the receiver in my hand and awaited someone to answer. I was so afraid of hearing the truth. This was truly the unexpected. I really didn't want to believe what I've just heard. Answering the telephone was my brother James.

"Hello," he answered.

"Yeah, it's me Paul," I said over-zealously. I knew something was wrong. I also knew that the truth was going to kill me. "James, what happened out there? Is it true? Did Billy get killed last night? James talk to me please," I asked.

"Yes little brother, Billy is no longer with us," James replied. My body weakened in the moment. I was angry from losing a loved one. My eyes went around the unit. I noticed Earl looking at me with sadness in his eyes, as if he has lost someone as well.

"James, I need for you to tell me everything," I said, now calm. "I want to know how and why this happened. I want to know who pulled the trigger." The moisture in my eyes built together heavily.

"You want me to talk about it over this telephone. Brother is it safe?" James asked. "Of course it's safe. Tell me what happened," I said as I was starting to get frustrated with James.

"Well, last night on the corner of thirty-First Street; Billy, I guess he was just driving through when he ran into Little Harvey. They exchanged some sarcastic words at each other.

The argument started getting out of control, from what I understand. Everybody thought it was going to be a fight; unfortunately, they were all wrong. Billy pulled for his gun, Little Harvey as well. The bullets rocked the community as they continued to fire at each other. As heart-breaking as this is to say, I feel real bad about what has happened. Geeze was unable to slip through that situation. He was hit several times in the body; once in the stomach, directly above the belly button, twice in the chest, just inched from his heart. He was also grazed on the right side of the face. As for Little Harvey, he was shot once in the chest. Fortunately, for him he was wearing a bulletproof vest; therefore, he didn't suffer from any gun shot wounds. I was told that no one even tried to help Billy; everybody just looked on as he called out for help. He was shaking and spitting up blood. He was pronounced dead on the corner. Some said that he bled to death, while others said that his gunshot wounds were too serious. I believe that if someone would've had enough decency, or courage to help him, then little brother, Billy would still be with us today.

At that point, I was in a complete emotional state. My mind was going in all directions. I just starting shouting, and calling everyone a bunch of muthafuckin' chumps and cowards. I felt scared. I felt as if I was going to hurt something. He was my main man, and now he's dead. I realized I was unable to do anything at that particular moment, but I also knew of my brother's work. They were some very revengeful men. I knew if James was unable to end Little Harvey's life, then it was most definitely going to be handled by Larry. First it was his father to testify against me, now it's his son who killed my best friend. Somebody just had to pay for this. I knew if Little Harvey was to come to jail for Billy, I would most certainly handle my business; however, if he was to stay on the streets too long, he would face the raft of unexpectedness.

So I asked James, "Where were you when all of this went down?"

"I was at home. The shootout took place around twelve twenty A.M. I was waiting on this young-girl to come over the house. I wasn't there if that's what you're asking, but Larry was."

"What! Larry was out there? I shouted.

"Yeah, he was. I even heard that he was the one Billy was calling out for, but I haven't gotten the opportunity to talk directly to Larry. I keep paging him but he never returned any of my calls. I want you to make sure you'll call me back later, and I'll have something for you to go on. Okay!"

"Okay James," I responded. I hung up the telephone and looked around my unit. My facial expression showed evil. I was placed in a state of shock. Everyone understood my lost, so majority stayed out of harms way. Some tried to make small talk, but they shortly realized that I wasn't in a conversational mood. I just sat on the edge of my bed and started thinking of Billy. I remember him all to well; now I shall never forget him. I remember one day we held a conversation about the neighborhood businesses. We talked about the younger brothers who were under our protection that had been getting into some unnecessary trouble, or losing their lives from not thinking clearly.

Billy asked. "Paul, I wonder who will be the next person to get killed. First it was **Moe, Eric, Main, Rodney** and now **Malcolm**. Man, life is getting real crazy. Every time we turn around we're making new funeral arrangements."

"Well Family," I said shaking my head. "It's not going to be me."

"Yeah Man, I know it's not going to be me either," he said. At that moment I looked into Billy's eyes with the look of deep concern. I spoke again.

"Look Billy, we must maintain our situation a little better then we have. We must be stronger, careful and less selfish towards others. It's a rough world we live in. I love you as if you were my own brother, and I don't want anything happing to you, nor anymore of the young niggas. You and I both know that we are some unwanted men in *Philly*. You know I'm sayin' the hell with everyone else except family, from them snake ass females, to them snake ass males. Don't know one like us as partners; furthermore, they will love to see us dead or in jail. Most importantly, they would try to become friends with us only because they fear us. They fear us as partners, as well as the ground we walk on." Bill just looked on and smiled. He spoke.

"Baby-boy, perhaps you're right. Your brother Deeze always spoke of you highly. He said that you were going to grow up to run your own empire, and be the man in charge. Your brother loves you. I truly cannot wait until I tell him how strong you've grown up to be." As he continued to talk I just sat there smiling. I remember those words made me feel extremely important. Who would have ever thought that he would be the next person to get murdered? Just that fast he was here and now he's gone. Many days after the death of Billy, I remained frustrated. Detention Center was a place where I put my foot down; therefore, everybody knew that I was capable of destroying something. I had no trouble coming my way for some time. I just rested back to take some of the emotional stress of my mind. Later that day, around 11:22am, I awakened, and was still a bit grouchy. I was definitely in a bad mood. I knew the thought of losing a close friend was eating me up alive. That thought has not completely sat in. I really didn't want to just sit back and except what has taken place; in reality, I felt the truth. I knew Billy was no longer with me. As a true warrior, I had to understand that fact. The fact that the ending of my friend's warmness and journey has finally reached its conclusion in life. My heart and soul was completely shattered. I felt bad because I wasn't there to get his back. Even though I was awaken, I just didn't move. I knew I was 80% of the blame. Billy knew we was up against some real move out men, but not once did he, nor I back down of what could take place as a consequence. I knew that he would be behind me on everything that was serious. Truthfully, the war with the Bells was with me and them. Something told me to take care of that business alone. What was I to do? I battered and questioned myself over and over again. Billy and I were behind one another on everything. How could I have told him to back down from my fight? Now, I feel as if I must be behind him throughout the rest of my days. I looked up at the unit lights. I started thinking more of Billy and our *last* encounter on the streets together.

. . . .

August 3, 1994,

"Billy pulls the car over," Paul asked loudly.

"Why? What's going on?" Billy quickly asked.

"I need something to munch on from that corner store," Paul said.

"Damn dude, you always hungry. You know we need to be takin' care of business first. I really don't understand why you always wait to the last minute to get hungry," Billy replied.

"Man, just pull the fuckin' car over," Paul responded. He was a little to hungry to be hearing Billy's bull-shit. Besides something else other then the food captivated his attention. As the car became closer to the curb of the small family owned department store, Paul noticed a bright pair of lights pulling over on the opposite side of the street.

"Hold on Billy," Paul said, grabbing hold to Billy's thin leather jacket.

"Man, what's wrong now," Billy asked, now getting fed up with Paul's nonsense.

"Billy, I think that car has been following us all night." Paul said in a curious way. "Yeah right Paul, you always spotting shit during business hours. I think your nervous or something." Billy said as he started laughing at Paul's crazy thoughts.

"Yeah Cuz, maybe your right." Paul was still unsure about the car behind them. Without allowing Billy to know, Paul continued to pay attention.

"Paul, are you going to get something to eat or what? You know I need to pick up that money from Bobby. You know how he be bitching' about us being late while he have all that doe in his possession," Billy said while smiling at Paul. Paul stepped out the car, looking in the direction of the suspicious vehicle. Paul and Billy both headed towards the small convenient store. They both went into separate directions, looking for something eatable.

"Excuse me sir!" Billy shouted from across the store.

"Yes! May I help you young man!" The short overweight Korean man shouted back.

"How much is these candy bars?" Billy asked, holding up two different types of candy bars.

"They are both one dollar!" The man responded.

"Common Billy! Why aren't you ready yet?" Paul shouted. Paul was now standing at the counter with his food already paid for and bagged up.

"Goddamn Paul, are you going to eat all that junk food?" Billy asked, placing his small items onto the counter top. Billy continued to look at Paul smiling gently. Paul just smiled to himself while shaking his head. The two men felt the security in one another. They both held their bags and headed towards the exit door. Suddenly! A long flash of thunder shot straight across the late night sky. Billy and Paul both jump out of their pants like two frightened females. Heavy rain started falling. The clerk on the other hand noticed a weapon of some kind in the front of

Billy's pants. He just stood silent, hoping they would go away. The two men walked forward, as everything stood silent in their minds. Billy became frustrated.

"God-damn-it! Can you believe this shit? He said roughly. Billy realized that they now had to run to their car, getting their expensive clothing wet, or maybe ruined. As they headed towards the car, a loud voice appeared from nowhere.

"Freeze right there Billy Green, and Paul Williams!" Paul and Billy stood surprised.

"Slowly, let me see your hands, and no one will be hurt!" A tall man believed to be in his early thirties applied.

"Drop the muthafuckin' bags and get your asses up against the damn wall!" Another gentleman shouted aggressively from the opposite side of his partner. Billy dropped his bag, and turned himself towards Paul. Making him face to face with Paul.

"Billy what the fuck is you doing?" Asked Paul

"I think these niggas is trying to stick us up." Billy whispered.

"What the fuck are you talking about? They have the drop on us Billy. Don't do anything crazy," Paul said. Billy started reaching down towards his chrome forty five automatic.

"What are you doing?" Paul asked

"The two men started walking closer. "Show us your goddamn hands now! We're not asking again! The well dressed men stated.

Suddenly! Run Paul Run! Billy shouted, pushing Paul into a different direction. Billy spun around with his gun in hand. The unknown men fired several shot as they noticed Billy's weapon. Paul reached for his nine miller meter while dropping his large grocery bag. Billy and Paul let the flames flow from their weapons as they ran off. The unknown men continued to return fire, as both of the now hunted men ran into completely different directions; allowing Billy's two door Acura, to remain untouched in its parking spot. However, the rain and wind blew stronger. Paul's adrenaline started rushing throughout his body. He was now nervously running threw a narrow, pitched dark alley way in the heatedness of night. Unfocused on what has just taken placed, Paul tripped over a trash can which sat in the alley way for several years. A huge splash, and a loud bang sounded as Paul fell to the ground. Another old trash can smashed up against his right hand, forcing his stainless-steel gun to entwine his grip. The gun slipped out of his hand and slid across the street corner into a huge puddle of muddy water. Paul was frustrated. He became upset as to what was going down. He cut his forehead on a sharp part of the aluminum trashcan, and it was starting to bleed heavy. As he fell, the concrete forced the wound to widen. Paul understood his time, realizing he had none to waste. He got up off the wet ground, and continued to move on. He knew the men was not that far behind. The cold rain ran down his broken smile and frightened face. The wetness from the rain ran blood down his cheeks, eyes and on to his new white dress shirt. This blocked his vision slightly. He looked nervously over his shoulder for any sudden movement. He was fortunate at that particular moment.

"Maybe the men ran after Billy!" He stated to himself. He felt as if the chase has ended. The men were nowhere to be recognized. Paul rushed towards his pistol. He placed his hands into the muddy water, pulling and grabbing out everything but what he needed. He stood in the street of a nearby intersection. People looked on as they drove up and down the intersection ramp. People would throw all types of trash out of their windows before entering or exiting the ramp, and now because of this Paul's situation in finding his gun was more of a difficulty. Again he placed his hands into the smelly water. A voice appeared.

"What are you doing out there in the rain son?" An old black man asked looking to be in his late forties. The old man was out on the town with his drunken female friend, whom sat beside him. Paul tried to ignore them both. The travelers had nothing better to do but to interfere in Paul's business. They drove in a 1981 smashed up, gray Caddie Cup Deville.

"Say there honey, you better watch yourself out there on this here road, before someone drive by without seeing your fine self standing there and run you over." The woman stated from the passenger side of the vehicle. As they started to drive away, the old man became upset at his drunken date, because she called Paul fine. He started to drive away, not before throwing a huge BBQ chip bag, full of garbage into Paul's direction; hitting Paul on the arm. The old man shouted as he drove away.

"Why don't you get your stupid ass up out the rain? What are you mentally challenged or something?" The old man voice was heard as he drove away laughing out loud. Paul couldn't believe the man's audaciousness. Paul was now even angrier, so he shouted back. "Fuck you, you half dead sonuvabitch!" The old man just put up his weak long middle finger and drove away. Paul proceeded to do as he was before he was momentarily disrespected and embarrassed. He now realized the lost of his precious time. Paranoid, nervous and still frightened, he started shouting at the muddy water,

"Goddamn you! Where in the hell are you?" At this point a shinny bright flash of lights flashed directly into Paul's eyes. On coming was a fast moving automobile, racing wildly onto his direction. As the car became closer, the sound of the cars loud engine told Paul that they were indeed picking up more speed. Paul wondered if it was the old man coming back, causing him more trouble; trouble he didn't need. He started digging harder.

"Common, common," he said to himself. The on coming car was approaching closer, and Paul needed to get up out of its way; but leaving his pistol behind was something he couldn't do. The gun was of sentimental value. It was passed down to him from his father that is now deceased, behind a robber that went mad. As Paul dug deeper and deeper, he started asking his father for help. The car was now almost a half block away. Paul looked into the mud with eyes of anger, his emotions started taken over, moreover he wasn't about to leave behind a precious part of his dad. As he continued to dig, he thought of his father . . . .

. . . .

Paul father was killed on his way home from work. His father would get up every morning at 0900hr., prepare himself carefully for work by slipping into his clean pressed pants and thoroughly creased dress shirt, race against the early morning sky, made his own breakfast and watch the news until it was time for departure. After getting himself dressed and having a small bite to eat, Mr. Ernest Williams, would say his goodbyes to his wife and be on his way. After separating from the home he would drive down to the corner liquor store for two bottles of thunder-byrd that he drank on a daily. He would have one before work, and one while coming home from work.

January 24, 1991; approximately, 6:21pm, while getting off a hard days work, and walking towards his car, witnesses said that it was a young black male somewhere in his mid teens; tall, with real dirty looking clothing on hanging around all that day, acting suspicious, however, they really thought nothing of it. As the witnesses continue to look on at the strange kid, they both simultaneously saw Paul's father walking up the street towards his car. The witnesses told police that when the boy noticed the older man staggering, he quickly walked up to him. At that moment one of the witness ran into the house to call the police, because the boy held a small caliber handgun up against Mr. Ernest's' chest and demanded his money.

"Give up your money old man!" The slim thug requested. "Please don't be stupid!" Mr. Ernest has always been a stand up person and at that particular moment the thunder-byrd was indeed marinating in his system, boosting his aggressive ways, making him completely fearless.

"Boy, why don't you just leave me the hell alone,' the old man stated. "Go on about your business," his said once again. The words slowly flowed from Ernest's mouth.

"Yeah, leave him alone!" The witnesses screamed out from across the street. Everyone who looked on knew that the old man was drunk and understood that he may not give the kid what he wanted. Mr. Ernest pushed the young criminals' gun away from his body, telling the skinny boy to go on about his business once more. The boy then became upset at the mans boldness, realizing that the only way he would get the money was if he shot the old man, or threw a hard, crispy right hook at the old mans chin, knocking him out cold, and allowing him to take the money with ease. So the boy placed himself into position to throw the hook. As soon he was just about to courageously shoot his short punch, Paul's father dangerously grabbed for the kid's gun. The tussle was in seconds, and the boy finger was still on the trigger. The gun accidentally went off, and the bullet stuck Mr. Ernest right above the left eye, leaving him helplessly on the curb to bleed to death.

"Dammit! I told you old man. I fuckin' told you!" The boy harshly shouted while ripping the man's pockets off. The kid took the few dollars he had in his right pants pocket for a sandwich and a cold beer after his hard days work. The witnesses screamed and shouted for someone else to call the police; unfortunately, it wouldn't have mattered none. Mr. Williams, an old slightly grey hair working man, was pronounced dead at the University of Pennsylvania at 6:53pm.

. . . .

. . . . Paul still thinking of his father. He wished that he could have been there to prevent the robbery from taking place. Paul promised himself that he would never stop hunting for the man who senselessly killed his father. The gun in the mud was the only thing left that could really remind him of his father. Therefore he cherished it as his favorite piece of weaponry, so he wasn't about to leave it behind. At this point it was either the gun or his life buried under a car; finally within seconds, he found the automatic covered in a huge lump of slippery mud. Wiping off the mud and looking into the direction of the on coming car, seconds before he could get up out the way, the car lost control via, disregarding the wetness of the rain. In an instant, Paul rolled his body to the right getting out of harms way. Whoever was driving the car never thought of the possibility of damaging themselves after making contact with Paul. The car had no real time to slow down, therefore, the driver slammed on the brakes, and the car continued to slide. It smashed loudly into a heavy street light pole stopping the vehicle instantly, forcing the driver to go head first into the hard window, ripping open his skull, killing him right away. Paul now recognized the two distinguished gentlemen as the men who were just chasing him just minutes ago. Not knowing if they were dead or alive, Paul lifted up the 9mm pistol, aimed it at the crashed up vehicle, and pulled the trigger one time as nothing happened. The pistol was still covered in mud, wet with small cracks around the barrel, making its discharge impossible. However, the loud click from Paul's gun alerted the one man on the passenger side whom worn his safety belt that Paul was trying to pull the trigger on his gun. The man opened the passenger side door with his thirty eight revolver in hand. He was a little banged up, but not seriously injured. He looked around the front of the totaled car and noticed Paul having some trouble with his weapon, so he reached his arm around the front head lights and fired the thirty eight special twice into Paul's direction. The loud sound, huge flames and long sparks placed Paul on point of on coming danger. Unfortunately, the skillful gentlemen bullets struck Paul almost simultaneously in the chest; causing him to fall backwards. Still placed on the ground, he looked at the 9mm in complete disappointment. Trying to catch his breath, Paul figured that the gun was the reason for him being shot. He started thinking that the gun now became bad luck. Thinking of how to get away, Paul wiped his finger prints off the 9mm and threw it back into the muddy water. The unknown man fired his gun twice more. Paul knew that the police would be racing towards the scene shortly, therefore, he only had seconds to react, or his life was over. He rolled over on the ground, now placed on his stomach, he reached deep into his highly expensive ostrich boot, that was now damaged from the heavy rain, and blood that flowed from his face. He pulled out a small nine shot chrome twenty five automatic pistol that was only used for situations as the current. The unknown assailant was now trying to reload his six shooter. Paul was on the opposite side of the car, therefore, in order to see where the man was he had to look from ground view. Quickly he noticed the man's leg, as he kneeled on one knee. Paul fired the twenty five four times at the man's leg, striking his kneecap, causing the man to fall to the side.

"OH, GOD!" The man shouted from feeling the hot metal flow through his kneecap shattering fragment instantly. The man now feeling the agony of pain continued to shout. He never succeeded in reloading his weapon; therefore, he was now helpless. The man now with fear of his life looked around, wondering from what angle the bullets came from. Looking towards the left under the car, his eyes lit up in shock, because he noticed Paul's gun aimed directly into his face; before he could make another move, flames from the gun lit up the dark street with two more mild bangs. The bullets stuck the unknown man both times in the head. The small sparks sparked as the little pop sounds exploded. Paul knew he only had seconds to get away before he maybe captured. So, he picked himself up off the ground, along with his six small shell casings that laid in his vision. Standing there, breathing heavy, Paul looked down at his hurting chest and just smiled in amazement. He was amazed because once again his bulletproof vest worn under his soft shirt has just saved him from possible death. Paul jogged into another alleyway on the other side of the recent shootout. While doing so, he noticed some police vehicles racing up towards the scene. He smiled once more, this time in disbelief. He realized that just like the other days before today, he was once again on the run from the law.

Later on the same night, Paul found out that the two unknown men whom were killed were indeed *Philadelphia Police Officers*. They were not in uniform and in unmarked cars. Paul was devastated; however, he was fortunate to be alive. As I remained in bed, I overheard my name being called; I didn't move. Hearing the calling of my name get closer, I then asked myself,

"Who could this be?" I knew one thing; they better had one hell of an explanation for this sudden interruption. I looked up, and it was a shocking surprise. Standing over top of me was my older brother James. He was finally captured in West Philadelphia. I looked on in a daze. As he became closer I smiled. Smiling, I began to realize that James was now in a situation no better than myself; therefore, I knew James was now not able to get revenge for the death of Billy. I spoke to my brother with happiness.

"What's up big brother? Damn, it's really good to see you family. So tell your little brother how you slipped up to get captured?"

I leaned forward, sitting up off my bunk. We started reminiscing about what has taken place. As James talked, my mind traveled elsewhere. I began to think of how audacious he was. James never really gave a flying fuck about nothing. Not saying that he's heartless, but this was definitely a person who lived his life day by day. Just years ago, he was doing time for another homicide with Billy. I don't know what exactly went down on that deal, but I do know that they were together when someone was killed. However, Billy and him were freed at trial after doing 2.5 years in the county prison. The homicide was won and the case was closed. My brother James wasn't your everyday rough looking brother; he was your laid back type, humbled and normally got his way whenever he placed his foot down hard enough. He was very well known in our neighborhood as the one to eliminate all the aggressive competition against us. He never talked about what he was going to do; in fact, nigga's like him is the most dangerous ones. James was one crazy cat. I just love his wildness/brotherly ways. As he continued talking, I just nodded my head. I continued to think of James and his cleverness.

. . . .

March 11, 1993; one year and five months before my arrest. My crew and I were in desperate need of some supplies, so we decided to pick up a couple of kilos from these small time hustlers that was on their way to an early grave. This was our only connection. We had plenty of hungry customers, so it was either we do business with them or fall behind on progress. It was Little Harvey, "The Real Deal "J"" (James), and myself Gangster/Paul. In order for us to pick up this package, we had to meet this guy named Travis Barnette and a few of his partners. The meeting was set up at a downtown hotel. Contact was arranged on the 11th floor; room 1124. James, Little Harvey, and myself all felt as if something might go wrong, so we decided to prepare ourselves carefully for any dangerousness that may be placed ahead. We drove slowly towards the building, approaching it with extreme awareness. Suddenly, we observed three conspicuous looking gentlemen entering the hotel building. Little Harvey shouted, "That's them right there; the ones entering the building right now. The one in the dark blue leather jacket is Travis!" "Well who are the other ones?" James asked. "They're acting like he's some kind of king," James said. "I don't know," Little Harvey said. I just sat there looking on in silence. The tension was definitely in the air. The shit was so strong; I smelt it heavier and heavier as we all became closer to making the deal. Either my senses were on point, or I was scared to death. The situation looked kind of funny, but we were already there.

"Everybody ready?" James asked. James opened the car door and we all headed towards the hotel. "If anyone has anything to say they better say it now," James suggested. "Because if anything goes wrong, I am going to kill everybody in that muthafucking room," James inquired.

"Common' James, lets just go do the deal and leave. Besides, I really doubt if any of them will try anything," Little Harvey stated.

Walking up closer to the entrance of the hotel, the bad vibes of uncomfortable ness started growing stronger; however, it was my duty to remain calm. I looked at the faces of my partners; I felt their safety surrounding me. I knew they were on some do or die thinking, so, I had to think that way as well. Arriving on the 11th floor, we stepped off the elevator one by one. I knew this was it. The anger James expressed in his eyes told me to be ready to go. He continued to say, "If anything goes wrong with this deal, I have no other choice but to destroy everything in the room." I knew he was serious, but I didn't want him to go in with that kind of attitude so I spoke. "James, won't you calm down a little. You do realize that this is our only connection; therefore, we cannot allow this deal to go wrong. I know you feel the attention in the air, hell, we all feel that. So take a step back and let's get this money baby. Besides, this isn't that type of party. We're just going in to do business, by getting the cocaine and leaving." James looked at me and smiled. He nodded his head and all continued on. Little Harvey just listened on; he stood motionless. Walking down the long hallways, I looked at the neat designs of mirrors on the hotel walls overlooking my team. We looked like tree kings on a mission for the impossible. Arriving in front of their doorway, I was no longer worried about our safety, I was now worried about theirs. We came prepared for the worse of things.

James carried a chrome forty four desert eagle with a twelve shot magazine. Bullets specially designed for a 99% death guarantee. It was with a black rubber grip handle, a fully equipped night vision beam, and a three inch silencer barrel made for special occasions.

Little Harvey was on his p's and q's. He was in a situation similar like this one before; however, the deal went bad and he took a lost on an unknown friend. Therefore, he had no time to pussyfoot around. He carried two blue stainless steel 9mm Rugers. Both with mild extended clips of twenty shots each, carrying cop killers and black rhino's.

As for myself; the baby of the bunch, I wasn't about to place myself into harms way. I was carrying a stainless grey steel thirty-two shot, baby semiautomatic mack-twelve. It held a dark grey rubber handle, with a 2.5 inch silencer barrel. It's the new technology of reliability.

We all had on bulletproof vest protection and carried extra magazines; besides, we held $54,000 in our possession. Being experienced in that particular line of work, I knew everyone wished silently that everything go as smooth as a good drug deal could. James knocked on the door, turned to me and smiled. I gave him the look of readiness. A voice appeared from the other side of the door.

"Yeah, who it is?" the man asked.

"Booking's," James responded using the code word we was giving.

"Well, Mr. Booking's, welcome to our place of business," the man stated as he opened the door allowing us all to enter. When James walked through the door, the man instantly stopped Little Harvey and me.

"And where do you think you're going?" he asked.

"Oh them!" James quickly responded. "That there is Little Harvey, your boss's connect; and truly, I don't think that he would appreciate your disrespectful hospitality."

"Oh yeah, well, who is the other one?" The stupid gentlemen continued to ask.

"Well, he is just a close associate of mine, and that should be all you need to know," James stated while moving the doorman out of the way to tell Harvey and myself to come in.

"Are you sure he is just an associate?" he continued asking questions.

"Yes! I am sure, now are you finished with your detective work," James asked, getting himself all worked up.

"Okay," the man said. "Little Harvey, you can go in the back, he's waiting on you; but the rest of you must stay here where I could see you."

Little Harvey walked towards the back room, while James and myself stood around checking out the surroundings of our so called professional drug dealers. In another room sat another man. The two of them was playing cards.

"Say, do either one of you two want to play the next game of spades", one of the men asked. He continued. "Why stand when you could sit at this table listening to these sorry jokes and have a drink." We both stood motionless. I wasn't in the mood for anything but making the deal. As for James, continued to look around the room, ignoring the man's offer entirely.

"So are you two muthafuckers going to just stand there looking like fucking traffic cops, or get into this card game?" One of the other men asked.

"Or what?" James said sarcastically.

The two men felt disrespected. However, so did James. The men unprofessional attitude and behaviors towards our business told me that they were way over their heads.

"What the fuck did you just say nigga!" The man asked, standing to his feet.

James began walking towards the table. I stopped him. "He just told me good luck," I said, interrupting the two so that James could calm down.

"Good luck for what? He asked.

"Good luck because of my bad spades game. He was just wishing me good luck." I looked at James indicating for him to watch my back. We started playing cards. The heavyset man out of the two asked James again if he wanted to play cards. That he was only showing a little better hospitality than his partner. However, James said that he would rather stand until the business deal was completed. I felt good that James maintained his self discipline. His patience was exactly what we needed at that particular moment.

After about another ten minutes has gone by, their boss Travis walked out from the backroom. He called for his man. "Eric get your ass over here right now!" The heavyset man jumped to his feet and rushed right over. "What's this shit? You bring this crap into my line of work? Mothafucker I should kill you right now! What's this?" He shouted over and over. "I told you to get nothing but pure. How could you bring this here?"

James looked at me as I looked at him. Things appeared to be getting out of control. But where was Little Harvey?" I questioned myself. He then walked from the backroom with anger expressed across his face. He spoke. "Common, lets get out of here," Harvey stated to James and I as we approached the door.

"Wait just a damn minute!" Travis shouted. "You mean to tell me that you're not going to buy any of my stuff after I've come all this way from across town. Little Harvey stood silently by the door, James and I as well. Travis walked up to Harvey and pointed his finger into his chest. "As a business dealer, I cannot allow you to leave with that money; fifty-four thousand dollars is hard to come by." Fortunately for us, we were all good at this kind of front. We peeped the go down.

"Hold on brother," Little Harvey said. "We didn't come here for any trouble. Harvey noticed that James and I were ready to reach for our weapons at any moment. "I've done what I was supposed to do on my end; it was you that fucked up the deal!" Harvey shouted. "Now you have the balls to tell me to my face that you're not going to allow me to leave with my own goddamn money!" Travis looked around at his partners and said. "Well this is all I have to say, "ALL YOU BASTARDS CAN DIE RIGHT NOW!" "Simultaneously, everyone reached for their guns. I guess they thought we were easy; however, all the guns were now pulled, it was complete silence. Harvey looked at James and stepped slowly towards the right. I slipped backwards, slowly towards the left. I understood their position. Knowing the game, sometimes words aren't needed. I knew once the bullets started flying around the room, we had to get out of there immediately. Everyone had a particular individual to go after. Me, I was after the one who was very talkative (The heavyset dark-skinned brother). James had the one brother who hasn't been saying much at the card table. Little Harvey had Travis on lock mode. It was now three of them and three of us. For whatever was about to go down, I was more than ready.

"Drop the guns and give up, you're in a no win situation!" Travis stated. Is these nigga's stupid or what? I question myself. They didn't even have enough sense to check us for weapons as we entered the hotel room. I really knew they were amateurs when I noticed their artillery. Honestly, I wasn't impressed with the small pistols they held in their hands. I knew death wasn't far from their futures, so I tried talking before the showdown. Unfortunately, I was too late. James aggressively grabbed the one man he was after by the shirt, pressing his chrome forty-four magnum thoroughly against his throat. It was an up close and personal cowboy and Indian movie, with me as one of the main characters. Who was going to have the biggest balls to pull the trigger first?

"Wait! Wait! Just a goddamn minute," Travis screamed. "I am begging you please. Please don't shoot my baby brother." Thanks to James, we now held a precious piece of Travis life. Furthermore, it was very clear that these men were ghetto experienced; they had a short range of understanding the true value of the game. It's a drug deal that's gone bad. Being uncertain of who we truly are, they were supposed to let us go completely unharmed. I guess they had other plans. Besides, this was my first pick up business trip. I was completely inexperienced on what words to use; however, I was completely well rounded when it came to gun play. Now that the guns are pulled and we had the upper hand, I just wanted to take their bullshit cocaine and leave.

James pictured a more realistic theory to my thoughts. They observed the large weaponry in our hands. They noticed our unexpressed facial attitudes. They now knew they were up against some major player's. Furthermore, James still held the boss's little brother. Travis told the other men to lower their guns. I was relieved; however, I thought of me being in their same situation and my brother was held hostage. I still wouldn't have lowered the only protection needed to see me through that ordeal.

A shoot out with these men was in the past and I was satisfied. A fast come up for some fast money wasn't worth the position they placed themselves in. It was indeed a bad day for these individuals. It was important to me because the learning experience can be identified throughout many more encounters. James was now heated to the point of no return. He was sweating and carrying on completely unprofessionally. Little Harvey and I proceeded in subduing them with telephone wire and gagging them with their own socks. James just looked on in complete frustration. While rounding up their low quantity cocaine and weapons, James never wanted to let the situation go. That was the only problem he carried in business trips. He could never be a negotiator; his place was to assassinate anyone without a second thought. That day, I knew he wanted to live out his reputation.

Walking towards the door of the hotel room, James suddenly froze. Little Harvey and I questioned his motives. "James, what are you doing? Common lets get out of here", I said. James stepped back and said. "These men just tried to pull a fast one on us; furthermore, they have seen our faces. It's no way I am going to let them survive this ordeal." "Damn!" I thought to myself. James turned and headed towards Travis little brother. He grabbed him roughly by the collar of his green satin shirt. The kid just laid there on the floor wondering what was going to happen next. I did as well. James placed a thick white pillow over top of his head. He turned and looked at Travis. Harvey, I and everyone else stood in silence. James spoke. "So you want to try some slick shit huh? Make sure you think about this for the rest of the minutes you have left to live." James placed the huge forty-four magnum against the boys' head. I looked on in shock, moreover, I almost shitted my underpants. James pulled the trigger. It wasn't a loud sound; it was sort of like a birds whisper. Travis closed his eyes as the moisture ran down his cheeks. He was unable to disregard the assassination of his baby brother.

"James what the fuck!" Little Harvey shouted.

"I'll explain later, James stated.

"But must you have killed him?" Harvey asked.

"Muthafucker, I am only going to say this once. You better shut your fucking mouth and do as you're told."

James dragged the still warm dead body in the corner of the small room. The dead kid's brains hung out of his head; thick chunks of blood were sliding down his face like melting ice cream. Everybody looked on in complete fear of my partner/brother's boldness. I also looked on in fear of what he was going to do next. Then he called for me.

"Paul, get over here."

"What's up bro", I said, speaking in a nervous voice.

"I want to kill the next one." I have never boldly killed a man before; never that close. But unfortunately, James reasons for doing this was starting to become more comprehensible. These men had to die regardless of who said what. Either they die or we worry about them trying to revenge their lost on cocaine. Therefore, I took the still warm forty-four gun from James hand. I placed it in the front of the heavyset man's head. I looked around. I noticed Harvey's emotion. He was frightened. Quickly, I pulled the trigger. The man let out a single sound as his life just came to an end. I dragged the body next to the other one. I realized my coldness. My heart was full of emptiness. Before I pulled the trigger; looking in the man's eyes I thought would be a challenge; however, it wasn't. Killing him wasn't as bad as I thought it would be. Before rolling him around on his back; just before he died, he looked at me with an unforgettable look of pleading-ness. A plea that I have never saw in my entire life of being in the game.

As for Little Harvey, his turn was next. He hesitated. He acted like he couldn't do it. He didn't have the stomach for this particular kind of killing. James took matters into his own hands. He rushed over to Harvey; the two are now face to face. James whispered into his ear.

"If you're not going to pull the trigger, then it's no way I can allow you to leave this hotel room either."

I thought, what the hell was going on now. James eyes expressed all darkness. His voice traveled throughout the room's atmosphere with the adrenaline to kill. My nerves shook beneath my skin. Harvey looked into James eyes, understanding his seriousness to us all. Harvey reached out his hand to receive the gun from James. James snatched his hand away and shouted, "Use one of your own weapons!" James spoke again. "It's all because of this low life that we're in this situation. Now I want you to kill him." Travis just looked on with an unexpressed emotion. He knew he was going to die; therefore, he didn't even try to plea for his life. After seeing his little brother murdered, he realized he never wanted his baby brother to get involved anyhow, now it's too late; he was ready to rest with his brother. Harvey put his nine millimeter Ruger directly in the center of Travis's head. Harvey froze briefly, and then pulled the trigger. He pulled the trigger not once but twice. I thought now we must vacate the scene. As we exited the hotel room, we separated into different directions. The playing cards that I've touched, I held them in my pockets. We held an inside connection with members of the hotel; therefore, no video recordings was ever found. The cocaine wasn't as good as it should've been, but it sold for a reasonable price. After the triple killing of the men, James and I later meet up to discuss his motives. I asked, "James, what was that all about in the hotel room?" He spoke wisely, "See, it's like this. That situation had to be done like that. Now can't anyone testify against you, Harvey, or me, because we have all committed first degree, premeditated murder."

"So killing them was our way out?" I asked.

"Maybe you'll understand when you do some prison time, but I have saved us from danger. I am not trying to go back to that place of living."

"Damn", I thought. Even though his actions were on point, the representation of his look informed me that afternoon that if I would not have complied with his actions, he would have killed me as well.

Sitting there thinking of James, I asked him more about his current situation. Just like I figured, James was arrested for another murder that I knew nothing about. As we continued talking, our delicate time came to a closing point. All of the nonsense that has taken place out in my neighborhood, I was still happy to see my brother James; however, I was in fact upset as well that he was in the same mind-blowing situation as me, but life must go on. I figured that if you do dirt, you'll get dirt. Now my brother and I are covered in a hole of dirtiness . . . .

It was his time to return to his block. He said he just wanted to see me before he got shipped to another jail; that he was going to the big Hamsburg prison tomorrow. Because of his homicide, they were sending him to the highest maximum security prison available; moreover, it's probably where he rather go anyhow. The wildest jails don't have that many snitches and most of the men in there have neutral respect for one another. As for myself, I was probably going to Hamsburg as well because of the two cop killings. My aggravated assault victim only got shot in the leg, and that was considered nothing towards brother's with double or triple killings. Because of my two murders on police officers, I was definitely Hamsburg status. Hamsburg was for men that put in some major work on the streets. From drug dealings, murders, contract killer's, organized gangs, and so on. The sad thing is that I was involved in all the above.

CHAPTER EIGHT

THE DOUBLE-CROSS

October 24, 1994; I received a pass to see my counselor. The counselor was the high powered brother or sister whom will tell you where, how, and why you were going to a certain jail. After I arrived in her office, I sat down greeting her with a soft nod of the head, acknowledging her respectfully. She reviewed my paper work with a stunning look on her face. She then told me that I was being transferred to Hamsburg prison. She explained that I had no bail, and all bail over $80,000 was considered to be a high risk dangerous offense.

I am Hamsburg material. I have heard a lot of crazy things about this prison; shit like brothers getting killed every month. A lot of people that was sent to this jail would go all out fighting the guards just to go to another institution. Hamsburg definitely placed its fear in people. This place had respect beyond competition. I felt a little pressure, but I wasn't about to bitch myself in front of Ms. Karen Heart abridge. This woman just gave me some dramatic news; however, I had to maintain and keep my cool. Besides, doing time with James wasn't going to be that bad. He has just done time in that place not too long ago. I knew that things would not be as rough for me as they would for many. I knew James was a wild individual, and with me he'll go to the end of the road. James really knew how to control rough situations very well. After leaving the counselors office I headed back towards the block. Getting closer to the block I ran into Newsy Earl. He has just returned from a visit; it looked as if he was crying. Sometimes visits with family can do that; however, that crying shit wasn't for me. I told him about the transfer to Hamsburg, his face showed some overwhelming fear. He explained that he has done time there before and was stabbed over his sneakers and commissary. I was thinking damn, this place must be really bad. He was also going on the next shipment to another jail; fortunately, for him, he was going else where and not the Burg.

Getting closer to our block, I started asking more questions about this so called dangerous Hamsburg. I wanted to know all that I could. If I was about to walk into a dangerous situation, I would like to know some things about it. He went on and on about the battles and wars over the smallest things. Not once did he speak of anything nice about this place. I began to think that this was a real rough stop for anyone. From what he was telling me and how he expressed his emotions when describing actual events, I'd better be ready for war at any given time. He gave Hamsburg its props. His voice cracked as he spoke. I was no coward; however, I continued to ask myself for my upcoming trip. I put my head down; I started worrying more about my case. After hearing Earl go on and on, I was starting to realize that maybe he just had it hard. Continuing to flow with our conversation, I noticed two dark-skinned brother's walking towards Earl and me. I paid them no real attention; however, as they became closer, I started looking a bit harder in their direction. I looked on so that I could speak to them. But things went totally into a different direction. As soon as I was to speak, one of the men reached around Earl with a tight fist; punching me dead smack in the eye. The sound was like raw steak hitting the floor. Only thing I saw was a quick flash of redness. Falling to the ground I didn't know what had hit me. Rolling over I saw Earl running, tripping over himself as if he was stabbed or the one punched. He ran in the direction of my counselor's office. I guess he was going to get some help. However, there I was lying on the floor while getting destroyed by these two unknown men. Only thing I could do is cover up my body to the best of my ability. I needed to prevent and protect myself from suffering too much facial damage. I felt the blood running down the side of my face. I tried to play possum, but they wouldn't stop pounding on me. I remembered one of them shouting, "DID YOU THINK WE WERE GOING TO LET YOU GET AWAY WITH STABBING A BROTHER FROM NORTH PHILLY. NO ONE GETS AWAY WITH SHIT LIKE THAT!!"

Just when I thought they were just about done, I felt some quick painless burning sensations throughout my body. I realized that I was now being stabbed. Just when I thought I had enough respect to be out of harms way and do whatever I damn well pleased; Tough Tony's friends finally retaliated on me. I have underestimated them all, now I am receiving a brutal ass whooping.

"Tim, Tim common! He had enough! Damn it Tim, I said lets go, he's dead! He's dead! The muthafucker is dead!" The other man shouted.

Little did he know, I was very alive and aware of what was going on. I wasn't at all feeling like I was about to die. The punches after the first punch to the face weren't that bad. The first punch was one of the hardest punches I have ever felt in my entire life. I've been punched in the face many of times; however, they were no where near as hard as that particular one.

Around the time the guards noticed me, the men were gone and I was just laying there dazed from the force of that first blow. I was bleeding, but nothing life-threatening; however, I couldn't seem to get my bodily functions to operate correctly. Indeed, them brother's has done a good job on me. After going to the hospital, I was released with minor injuries. I was handcuffed and taking once again to solitary confinement because I told the police nothing. It was in their job duties to protect the system, the assaulter, and myself from trying to get revenge on another inmate; therefore, I had to be placed in protective custody. Because of my transfer, my property was brought to me. Most of my things were missing; however, I didn't really worry about it. I had a knot on my eye the size of an onion, my bottom lip was split open and I was experiencing some major back pain. I was hurt. I just sat back on the bed and laughed. I laughed because I was not expecting them cowards to move on me. "Oh well," I thought. "Let's see how this Hamsburg situation goes."

MEANWHILE, Connie was sitting up, awaiting Paul's telephone call. Not knowing that Paul was suffering from a brutal beating. Connie has been trying desperately to get Little Paul to fall asleep. She was tired, exhausted, and lonely. She desperately needed some company. Paul was too far away to satisfy what she really needed. So, she sat there thinking of him. Holding tightly to a pillow, he brought her as a birthday gift. She thought so strongly. She began to feel the moistness between her smooth legs. Before she could go on, she was interrupted by a heavy knock on the door.

"Just a minute!" Connie shouted. When she opened the door, her eyes lit up in surprise. Standing there was Little Harvey.

"Hello Harvey," she said.

"Hello Connie," he sharply responded.

"Well, come on in, make yourself at home." Connie let go the doorknob and walked further into the house. He watched her patiently as her unconscious erected nipples perked at a standing salute. Paul was not fully out of her mind when the door was knocked on. The large nipples captivated his compassionate male hormones, giving him a silly smile like an overwhelmed school yard kid. Connie had a loose behind that was soft and very firmly shaped. It often jiggled, or shook wildly as she walked. Little Harvey looked deep at her lips whenever she would speak. Her lips were often moist, but today they were mildly dry, causing her to lick them sensuously and passionately over and over again, giving them a silky wet shinny look. Harvey realized that it was no second guessing that Connie was hungry for love making, but making love to Connie wasn't what he was there for. He needed to talk to Connie about what was happening to the men who once called themselves brothers.

Connie's pigeon-toe stance, her long lean legs, and beauteous womanhood, could give any humanly male an instant hard-on. Harvey knew he was thinking stupidly. However, his mind continued to travel down that dark road to enemy territory. He photographed her nakedness in his head. Her caramel coated complexion gave her a highly recognized sex appeal that most women need make-up for.

The cry of the baby's voice plunged away his thoughts of negativity. The knocking of the door must have awakened him. Connie walked up to his crib, crouched down to maintain Little Paul's wild cry for his bottle.

"Here I am, my love," Connie said. "It's no need to cry, mommy is here," she continued to say while placing the warm milk bottle into his mouth. She fluffed his baby pillow so that he was perfectly comfortable while drinking. Little Paul curled to the bottle and his small lips puckered as he slurped the warm milk from the bottle. Harvey looked on observing her womanhood. It flattered him completely. Again his mind started wondering around wildly. In the heat of the moment, a sexy woman and an overheated male can easily lose control of their emotions; emotions that's surrounded by passion and desire. Nevertheless, it can plainly overpower the male attitude, and any of his positive thinking. He knew that portrayal was never his style; but has been accused of such accusations.

"Damn, Connie is so beautiful," Harvey mumbled under his breath. "She could have been the next Tyra Banks or Naomi Campbell." Little Harvey continued to be fascinated behind Connie's sexuality. Connie looked back at Harvey from the corner of her eye. She realized that he was thinking deeply about something. Open-minded, she spoke.

"Harvey, what are you over there thinking about in that hard head of yours?" She said smiling at her own brief humor.

"I wasn't really thinking of nothing," He openly replied.

"Nothing, huh," Connie said in a disbelieving way.

"Well, you sure do have a troubling look on your face that only a mother could adore," the two laughed loudly.

"You look as if you've done something terribly wrong."

"Not yet," Harvey mumbled beneath his smiling face.

"What was that you say?" Connie asked crisply.

"I was just thinking out loud about all the good times we all use to have as a family. Now we may never be as one again," he said while putting his head down in disbelief.

"Well Harvey, what's done is done," Connie said. "Only thing we need to do now is try to fix some of our mistakes," she maintained her words. "Mistakes that has been bitterly and painfully experienced through us all."

"Yes, perhaps you're right," Harvey answered back. Even though Connie was well over do for a romantic night of her own, she was well educated and showed no signs of her needs. She was determined to fight, as long as she was not overwhelmed and aggressively encountered with seduction. Other than that, she could make it over whatever hurdle, building, or roughness that stands in her way. Besides, she wasn't the forceful type, who would just openly throw herself to a man. However, whenever Connie is seduced properly, it's no stopping her aggressive craving. The deep dark tunnel that sits below to climax. To satisfy her thirst in having multiple orgasms, Connie walked back over to check on Little Paul, he was in baby land.

Little Harvey looked excitedly on as Connie bent over to place Little Paul on to his side. As she bent over, the wideness of her caused her buttocks to open. Her long red robe moved passively as she moved. She stood back up and her petite buttocks captured the long robe directly in the center of her, causing the robe to become tighter. Her bare nakedness showed excitedly through her soft silk pajamas, that she wore underneath the long silk red robe. She flinched a little and let out a small giggle. Then she pulled it from between her.

"Oh my God!" Harvey thought to himself, as he captured the quick view of Connie's nudeness. "Why would a man leave behind something so damn beautiful?" He questioned himself. Even after Little Paul's birth, Connie continued to maintain her wonderful modeling figure. Harvey knew that even though her modeling career was well behind her, she could still walk the long runway and battle with passion and beauty, and come out on top of the best ones out there today. Little Harvey have never looked at Connie in the way he was examining her at that moment.

"Harvey, would you like something to drink?" She asked.

"Yes . . . . please," he responded shyly with a dry mouth. Connie walked towards the kitchen and had suspicions of her own. She hasn't been with a man in months, and the thought of Harvey was becoming distasteful because of his family like behaviors.

"Girl . . . you better get a grip of yourself," Connie said to herself while shaking her head in disbelief. She continued to stand by the refrigerator door, wondering what Harvey was thinking about moments ago. She shrugged her perfectly round shoulders and headed back towards the living room, with a large juice jug of raspberry punch.

But before her return, Little Harvey stood up and walked towards the baby's crib. Leaned over and looked sadly at Little Paul's warmness. Little Paul was cuddled up softly with his tiny mouth open. Harvey smiled, remembering a night very long ago, when Paul was drunk and asleep after a long party at his house. Paul's mouth was open as well, and everyone was trying to shoot corn chips into his mouth as if they were playing basketball.

Harvey continued to smile. He leaned over and gave the baby a little peck of a kiss on his forehead. Then he spoke.

"Sorry kid . . . or should I say nephew. Your father is the one who caused this sadness upon us. To challenge me in a war that I never wanted. I never wanted war son, but it's nothing anyone could do about it now. I hope my father allow Paul to reunite with you. You need Paul and Paul needs you. May God be with us all," Harvey said, while still standing over the small child. Connie observed Little Harvey standing over the baby's crib, whispering some words.

"What a good man," she thought. She continued. "I only wish that my man was home to comfort us the way Harvey is doing." Her mind stood flat and silently fulfilled itself with images of what could have been . . . . Only if's and how could's. She walked to a small table in the living room, sat down on the soft sofa, and began to pour them both a tall glass of over-sugared juice. The conversational terms of questions and answers thundered through their ears, with drum-like beats, sounding off like little cannon balls.

Connie asked,

"Harvey, what were the troubles between you and Paul? I mean, it can't be that much of a big deal because you and Larry are still good friends." Connie continued. "Larry is Paul's older brother, and I know that he would never bring any intentional harm in his direction . . . that I am sure of." Harvey looked down at the dark punch as he realized that it was too sweet. He shook it gently to defrost the ice.

He began to speak with words of a sad state. He looked up at her and gave her a friendly smile, and added, "You really do love and miss Paul a great deal, don't you?"

"Of course I do Harvey. Why would you ask me something like that?" Connie said. She let out a loud gasp sound and bit down on her bottom lip gently. She spoke pleasantly soft. "Yes, I really miss my baby, but it's been so long already . . . I mean, how much longer must I be all alone. I ca-."

"CONNIE! Please don't bother upsetting yourself," Harvey said as he quickly interrupted her impatiently. The tears gathered in Connie's eyes; they flowed down her cheeks like rain fall off a plant in the rainforest on a beautiful sunny day. Paul showed no hesitation in comforting Connie's time of needing him.

"Well Connie," Harvey said in his saddest voice. "Paul and I have experienced some overwhelming times together as friends. Many people looked upon us and thought of us brothers'; regardless of our completely different identities.

Harvey continued. Connie looked on with curiosity in her eyes. Her eye's sparkled from the moisture that gathered minutes ago.

"Only GOD can understand the many times I have wished we were actually brothers. Now Billy is dead. Paul is in jail behind our own stupidity; our arrogant behavior and foolish thinking. We were supposed to conduct ourselves as intellectual business partners." Connie looked on in amazement. She showed no serious signs of hostility, or hatred. Little Harvey placed his well manicured right hand onto Connie's left knee. He rubbed and caresses it like a big brother would do his small sister. Connie listened on as he spoke. She placed her soft, left, fragile hand on top of his hand that lay comfortable on her knee. Even though Connie was well in love with Paul; Little Harvey, James, and Larry were all very close to her. If any of them stopped by to see Little Paul, Connie had no problems with that. Harvey's words flowed nonstop.

"Connie, I really believe that Paul has made a bad decision in declaring war against me. I would have never done or thought of doing such a disrespectful thing towards him or his family," Harvey continued.

"However, I will always have love for Paul. Unfortunately, I have no control over my father's attitude toward him."

"Would you at lease try your best to talk with him, in allowing Paul to come home?" Connie asked, with another build up of watered eyes. "Harvey, I have been really struggling . . . you know, with the baby and all. I mean, I am having some serious financial issues. My mother is attacking me about what I should do and shouldn't do with my life. Paul used all that we had left in our savings for that expensive lawyer. I really don't know what else to do."

"That stubborn bastard," Little Harvey said under his breath. Connie continued. "Paul is all that I have." Harvey sat there silently looking at her, noticing her eyes becoming a darker green in color, when she became really emotional. "I miss him oh so much," Connie's eyes looked towards the floor. "Harvey, can you understand that I have needs?" Harvey nodded his head. He understood her needs all too well. Harvey stood up, grabbing her hand to pull her with him. He gave her a tough squeeze. "WAIT!" He shouted. He quickly pushed back. He placed his hands into his cotton pants pockets. He started digging into them, pulling out a huge stack of $100 bills. Connie's eyes showed suspension, as to what he was doing.

"What are you doing Harvey?" Connie asked shyly.

"Connie, you don't have to worry about cash anymore. As long as I'm alive, you and the baby won't strive too hard for anything," Harvey said. Harvey handed her a healthy stack of hundreds. Her eyes narrowed down in receiving the gift. She suddenly realized that it had to be well over one thousand dollars.

"Thank you Harvey," she said as she gave him a loving look of deep appreciation.

"You, Larry, and James are always so nice to me and the baby," Connie said happily. She placed the heavy lump of money into her jet black crocodile handbag. She leaned forward and gave him a tighter hug than he gave her. Much more then she was supposed to. Harvey stood emotionless and a bit stunned from the tough hug. Harvey understood very well how loneliness felt. Harvey and his girlfriend Keisha was having some troubling times. Harvey left the house and hasn't returned or called in three days. He wanted things to simmer down, or maybe just go away. Harvey was never the arguing type. Therefore, when anything would steer up in their relationship, he would just leave.

Connie and Harvey continue to hold each other with the warmth of compassionate charm. Harvey rubbed her soft sensuous back, caressing her time of emotion. Connie hung on as if she was with Paul. Harvey leaned back and looked deep into Connie's large marble styled eyes. He smiled nervously. The moment was overwhelming for them both. They stood briefly in silence, as if their eyes connected momentarily. The moment of the daze was the moment of truth. Connie felt the dangerous vibes creeping up. The feeling cuddled and covered her dark hole. The hole she thought could never be replaced without Paul's touch. It gave her a warm, tingling feeling that vibrated her thighs. Her blood started flowing rapidly. Her heart pumped faster, causing it to pace at an abnormal rhythm. Harvey felt the thump-ness of his erection. Pleasure was definitely rumbling their wicked thoughts.

"Would it be so wrong if I?" Connie began to ask herself. She placed her head on Harvey's chest. She hasn't been with a man in so long she thought; but the moment felt so good. Her fight was becoming weakened as the moments progressed. "I CAN'T DO IT! DAMN IT, I CAN'T DO IT! I mustn't go against the man I love," Connie said beneath her breath, over and over.

"I know Harvey will make love to me; but do I really want to experience making love to him?" She questioned herself again and again. Harvey just floated in the moment of truth. Having some of the same thoughts he calculated his thoughts mathematically. He continued to rub her back, while also enjoying his captivating surrounding. Connie continued to question herself. Furthermore, a strong man is what she needed. A strong, hard man Little Harvey was indeed. Her child's father was very powerful. He stood firm intellectually, sexually, and his supportiveness was unmatched. He builds an empire from nothing. A large chunk of a man she thought. However, he was one man she needed, and he was no where to be found.

Harvey on the other hand was a man who was definitely around and in the right place at the perfect time. Connie was unable to hold back her craving for passion.

"Harvey, would it be wrong if . . . I mean, if we were to make love?" Connie asked, while looking down at his feet. Harvey lifted up her head moderately to get the face vision. Looking into her eyes he massaged the passion that hung in their souls. He held her chin to whisper softheartedly,

"No, not at all would it be wrong. Not at all should we be wrong," he repeated. Connie's eyes gathered another batch of sparkling clear tears. She smiled prosperously.

"Thank you Harvey," Connie said as the mood became even warmer.

"Thank you for not looking down on me because of my weakness. God knows I am trying." She leaned forward and placed her lips onto his. The two kissed passionately. Connie reached for the light switch and the two covered themselves in the heated darkness of pure lust.

CHAPTER NINE

TRIP TO HAMSBURG

Dealing with the pain, I continued to laugh throughout the night. I was awakened by a voice.

"Wake up boy!" I heard, while laying there looking up at the lights.

"Mr. Paul Williams, would you please get up out that bed, we're on an important schedule if you don't mind," he stated. I turned and looked at the officer. He was very short; around 5 feet even, with curly jet black hair. I thought he would be tall and heavyset because of his deep voice. However, his words were very coherent. I rolled over, now standing to my feet and asked,

"What time is it?", while walking towards the cell door.

"Well, it's now 4a.m . . . Jesus Christ! What in God's name happened to your face son?" The officer asked while jumping backwards, and then hopping back forward to get a closer look at my face. "You must be the one whom I am supposed to keep a close eye on. Well what happened son?"

"Oh, it's a long story and I rather not talk about it," I said. I gathered up my things and prepared for the trip. The guard walked away shaking his head. After I finished gathering my things, I sat on the end of the bed and thought heavily of my family. It's so much I remembered, but it carries so much pain. Why must I always remember the good times that brings upon so much hurt, I asked myself. Family isn't supposed to have so much wrong in their lives amongst each other. Why is life so difficult to understand? Can someone explain to me why? I sat there having no choice but to think of my family.

. . . .

"THE GREAT BANK ROBBERY"

December 4, 1990. Six months after my parents' Anniversary surprise party. It was patients of this occasion that brought us together. Our determination and skillful planning to rob the "First National Bank," has ended. The time has come to complete what we have plotted on doing for months. It was me Paul, James, Little Harvey, Larry, and Billy. Men who expressed great tenacity in the underground world of criminality.

To complete the robbery, we had to rent a small room on the sixth floor at the "Random House Hotel," located on the east of 11th and Chestnut Street, in Philadelphia. The reason for the room was so we could overlook the banks view. The bank was located on the west side of 11th street, on the corner of the old "Antique Train Station Museum." As we sat in the hotel room awaiting the time to move out, Larry figured, being as though we still had plenty of time to spare, why not go over the strategic plan once more. Larry spoke before the extremity has taken place.

"Okay gentlemen, this is it." I felt the protection and assurance of Larry's plan. "Listen here Quartos," Larry said. Quartos were a name we called ourselves. It was a Latin terminology for the number (4) four.

The men who over protected me was considered to be one as brothers. Therefore, the letter "B" was the most preponderant for our name. Now we needed to use, four B's and involve it into something we was doing. At that present time we were bank robbers; therefore, we call ourselves the "***Big Bill Bank Believers***." We was all young, self-centered, and totally over-zealous to commit a felony. However, we were all willing to listen to ones plan. We all faced the hands of cruelty. Now we must maintain our own physical abilities in order to adapt in this society of wrong and corruptive doings. So if we were going to rob people for money, why not go after the big scores.

Larry continue to speak,

"Look here everybody. We all agreed to go after this banks money. It was either the "Brink Truck, or the Banks Vault." We all understood that the bank held the most cash. Now we must subdue this bank with overwhelming intensity to succeed. Okay, to go over the plan once more, we must all meet up into the bank at 2:45p.m., a quarter to three. I want everyone here to state to me their parts in the play. Billy you go first." "Well, I will go into the bank first. I will walk up to the desk and ask for a "Bank Book Savings Account Information Form," while I'm filling it out, I will wait for you and James entrance. Meanwhile, I will scope the place, while in position to perform my attack on the nearest guard."

"Good job. Now Paul, what's your position?" Larry said.

"Well, my place in this matter is simple. I will stay in the hotel room, watching everything at all times on the outside. I will only use the 30-30 long range riffle if necessary. If things get heated, I will point aim and shoot only at the chest and head. I have four extra magazines. My job is to protect y'all when coming out. I must not stop watching the bank until I see that everyone has made it to the Monte Carlo that will be parked across the street from the bank. If I fail, then the entire operation my fail as well. Therefore, I must not fail."

"Okay Paul, good job little brother." Larry stated. "James, tell us your part," Larry asked.

"Well, you and I will walk into the bank directly two minutes after Billy's entrance. I will focus on the entire scenery. At the same time I will strategically attack the second and last guard, take away his weapon, and watch for any sudden moves of bank tellers trying to push the silent alarm button. I must stabilize and control the vicinity." "Okay, James. Good job," Larry said. "Well Little Harvey, your turn now."

"Well, I must enter the bank two more minutes after you and James. I will shout that it is a stick up. The attention that I will bring towards me will give everyone time to put on their disguise. I will enter with my mask already on. In a large duffel bag, I will have four extra backpacks, a backpack for each of us. While Larry will be in the control room subduing all the video recording cassettes that is next to the vault, collecting all fifty, twenties, and one hundred dollar bills. Billy will watch James. James will be looking over me. I'll watch Larry and Larry will be watching Billy.

"Okay, the plan sound great," remember that everyone have on bulletproof jumpsuits, suits that cost us an arm and a leg to get. I must state that if something goes wrong because of our own unfocused behaviors, I will personally put that individual in the ground. If we happen to run across any unsuspected hero's; then whoever got the shot, must take him or her out with one shot, and one shot only. The silencers will protest us from the loud sound. Here are the guns everyone requested. Billy, you got the 36 shot, double clip, fully accurate Mack Eleven. Your side arm is a nine millimeter. James, here are your 150 shot Calico and nine millimeter pistol. Little Harvey, you have the baby AK 47 assault riffle, with 100 rounds, and your back up piece is also a nine millimeter. Paul, here's your long 30-30 riffle and nine millimeter. You all know by now that I will have my M.P.1., Simi Mack machine gun and nine millimeter. Here are the masks so our faces won't be discovered. Four we'll put together "Cartoon Celebrities." "Everyone laughed at the colorful disguise. Larry, he was a very on point person; a solider who I have been admiring all my years of growing up. I just looked on. Everyone was silent and listening as well. I was very young and I was already giving the know how to act on instinct. I was ready to move.

"Okay, each and every one of you men has a very important duty to do today. It's your responsibility to be very careful, so watch your asses, and everything will go smoothly. Everyone was now ready. They all walked towards the door and I just sat there. I sat there concerned about the go down. I was sweating, shaking slightly, and my mouth was very dry from the anxiety. Time moved along. It was now a quarter to three and the robbery was in progress. I observed the bank closing sign getting placed onto the doors window. I looked on like a professional with some expensive army type, crystal clear glasses. My palms were wet and slippery. I had to persevere my condition. I must retain who I am and what I stand for. I inhaled and exhaled deeply. I was ready to kill for the security and defense of my family; therefore, I prepared myself. My faith was being tested. A shinny, dark-bluish colored Mazda 626 drove up and parked right in front of the bank. A chubby white man got out. I placed the riffle in position to strike at any moment. He walked towards the bank door. He pulled on the doorknob, and expressed some anger because of the door being locked. He then realized that the bank business hours was from 9a.m. until 6p.m. Monday-Friday. He looked at his watch and placed his hand onto his head in disbelief. I was hoping that he would get back into his car and drive away, but he was too self-centered. He looked into the banks window and saw that people was inside. He turned a bark-red and he wondered what was going on. In a wired way, he continued looking in the window with one hand onto his hip and one on the glass. He must have had detected something going wrong inside. He rushed back towards his car. I noticed a hand gun on the side of his waist. I was hoping that he was not a hero. I hoped he was an innocent man that I had to kill for his belief in justifiable justice. I began to panic, asking the man to go on about his business. The man was holding a walky-talky, or some kind of communicating device. I realized that the boys only had 30 seconds left before coming out of the bank. My finger gripped the trigger. I was breathing rapidly in fear, but I was not going to ruin the plan.

The banks doors sprung open. All four of the men walked out with calmness and tenaciousness of great men in unity. The panicking white fellah shouted at the top of his voice. "STOP RIGHT THERE, THIS IS THE POLICE!!!" All four of the men fired their guns, ripping large diameter holes in the man's vehicle instantaneously. The death encountered man was able to fire once at the men before he jumped in the car for cover. But before he jumped, I fired two shots at his face, missing his head by a centimeter.

My accomplices were well on their way, speeding off and turning the corner in the "Monte Carlo." The banks alarm rung out. I smiled at our accomplishment. I broke the long thirty-thirty weapon down into six pieces. Placed it into a brown suitcase and headed towards the getaway shelter. When I finally reached the shelter, the boys were expressing some down-ness emotions between happiness and sadness. Apparently, the bank has just given most of their money to the brinks truck at 12 noon. We missed out on most of the cash. We only succeeded with $125,000.00. $25,000 a share. We all were disappointed, but at the same time, we were appreciative that no one was killed or injured. After another attempt to get some bank money, and again not as successful as a turn-out, our bank robbery days was over. It was too risky; therefore, we all came to the conclusion of taking contracts, jewelry pick up's and delivery's, and partial cocaine distributions anywhere in the world. If it was about some money and sounded workable, then we were going to take it. Regardless of who or how well their reputations was.

Billy, James, Little Harvey, Larry, and I were a good team of thugs/hoodlums. Men who was young and ruffian. Men who came from the bottom of the ghetto with nothing. Men that had no other choice, but to carve their own destiny in life. How long it will last was the question that couldn't be answered. But for the time being, I will, and they'll protect the family proudly. We laughed and drank some mild wine, in celebrating the night of the first robbery. We expressed a lot of love for one another that night. I couldn't imagine anymore men greater than the few who sat feet away from me. I felt as if the world was just beginning to be at our mercy. I will never turn my back on these individuals. I know for certain that they will never turn their backs on me.

. . . .

"Well okay, you can suit yourself, just make sure you pack up all of your belongings; roll your sheets up tightly in your pillowcase and place them up against the wall. That way when the other inmates come around to clean up after you, they'll have an easier job." Those words traveled from the officer's mouth as he walked down the hallway. His words snapped me from my moment of daze-ness. My head started to ache painfully. I just sat there awaiting the guard to return. After about fifteen more minutes or so of rough thinking, the correctional officer returned.

"Mr. Williams, are you ready?" The officer asked.

"I am as ready as any of the other men," I responded. I walked towards the cell door.

"I wouldn't say everybody is thrilled to be going over there. Hell, it's a moron upstairs right now, bitchin' and carrying on about how we made a mistake, that he was supposed to go to another jail. Some men shouldn't be criminals if they can't handle their own shit . . . you dig." The guard stated while cracking my door just enough for me to squeeze out.

"Why must we get up so early sir," I asked.

"Well, we have to wake you guy's up early because if we don't the entire shipping trip will be off track. I get y'all up early to protect the schedule and mainly to protect my own ass understand," he said.

"Yeah, I understand," I stated while walking by his side.

Suddenly, I heard a loud shout. I thought someone was being beat or some nigga's up early in the morning arguing about nothing. The whole line of transferred men turned around to see what was happening. We saw nothing so we paid it no mind; however, we had to return around a second time because of the same loudness.

"Wait please! Please wait! You're making a mistake, I am not supposed to be on this trip!" the man shouted, pulling and fighting to be heard. I said to myself, "If a jail can have a brother belittle himself like this, then Hamsburg must be hell on earth.

"I am supposed to go to another jail, not Hamsburg!" he said as the teardrops flowed down his cheeks.

"OH SHIT!!" I thought. Screaming and shouting like some pussy was Newsy Earl Wilson. I was shocked behind his coward-ness. Newsy Earl was now on his way back to Hamsburg. He explained the burg to me in complete fear. Therefore, I had to stay close to him, even though he was no real friend and definitely no killer. He mainly stayed to himself; besides, I really did appreciate his information on Billy's death. At that point I couldn't see him carrying on like some, (going to jail prostitute). So I spoke loudly.

"Earl! Earl, calm the fuck down!" I said. The guards and the other inmates stood silently, looking on awaiting my next words. "Hell man, we're going over this muthafucka together and we'll stand up together. It's nothing but another Goddamn jail for shit sakes; therefore, you better straighten your back up and take this shit on the chin. On top of that; I can't believe your standing there literally crying about not wanting to go over to this place of lock up." His ways was becoming more upsetting as I talked to him. I shouted, "GET THE FUCK IN LINE AND SHUT THE HELL UP, SO WE CAN GET A MOVE ON!" Everything stood motionless, as Earl got back in line without another word said. I spoke to him again. "Earl, just be cool blood, everything will work out, trust me." Getting back in line, I looked down at my feet and shook my head. I couldn't believe his spineless ways. You never can tell who's that chump and who's not. I understood now, that I was left for dead when those men jumped on me. He left me because he was afraid.

"Yo, my man! It's not like you got his back!" an unknown voice stated. Everyone turned around.

"Hell, have you looked in the mirror lately, or have you not noticed that someone fucked you up recently!" a tall man shouted from the back of the line. The other men started laughing at his statements towards me. Even that punk mauthafucker Earl, found his words a bit amusing. However, I laughed as well and then spoke.

"You better make sure you don't be the next person to get fucked up, being as though we are going to Hamsburg." The oozing and ahhh's started as everyone tried to instigate the situation much bigger then it was. The man realized maybe he said something to the wrong person that morning.

"Sure you right pal, sure you right," the tall man stated as his words was barely heard because he murmured them out in a shy like way. We finally started walking towards the door of the outside. I heard brothers taking deep breaths of the fresh air from being inside for such a long time. The fresh air was overwhelming to most of us. Walking towards one of the three correctional vans, I felt like an extreme person. I was hand-cuffed and ankle braced to some sick looking, undernourished gentlemen. Again, it was that time to hold my head up and put my chest out. I did proudly. I just looked on out the window as the van's engine started.

The driver of the van spoke, "Are you men ready for Hamsburg!" I smiled and spoke to myself. "Shit, I hope Hamsburg is ready for me." We drove away.

"HAMSBURG COUNTY PRISON"

Arriving at this prison, it was the view of oldness. It looked like a place that has been recently in a somewhat catastrophic episode. It was nothing like I'd expected. In face, the conditions was more worse then what people gave it credit for; however, unloading the van, I could almost hear the pounding of the men's hearts as we all walked into the prison doorway side by side, couple by couple. I looked around with hunger to find Earl. Just like I expected, he stood in the back; hands behind him folded together, as he leaned up against a old dirty wall, silently looking down at his feet and ground. He was afraid of something, what? I had no idea.

Meanwhile, we all got checked in. It was not that many of us at Hamsburg, because those other two vans went elsewhere, other prison. Everyone in that small unit was giving separate blocks to go on. Earl looked at me as if he was being apprehended for a wrong conviction, and I was the judge to do the sentencing. I couldn't understand his emotion. I figured he better been glad that I wasn't into homosexuality; because, if I was, his weakness would have giving me the opportunity to prey on him heavily. He acted in the manner of weakness, however, I felt sorry for the dude. I knew if a person would push up on him aggressively, he would cave in without even given up a fight for his dignity, self-respect or even his manhood. So before we separated, I walked up towards the guard whom has place us on different blocks. I spoke.

"Officer, may I have a word with you?"

"Sure kid what's up?"

"I understand that you have a very important job here. Therefore, I'll only be a minute." The Jamaican looking officer placed his clop board down and listened on.

I continued.

"I would like for you to prevent a serious situation from getting bolder."

"What's the problem?"

"Well, see that brother over there with his head down. He's a little frightened about Hamsburgs' reputation. I would like to know if you could somehow place us on the same block." The guard looked at my bruised up face and thought of me as no real protector. Realizing how he was looking at me, I spoke again. "I am no tough guy, and I am no freak, however, I feel as if I could look out for his well being." The officer just looked at me with complete understanding now. He knew exactly where I was going, furthermore, he see matters like this all the time. Finally he felt good that someone had enough courage to say something about the problem before it was far too late. The other inmates stood there saying nothing. Most of them didn't want to go on anyhow.

"Well, let me see what I could do. What's his name?"

"Earl, Earl Wilson," I said.

"Bring him over to me," the officer said looking down at his clip board.

"Thank you sir," I said while waving my left hand for Earl to come over. Some of the other men looked at me as if I was some kind of a hell-a-fied hero or something. I knew they wanted me to do the same thing for them. All of the men weren't afraid, but majority was. The ones who weren't had my respect. The ones who were must stand their own ground. Earl and I were now placed on the same block. Arriving to our block everything was quiet. The jail was on temporary lock down, because someone got stabbed previously to us coming over. Therefore, you heard small voices of men's conversation coming through the bars of the cells. Some inmates stood of the doorway bars just to see who the new kids on the block were. "Fresh meat!" Suddenly, a loud voice appeared.

"Yo, looks whose back in jail! Yo, Chubby, get on the door! Look whose back in this bitch!" A man shouted from the inside of his cell. It was kind of strange to me that Earl would be acting so afraid of Hamsburg. People sounded real happy to see him. I looked over at Earl, with a questionable expression. He turned his head away and continued walking forward. Arriving at our cell, we entered. Several other men shouted Earl's name. Earl just ignored them. Slamming the cell door shut the officer walked away.

"Is there something you want to tell me?" I asked.

"What are you talking about? Earl responded in a humbled way.

"Do you owe anybody drugs, money or your mutherfucking life, that's what I am talking about nigga?"

"No, I don't owe anybody anything," Earl stated, looking at something other them me,

"Okay Earl," I said. "If I get stabbed over your old foolish behaviors and live to see another day, I am going to kick your ass up and down the entire jail. Do you understand?"

"No!" Earl shouted, throwing his belonging down. "You are the one who don't understand."

"I don't understand what? I asked. "Well, whatever I don't understand, you better make it understandable, you dig." I started getting upset. How could I not understand I thought? Hell, maybe I should've left him in the arms of the gorillas. I bet they would have understood his ass.

Our cell door was being reopened. They found the men who did the earlier stabbing. We had to prepare for chow; I paused our conversation.

"Earl, when we return from lunch, or maybe when we lock up tonight. I want you to tell me everything, and I do mean everything your involved in concerning this jail shit." I gave him the look of a man who wasn't playing any games. Hamsburg was a very serious place. I damn sure wasn't going to fall victim to its reputation because of Earls' old ways. I turned and walked away. Earl stood behind making his bed. I headed towards the chow hall. I looked around for my brother James in the mist of the many crowds of men. I recognized no one. Earl on the other hand didn't even eat chow, and I knew he was hungry from the long wait of being checked in the institution. Earl was definitely holding something back from me; however, I was going to find out that night what it was, even if I needed to beat it out of him. Everyone who stood in front of the chow hall looked really serious. I couldn't express too much seriousness, because of my recent ass kicking. It showed on my face. Most men looked at me as if I was invisible. I felt the tension of their eyes focusing on me. I didn't even look back. I continued on about my business. My heart was banging hard and slow and slow and hard again. Fast and then slow, slow and then fast again. Even though I felt afraid, I felt calm as well. My mouth was very dry. Hamsburg was all of what people said it was. Suddenly!

"THERE'S PAUL!" A man shouted. Hearing those words, I sharply looked around. "OVER HERE GANGSTA! OVER HERE!" Another voice shouted. I knew that voice anywhere. It was my brother James. I looked on and saw other men from my neighborhood. Some was even our enemies on the streets; however, in jail enemies from the same community somehow came together. The more men in your click, the better your chances are surviving difficult wars. Everyone called out for me. Most of the men who were from my neighborhood called themselves . . . YOUNG *GUNS* . . . . Men who lived their lives behind money, drugs, murder and extortion. Among these few men, you had . . . ***Cappri, Gee, Manny, Vence, Johnny, Kev, Prime, lil TY aka Pee-Wee, and Rell.*** I was no longer hunger, I was excited to see everybody; therefore, my craving for food was of no more. Walking closer, this kid name George spoke.

"James what happened to your brother face?"

"I don't know, but I'll soon find out," Getting closer, they all noticed my face. "Little brother, what happened to you face?" James asked.

"Oh, this. It's nothing. You know me big brother. I got myself into a little altercation in that other jail." The other men stood around listening on. I continued.

"A fist fight and I caught a clean one, as expected in a fight. Seriously, it's nothing.

"Are you alright Paul?" James asked.

"Common James," I said. "How long have you known me? When have you ever known me not tell you when I am hurting? Seriously, this is nothing," James looked sad and angry at the same time, fortunately, he and everyone else knew I was about my business; therefore, my face was no longer a major concern. I stood there completely zeal in the moment.

"Little brother, what are you doing over here?" What block are you on? Do you need anything?" James asked, while throwing soft punches at my body to show his happiness in seeing me. I stated that I was on B-Block and that I needed a weapon, some writing paper, pen, pencil and some junk food. The junk food was for Earl. I still thought of him in my moment of being comfort. James smiled, stating that he was going to send me over a welcoming package. Furthermore, he was going to see to it that I receive my right amount of telephone time. Over the "BURG" no one man ran the telephone time. Hamsburg had no telephone monitors. You got in where you fitted in. It was the capital of criminals. South Philadelphia had their own telephone. North Philadelphia had their own telephone and Southwest and West Philadelphia was considered as on neighborhood, therefore they had their own telephone as well. After being introduced to many men, chow was then over. James went back to A-Block and I returned to B. Some of the men who sat at our table were on my same block. I was now comfortable. People who normally had problems were the ones who had none or little back up. I understood my jailing situation would be much different then most. I wanted to tell Earl what has just happened. Arriving to the cell I saw Earl standing in the back of the cell. He was sweating heavily, and held his clothing in his right hand.

"What's going on?" I asked.

"I am moving to another block Paul. I have a cousin there and I think it will be better for me to move over there with him" He said while grabbing up the rest of his things. I knew something was shady, but I said nothing. If he wanted to be on his own as a man, then so be it.

"Okay Earl, just remember, if you need me for anything, just send word over and I'll make sure I get to you." We walked towards the cell door and Earl walked farther out. We shook hands; he turned and walked down the block. Looking on, I noticed a heavy set brother approaching him. I continued to look on. The man was angry looking. It looked as if they were arguing about something but I thought maybe not, that maybe the gentlemen was his cousin, therefore, I paid it no real attention.

"**What took you so long Earl?**" Jeff asked crisply, Jeff grabbed part of Earl's things, and they both headed towards the top of the block. Earl turned around to look for Paul, but he was gone.

"I came as soon as I was notified that you wanted me," Earl said.

"But did you miss me," Jeff asked.

"Of course I missed you." Earl replied with delightful eyes. The two men arrived on J-Block where Jeff housed. Everyone looked on at Earl, as he entered the block with Jeff. They shook their head in disbelief; but already knew his homosexuality was no surprise.

"Earl, I never knew how lucky I was having you in my life," Jeff's voice cried out. Arriving at Jeff's cell. Earl knew that everything was just how it was when he left.

"All those stupid little men you been running around with, do you think that they can give you a better time then me?" Jeff said aggressively. The two walked into the cell. Earl's, property was still on the outside of the cell while the two talked in.

"You will, and always will belong to me Earl. Is that understood?" Jeff asked with a child like smile.

"Yes Jeff, I understand." Earl nervously replied. Jeff moved swiftly towards Earl. He came and stood directly in front of Earl, as Earl placed down a small bag of clothing he held in his right hand. Jeff muscular chest stood out firm. His dark brown eyes glittered from the over head cell light.

"Have you forgotten me?"

"No. The question is have you forgotten me?" Earl asked. "You forgot how much you needed your sweet Earl, did you not," Earl asked. Earl put his arms tightly around Jeff's waist. Jeff pulled the curtain on the cell door, so that they could have a little more privacy. Earl thighs slipped between his legs. They stood beneath the overhead light in the cell Hugged up like a man and a woman who's deeply in love. Earl's body was moving slowly backwards and forward, feeling Jeff's hard on against his leg, Jeff looked down into Earl's eyes and stood silently. Earl started flicking his tongue along the massiveness of Jeff's chest, down to his neck and then along the brim of his huge, soft lips. Jeff stood without resistance. Earl removed his female like leg from between Jeff legs to release some pressure on his waist. Then Earl pressed his rock hard dick roughly against Jeff's groin. They felt the hardness of each others erected blood thumping penis.

"Please don't stop . . . pleas," Jeff groaned.

"Tell me something honey; do you like it when I do you like this?" Earl asked, while undoing the buttons on his county blues and drawing his large thickness out with skillful and experience hands. He stroked his thickness and cupped his balls. Clutching and un-clutching them gently until he was hot like raging bull, and ready for love making. Jeff looked down at Earl watching his small girlish like hands with slim fingers, masturbating him in a circular motion. Jeff moaned out loudly, as blood of excitement flowed through his bloodstream, sending sings of passion to his brain. He leaned forward, buttocks clenched tightly. He was terrified that Earl was going to stop. He rubbed his hands on Earl's curly hair and massaged his skinny shoulders. Jeff looked on when Earl placed the long black penis into his mouth. The warmness suddenly relieved all stress that Jeff held inside his mind. It made him lean forward in pleasure. His hands clutched Earl's head tightly as he pressed his head to him, giving him every inch of his hardness.

Earl was a homosexual since he was thirteen years old. Now he was twenty eight. Earl sucked on him deeply, as a professional would, while feeling his long-ness at the back of his throat. He moved wildly so that his tongue could flicker around him. It drove Jeff crazy. That's what he loved about Earl. No one could make him feel the way he did. He shook, slightly as his toes tighten. He was ready to climax. His words flowed smoothly.

"Oh . . . yes, Earl . . . Oh . . . God . . . yes! A large splash of bursting cum gusted out of his penis. Earl held him tightly as he swallowed every drop to drain the man he had known, and cared for, for many years. Earl stood up, and looked Jeff in his colorful eyes. He gave him a small peck of a kiss on the lips.

"You see how much love I can give you Jeff", Earl asked. He tucked the relaxed, but still erected penis back into his lover paints. Fasten the buttons and walked on side by the door. He reached up to remove the curtain, and continued to bring in the rest of his private things. Jeff just smiled. He realized that he was never going to let Earl out of his sight, nor ever out of his life. Jeff was blinded by love.

Still shaking my head about Earl's separation, one of James friends that I didn't know walked in my cell un-announced and started a conversation about Earl.

"Yo, little homie, I know you're trying to get yourself situated, but you need to be careful of your surroundings." Instantly, I became angry. I started wondering why he was all in my business. Was it because of James or was it for general purpose.

"That dude Earl is bad business. It was here in this same jail when brothers were getting sliced up because of his homosexuality," he said, looking at me up and down as if he were questioning my motives.

"A homosexual!" I shouted. "Man I was just doing time with that brother in another jail and didn't anyone say anything about him being gay. I seriously doubt if he's a fruit-cake."

"Brother I am trying to tell you that the dude is . . ."

"I don't give a flying fuck about what you're trying to tell me," cutting him off. "I don't even know your name first of all; furthermore, I think you better get to going up out my cell." My teeth locked. Even though he noticed the huge knot on my eye, I was hoping that knot for granted.

"Damn! What's your problem?" He asked. I noticed his fear. His voice rumbled out.

"First of all, you just waltz in here un-welcomed, secondly, I don't know who the hell you are, and third I really don't like the fact that you just assassinated the character of that man for nothing. If he was gay, which I serious doubt, and it's none of your business. I wonder why it is your concern to run in here to tell me to be careful of my surroundings." The man just stood there. He realized I was no chump, nor was I gullible to run with his words about somebody. "Now get up out my cell." I pointed towards the doorway and without another word said. He exited the cell. I knew he would run back to inform the others about my aggressive behavior towards him, but honestly I loved every bit of that scene. He just looked at me as he stepped out the cell. As he left, I started thinking of Earl being gay. "Gay, no way." He being gay never once stuck in my head. I started thinking. "Damn, sometimes he does be acting . . ." Naw, I can't go for that. That recent dude was just trying to make small talk. I ignored the thought and continued to clean my cell. After an hour has gone by, I sat on the end of the bed and started thinking about my baby Connie. "Damn, what I'll do to be in her arms right now? I wish her and the baby the best."

CHAPTER TEN

FRIENDSHIP

After time continued to grow wildly, my days turned quickly into months. It was now **March 16, 1995**; I've been on locked down for over six months. The day was Friday and I've been looking forward to my visit all that day. Connie was suppose to bring up little Paul. She also stated in her letter that she had something important to tell me in person. I was hoping it wasn't any bad news, even though I have been hearing some upsetting things about her while my incarceration. I still wanted to see her. However, I am not at all thrilled with how she's maintaining her duties as a woman (Hangin' out late, being with bad reputation women in my neighborhood, and not keeping in touch with me as much as she should). She was starting to fall and I haven't even been sentenced or found guilty yet. It was now 4:27pm and she supposed to be up here first thing in the morning, (9am). I wanted to call to find out what was happening, but I didn't want her to know how angry I was at her. Therefore I needed to do something other than sitting around awaiting her visit. Walking out my cell, I noticed a group of around twelve men hanging in the back of the block reminiscing to something and moving their heads rhythmically. I figured; why not see what the deal was, to pass up some of this emotional time. As I got closer to the men, I heard what sounded like a rap song. I started walking faster. The person who was entertaining the men sang about his situation in prison. His name is: **RAHEEM MUHAMMUD AKBAR ALI**; he was only twenty years of age. He reminded me of Larry. A slim brother who always stayed to himself. He wore the best of county clothing. Always placed his head into books or surrounded himself with knowledgeable men. Most people called him **RAY**; I guess that was short for Raheem. He came down from an upstate prison to face a first degree murder charge. However, he was sent upstate on a ten to twenty year sentence for armed robbery and assault. From observing him on the block, people stated that he would be in prison for the rest of his life because of that homicide charge. But, what do they know? Just maybe he would beat it. I hope so anyhow. Finally, I got to where they were. All the men gathered around while he was saying some strong words about his personal experiences in life. I only caught the ending of what he was saying. And it was perfectly put together as he flowed . . . **Because everyday revenge was on my vocabulary, now I'm getting' up getting' in line every week for some commissary . . . As I wake-up sweatin' for the fear of my young life, they got a brother on lock down now thinking twice . . . I pray to God everyday for him to help me please; help me rewind the time so I can call it truce with my enemies . . . Through this system I ride, with my pride I put a side, then I asks God to please help me with this homicide. As a small kid, I did what I did; now I'm sittin' in prison asking why off a ten year bid . . . . So if you got another chance in life think for you and for all the young brothers that just come through; "As-salaam-ulakum" peace beyond to you . . .**

Everyone started shouting and carrying on about the rap song. Overwhelmed at the small part I've heard, I fortunately departed because my visit has finally arrived. It was now 5:11pm, and I was upset. I even wanted to turn down the visit, but I couldn't do it because of little Paul. I was disappointed in Connie's behavior. I felt each and every crushing blow of her cleverness. Walking back to my cell; I brushed my teeth and re-groomed my hair. That's when I was approached by Raheem. He was finished with his entertaining.

"Excuse me family," he said in a low voice tone. "Do you mind if I could ask you for a favor?" He stood in my doorway. I soft stroked my hair with the soft brush, laying my waves down smoothly, as I listened on. I answered him.

"Sure, what can I do for you?" I stopped grooming my hair and just looked at him.

"Well, if I'm not mistaken, they just called you for a visit, right?"

"That's correct," I responded, wondering his point.

"Well, I would like to know if I could have half of your telephone time tonight." My eyes narrowed in on him. "I mean, being as though you're not going to be using it." He asked, while looking me directly in the eyes.

"How do you know if I don't have someone maintaining that responsibility in line already?"

"This is why I am asking you for a favor."

"What's in this for me," I asked.

"Look, I just come down from an upstate penitentiary, and I really need to call my family. It's very important to me that I do so. Even though I've been down here for some days now, I never once asked anyone to use the telephone until now. Furthermore, I would appreciate it gratefully if you could handle this one thing for me."

"Damn," I thought to myself. I understood the brothers' situation all too well. I was in a crazy situation quite similar not long ago. However, I was forced to handle my business. What the hell, it was only a one shot deal; however, he better not make this a habit.

"Sure you can brother. Let me first clear things up with my partners." Walking out the cell, I closed the door behind me. Raheem and I walked down the block towards the front gate, near the telephone. While walking, I continued our conversation.

"How did you know that was my telephone time tonight?"

"Because I see things. I mean, I see you all the time on the telephone. I knew you were a pretty thorough and understanding person. I've been meaning to ask you for some time days ago, but you looked a little stressed about something."

"Oh, yeah," I said. Maybe he thought I was gentle or kindhearted to meet all of his demands, if he applied them the right way. Besides it was plenty of other neighborhoods with telephone time; men with just as much time as me. The question was. Why didn't he go to them? Oh, yeah, he said he knew I was thorough. I guess flattery always work.

"I never wanted to disrespect you in any way", he said.

"Naw! I said shockingly. I just looked at him comfortably. We finally reached the top of the block.

"By the way Raheem, my name is Paul Williams, but most people call me Gangster. Because of how you approached me, anytime you need a favor, please feel free to ask. One more thing, what part of Philadelphia or should I say the city of brotherly love, are you from?"

"Hell, I'm from South Philly," he said sharply.

"Oh, yeah", I said quickly. I knew from that point on the entire conversation was looked at differently.

"Well you go right ahead and use that telephone, and when I return back on the block, we'll discuss your private telephone usage.

"Okay, okay family. I'll be looking forward to it," he said smiling away, before we departed.

"By the way Paul, thank you. This is really good looking out." He walked over to Pee-Wee, whom were standing on point near the phone room. I guess it was because of the new female correctional guard. He looked over at me and I just nodded my head. I departed for my visit. While leaving, I looked back, as Raheem and Pee-Wee were shaking hands. I just smirked. Pee-Wee was being very polite to the brother I sent to him. I really did respect that kind of loyalty.

Getting checked in for my visit, I started thinking of the recent Raheem. I even thought of giving him that telephone time permanently. I knew if I was going to give him any time, it had to come from my very own. I personally felt him; you never know what a man will do in a situation as simple as wanting to call their family. Moreover, I wasn't going for my king of behavior, so, before it came to the point of fuckin' him up, I thought why not try and work things out first. Compromising was something I was good at when it came to being compassionate for others. "Welcome to the family Mr. Raheem Muhammad", I thought. "I'm really hoping you're all that I think you are." Walking up the steps towards the visiting room, I sat down on a small broken down bench to await the calling of my name. Looking around, I really had a chance to observe the old structured building. I was impressed that it was still holding its ground. Hamsburg was like number three in the state for the most serious and hazardous county correctional facilities in Philadelphia. Its paint job was all chipped up. Most of it was falling helplessly to the ground. Debris fell all over the floor, on top of people heads, and sometimes in their food in the cafeteria. Some people complained about chips of paint being on their food tray, but nothing is ever done about it. I just sat there looking up at the top of the building. I observed three small birds flying around, as if they were playing amongst them like a mother of father would do a smaller child. This place was completely unsafe and unsanitary. Suddenly, my eyes flinched. Apparently, one of the smaller birds whom flew around freely took a shit directly in front of me as if she was aiming for me. Degrading as that was I laughed at the disease infested animal as they flew above me. Looking around at this dehumanizing environment, I saw the birds dumping. While shaking my head, a small mouse ran up from under a large table that sat nearby. As it became closer to the birds feces, I lifted up a chair and slammed it back down. The loud sound should've frightened the small creature; unfortunately, it just stopped, looked up and continued on. Again, I shook my head in disbelief. I suddenly couldn't believe what I've gotten myself into.

Finally, my name was called. Walking into another room, I was acknowledged by a female guard. One I've been admiring for the last three months.

"Hello, Mr. Williams," she said. I started blushing as I tried signing my name on the check-in sheet and admire her at the same time.

"Hi you doing, Ms. Johnson," I shyly replied.

"I hope you enjoy your visit," she said.

"I hope so too," I stated, as we both made strong eye contact. Before I walked out into the visiting room, I looked back at Ms. Johnson and smiled. I knew it was more there then just wishing me the best on my visit. The visiting room looked like someone tried to cover up the dirtiness. I guess they wanted the visitor to enjoy their half hour with their loved ones. Giving the guard my pass, minutes later Connie walked through the doors. Seeing her, my heart fell into pieces; however, knowing her as well as I do, her face expressed am image of fright-ness. She held little Paul in her arms; I looked down at him.

"My baby boy," I said to myself. I reached out to take him from her arms. Connie's eyes connected with mine, she turned her head away. At that point I knew something serious was troubling her and I wanted to know exactly what that something was. Without wasting anymore time, I went straight to the point.

"So, Connie, what was it you wanted to talk to me about?" She just sat there looking stupid and saying nothing. I felt the dissatisfaction between us. I knew she was sexually involved with someone, but who that someone was I held the slightest idea. I spoke again.

"Connie, what's the problem? Am I sitting here questioning myself?" I aggressively said.

"Once again, what was so important you couldn't tell me over the telephone?" Little Paul started crying mildly because his bottle slipped out of his mouth; I placed it back in and held him firmly.

"Okay Paul," Connie said. "I want you to know that you've always been and still am a very special man in my life. You know that I've never been dishonest towards you, nor have I ever thought of cheating on you." As she talked on, I started feeling dumbfounded. I now knew the main topic. I sat there realizing how much I cared for her and the baby. The moment was just right. I was deeply in love with Connie. I understood that I may never be with her again. I listened to her explain herself.

"One day the telephone rang and I never answered it. I had a hunch it was you, and yes I was still upset with you. However, the next day when we talked, you confirmed that hunch. I didn't answer the telephone because Little Harvey and Larry were there. I wasn't going to tell you because I have nothing to do with the miscommunication you two are having, neither does my son." My face turned dark red. She continued.

"We started talking about you and this unfortunate situation." I started shaking my head. I was hoping she wasn't going to say what I thought she was going to say.

"Harvey said he still love you as a brother. He stated that things could never be the same between you two. Paul, as time went on, and because I was emotionally destroyed behind you leaving me, I started crying and he held me like a true friend. I was lonely, and one thing did lead to another. Before I could realize what I've just done, it was far too late."

"What the hell you mean, one thing led to another, you stinking bitch!"

"Paul please," Connie said.

"Please my ass. Are you sitting here telling me that you fucked the one dude that killed Billy and placed me here?"

"It wasn't like that." Connie said while crying her beautiful eyes out. "Don't blame me, don't blame me!" She shouted.

"Connie you are so fucked up. I want you to leave," I said as Little Paul almost slipped off my lap. "I cannot believe you Connie, you were dead wrong." I grabbed her by the top of her shirt, pulling her closer to be face to face. "I am going to kill the both of you double crossing snakes!"

Connie jumped to her feet. She knew she may have made a mistake, but she never thought of Paul saying he would kill her.

"What you mean you're going to kill me!" she shouted. Everyone looked on in the visiting room. "Maybe I was dead wrong Paul, but you're the one who placed me in this wrong doing by leaving me and your son stranded. You're the one who got yourself into this bullshit and now you are blaming me for needing some comfort. If you must kill me then so be it. But you will always remember what's done is done, and killing me won't do anything to change that." She took Little Paul out of my arms and walked towards the exit. My eyes then watered. I just wanted to get right up and punch her face, but in more ways than one, she was right. However, that still doesn't justify her sleeping with the enemy.

The individual has now become a priority in my life. He was once like a brother. I was in a killing mood. He has crossed me again. First it was my hard earned currency. Secondly, he killed my closest friend, and now he stuck his dick into the woman I loved, (My son's mother). I wonder what's next. Just maybe he would gain custody of my son.

"Oh yeah," Connie said, stopping at the doorway. "Your brother Larry drove him there."

"What!" I said. I had forgotten all about Larry being there. "Connie you mean to tell me that Larry brought that bastard over to your house after what has happened to me?"

"That's right. You want to know something else. The two of them be together all he time. Your situation never stopped them from being friends," she said, turning up her lips, looking at me as if I was a complete ass. "Another thing, Little Harvey is locked up for the murder of Billy." My heart stopped momentarily. I felt like I've just died and came back to life. I walked up towards Connie. She stood in a questionable state as to what I was going to do. I looked at my son and kissed him softly on the forehead. I looked up at Connie. She must have thought I was going to smack her repeatedly. I wanted to badly; however, I leaned over and kissed her as well. I whispered my goodbyes. Walking back towards my chair, I heard Connie cries as she walked away. My legs felt weak so I sat down. I didn't know exactly what was happening, but I was feeling quite strange. I realized I had a lot to do when released. Connie, on the other hand was someone I must overlook for the safe being of my son. It was somewhat funny because at that moment of her telling me this devastating news, I finally realized how much I loved her. In reality, she was nothing more than a modern day, two timing prostitute. Connie was now gone. I just sat in that chair. I thought of Larry. I wondered why he was being so ill-mannered towards his own flesh and blood. I couldn't remember if I have done anything to him to make him want revenge on me so badly. I admire him, yet and still I am the one whom he rather hurt. I remember a time when we were all un-separable . . .

. . . .

"THE HIT"

The Dominican Mafia. Location: The country of Santo Domingo in the West Indies. Total population 7,632,000. This trip consisted of everyone's attendance: James, Little Harvey, Billy, Larry, and I. This was an important mission for a nice piece of paper. We put most of our saved up cash into this trip. The contact was rich and powerful. We needed to impress him as much as we could with nice expensive clothing. We even tried renting a private jet, but our pick up arrangements had that all in play. Arriving at the airport in Larry's jet black and chrome Benz; I couldn't wait until I got aboard the expensive plane. The jet was a 1989 Lear 35A s/h 25A-386, N850mm. It had in 2150 ft, cargo doors, de Marcus thrust reverse. Century III wings w/ soft-flit, drag chute, dual f/s 84 w/ehsi-63 Jet fc-520 Auto pilot, uns-la, Gns-1000m, tnl-2200, king khf-941 w/selcal, Wolfsburg flitefone VI. Excellent paint and interior in a standard eight-passenger configuration w/optional video entertainment center, with ipeco crew seats, all in a money green and white coloring. This jet was comfortable.

Several hours later we arrived in the *Dominican Republic*. We were welcomed by a couple of native women. They showed us good hospitality and we all enjoyed their unique ladylike behaviors. I was very impressed. Some people looked at us as if we were un-welcomed; however, we ignored them. Before exiting the jet, we held a conversation about our possibilities in never being seen alive again. It was a chance we all wanted to take; besides this was the opportunity to see a different part of the world. The way they ate and slept. Pussyfooting around wasn't what we were there for, so without anymore sight seeing, we headed straight for the person who sent for us.

Arriving to our destination, the business negotiation started. We were offered to kill four individuals for a total of one million dollars. That's 250,000.00 a kill. 200,000.00 for each of us. Everything was going accordingly; that's until he spoke some words in Spanish. They were translated by his interpreter . . .

"As much as I hate Americans, I'll allow you ape's to do this for me because you are Americans. I sent for you because all of you are easily replaceable. However, the job is very easy".

"If it's so easy, why don't you do it, you fucking bastard," I said underneath my breath.

"You must hit the target and their children. If anyone is left alive, you will not receive any American currency. For each one it's 250,000.00; however, you will only get 250,000.00 up front and the rest when the job is done. Get them out of my face." We were directed out. Me personally, I didn't care about killing their kids, neither did Billy, nor did James. But Larry and Little Harvey wanted to talk about it more. They never wanted children involved. Bad enough a woman was involved. I figured it was business and nothing personal. 250,000.00 were given to us along with the location of the targets. Apparently, the large lump sum of money placed

Larry's and Harvey's mind into financial stability. Going after a child was a very bad thing, but it was their tradition. For them it was the way things went. If a hit was placed on someone for whatever reason or reasons, their young was murdered as well. I say we should live by those values back in Philadelphia. It's an old saying of theirs. "If you're trying to cut off a person's blood line, then you must destroy everything that carries out that blood trait." These people betrayed a very powerful man; therefore his family had to pay. We held another meeting about the same situation. The ruling was over powered. Therefore, the job was to be carried out.

Larry stated that the so called boss-man's attitude was ridiculous. Billy stated that most faraway countries act that way with out-of-town people, especially Americans. They call us townies. They realize it's a sad thing when they need outsiders to do their dirty work. I just wanted to get it over with and count my money. Later that same day we were provided with some of the best artillery available. Even though, I felt as if this was only a two man job, it was no telling how this thing will really go down. Only time will tell. Nine times out of ten, he understands by now that his life is in serious danger. Perhaps, other miscellaneous people had to be killed as well; furthermore, the boss-man knew of something else. We really needed to stay on point. This was something I felt when he spoke. Only thing I wanted was an AR-15 with a night vision scope; long range striking ability, and silencer. A nine millimeter with 16 shots; prefer German Lugar. Just in case something up close and personal jump off. What the others carried was unknown, but I was more then sure it was something good.

Three days after receiving the guns and looking over the scenery. The assassination of Ricardo Melendez, and his family, day has arrived. Larry was a bit frustrated about the children and the 25% down payment received. He felt belittled and disrespected. The leader who placed the mark, his name was Mr. Leonardo Rodriguez. He was short, fat and a true enemy of Americans. Especially African Americans. We understood that getting back off the island without a war would be a risky task. **June 4, 1989**, 5:47pm. The day of the hit. We were all covered in black army typed clothing. We were informed that it was only the target and his family, or maybe a few other soldiers. We had to work with extreme caution; because I was the youngest I was placed on a nearby hilltop with the AR-15 to be the over-looker. The positions are Larry come from the **East**, James from the **West**, Billy from the **North** and little Harvey from the **South.** I watched silently, and James sneakiness appeared. His creeping skills were perfectly done. A fearless guard sat freely in the front of the large house smoking a cigarette, and reading a magazine what looked like a New York Times. Like a magical magician, James struck like thunder in the mistiness of night. There weren't any sound when the bullet made contact. One to the back of the head, and the man was of no more. He entered the house through the front door, and was no longer in my vision . . . .

.... Billy and Larry appeared simultaneously from each side of the house. Larry made contact with one guard on his way in. The guard was no longer of a threat. Unfortunately, the guard partner saw what went down and ran to get help. Running wickedly through the kitchen, he bummed into Harvey who was waiting patiently in the dark. The man's body fell helplessly to the floor, when the bullets struck his chest and face. It was the element of surprise. However, the sight of a murder frightened someone. Harvey was attacked by something that also sat in the dark. It gripped him tightly, hanging on to his back and neck; choking and scratching him compulsively. Hearing the commotion, James appeared heroically to Harvey's response for help. On arrival he noticed a small girl no more then seventeen swinging around wildly on the back of little Harvey. It appeared that the girl and the guard was freaking and fooling around when they both witness the death of their fellow friend. When Harvey killed her boyfriend she became crazy, however, James grabbed the girl by the hair and threw her roughly against a refrigerator door. The fragile child banged her head. She stood dazed and incapacitated. James raised his right hand with chrome 357 Magnum, placing it to the face of the helpless girl. Before he pulled the trigger, Little Harvey noticed it was a small child and he shouted.

"No James no! Please let him go!" James looked back at Harvey and pulled the trigger. For Harvey, everything moved in slow motion. James shattered her fragile brains all over the kitchen. She sat there slumped over; as her eyes remained opened. Death has called her name. Still looking into her eyes, Harvey couldn't believe the cold-heartedness of his partner. He looked back at James, and James smiled. At this point Larry and Billy entered the kitchen, noticing the two dead bodies. Larry looked on and saw the girl, recognizing the still smoking weapon in James hand, he looked at Harvey, shook his head and he walked away with disappointment. Billy looked at James, and they both walked off. James looked back at Harvey and smiled once more. Little Harvey just sat there asking himself if he was in the right line of work. He looked at the small girl's dead body, and closed his eyes. He realized that the mission was yet over. All the men started searching the area for the main target .....

I noticed a woman and man with a small child crawling from underneath the house. It's were they would hide if something would go wrong. I instantly realized it was the mark and his family. I placed the long AR-15 up against a small rock, aiming it in their direction. The escapists were now in my sight. Aiming at the man first, I pulled the trigger. It wasn't a sound or whisper from the riffle. The man just fell to the ground. He was killed instantly. I pulled the trigger once more at his head, making sure the target was gone. The woman screamed loudly as she not knew what just happened to her husband. She grabbed the child's hand and ran towards an automobile. Before reaching it, I fired the riffle at the ladies heart, striking her in the back. The bullet rushed down powerfully, as it forcefully ripped threw her back, exiting from the front of the slim woman's chest. The small boy who was around nine or ten, just stood there crying while watching his mother reach out helplessly for her last breathe of oxygen. The boy got down next to his mother. He pulled for her to get up, but she slipped silently away. He sat down next to her dead body and watched his mother as if she was sleeping. I placed my head down. I didn't know what to do. I didn't want to do it, but it was our job, and it was nothing personal.

"Sorry little friend, but your family caused this to happen to you," I said before pulling the trigger onto the child's head. Unexpectedly I noticed someone else coming. I looked around through the scope of the riffle. I realized it was Little Harvey. I placed the gun down, to watch Harvey handle the assassination of the child; besides, I didn't think I could have done it. At that moment Larry appeared, and they talked amongst each other. Harvey held the hand of the small boy. I was curious as to what he was doing. I fired a single shot at the window of the nearby car, shattering it instantly on contact. The two men jumped and looked around for me. Larry pointed in the direction of some trees, and Harvey picked up the small boy and ran off. I became devastated at my teams stupidity. I fired at the little boy, hoping to hit him without injuring Harvey. I knew if the boy wasn't killed it was our asses for showing disrespect to the Dominican Mafia. Not only will they try to murder us, but we will not see anymore of that million. Larry rushed towards the dead lady. I just looked on at our fatal mistakes. I couldn't believe my brother (the Thinker). I placed the riffle down as Larry rampaged through her pockets looking for something. Finding what appeared to be some car keys, he got into the car, drove about fifteen feet near some trees to pick up Little Harvey and the small boy. They then drove away. While driving off, James and Billy appeared. They fired their weapons at the fleeing car, thinking that someone was getting away. Minutes later, I informed them of the news. The two of them stood in disbelief. We all understood war with the Mafia. We believed it was unavoidable.

The very next day, the three of us sat back in a small village awaiting Little Harvey and Larry's telephone call. That's when the door bell rung. At the door stood two of Leonardo's men. We were to meet here after the hit to receive the rest of the money. Apparently the men came with no money and started asking questions about the murders. They stated that it was a man in the woods watching the hit as it went down. He called us amateurs, and weak assassins. I looked at Billy and Billy looked over at James. We all knew what had to be done. So before debating on the matter any longer, James jumped up with his 9miller meter and fired at the man closest to him. With hatred, so did Bill and I. James dropped his clip from the smoking gun and quickly replaced in another. I realized it was something that had to be done. The next steps was for us to get the hell up out of Domingo as quickly as possible before the news got back to Leonardo about what has just happened to his two soldiers. The door bell rung again and a voice appeared.

"Telegram for one James Williams!" We all held out guns close. It was a small child with a message from Larry. It quoted.

"Come to the nearest boating docks . . . Larry!" Knowing what the two pulled the night before, I was still concerned about their safety. Without Leonardo's men reporting back to him, I knew he would have the air ports and train stations blocked off; therefore, we made a detour and looked for the nearest boating docks as Larry requested. We approached a small private yacht. I observed a man with a small child walking freely. Billy shouted.

"Oh shit, there's Larry with that fuckin' kid!" Everyone in the vehicle leaned forward. I saw Harvey walking with an old Cuban looking gentleman reading what appeared to be a map. I started laughing loudly. I realized that Larry still held enough sense to go in the opposite direction. Even though I didn't approve of their recent tactics, it was too late to go back. The Cuban looking man was Larry back up plan. Larry thought of something going wrong so he prepared. Because of him, we may have avoided a war. Billy spoke.

"Man when I get my hands on that coward Harvey, I am going to kill that sorry bastard."

"Yeah, I never liked that chump anyhow," James replied while holding on to the steering wheel. I quickly spoke.

"Listen. What you two are going to do is sit back and do nothing to Harvey. I mean, I don't agree with either one of them, but it's because of them where getting away. What's done is done. Just think. Back in the states we were killing mutherfuckers for nothing. I believe them two fucked up something good for us out here, but that doesn't mean it was done intentionally, besides, we do have 250,000.00. Even though it's really nothing for what we been through, it should be treated as if it was everything to our lives." While talking to James and Billy I honked the horn several times before Larry noticed us. He called for Harvey. The two of them with the small boy and boating captain looked on. I continued to soften up my friends. "We're going to get on this boat, and were going to do our best in getting home safe. I love all of you ugly bastards the same, therefore, I don't want any to go down. Not right now anyhow. Can we be clear on that?"

"Yeah, you got it Paul," Billy said. James just looked on as if he wanted to kill something.

"Is that clear with you James or what?" I asked again. He just knotted his head in agreement. Stepping from the automobile, we walked towards the boat. Larry smirked at me and said.

"Welcome my beloved brothers'. I hope you niggas trip here wasn't as crazy as ours last night." Crazy as it was, when Little Harvey and Larry made their get away with the small child they were under-attacked by a small army. With the exceptions of a couple more lives they took, they made out alright. That sorry fuck face Leonardo had his men waiting for something to go wrong, and when it did, Larry and Little Harvey drove right into their trap. Walking closer to the boat, Harvey pointed his forty five automatic into our direction.

"I will not repeat myself. Nothing will happen to this kid. If any of you try to harm this kid we will have some trouble." James and Billy reached for their guns as well.

"Harvey! You better holster that fucking weapon before you be sorry!" Larry looked at Harvey and said.

"Cool down Harvey, it won't be any of that going on here. So put down that gun." Harvey put his gun at ease and walked away with the small boy. James and Billy looked at Harvey very aggressively, wanting to speak, but said nothing. Harvey on the other hand applied a smirk as he walked by James as James did him in the kitchen when he killed the small girl. The men made strong eye contact.

After a long trip back to the good old U.S.A., then to Philly, we split the small amount of cash, which gave us 50,000.00, a piece. We all went our separate ways, just to cool down and think. As for the small child, he was burned beyond recognition in a fire two month later in an American Welcoming Shelter. It would've been one more month before the child could've been a full fledge legal Alien of the United States. He was going to be adopted by Harvey and his fiancé Kiesha; however Larry, Harvey, James and I all gave the young boy a proper burial on the boarder of the United States and Mexico. We labeled this tube stone as **_Familia!_** (Family). Under that it read off, **"<u>The boy who's a part of us</u>"**

· ·

"Excused me sir," the prisoner guard said to me while I sat there in a complete mind blowing daze.

"Yes," I responded with the look of a depressed prisoner.

"Is your visit coming back into the visiting room, because you have been sitting out here alone for some time now without the company of a visitor? I understand that you may be a little upset about your visit leaving, but we need the room out here for other families. Therefore, if your visit doesn't return in the next two to three minutes or so, you must return back to your housing block." The lady was short and stocky. I just smiled and nodded my head at her words. I understood completely. Knowing the Connie wasn't about to return, I got up and walked slowly towards the door to return to my block. After I was stripped searched by two male officers, small tears started to fall down my face. I wiped them quickly. I was so upset at Larry and Connie, I could have killed somebody. I looked on A-Block for James, but I couldn't find him. I needed to talk to someone. I needed to find out why Larry would betray me. What was the reason for his disrespect? It was not doubt in my mind that Little Harvey was like family, but once we had a fall out Larry shouldn't continue the bound of their friendship. I walked on B-Block with the face of a hurt man. Waiting there for me was the new kid Raheem. I guess he was waiting so that we could finish talking about that telephone time. Larry, Connie and Harvey's disrespectfulness was beyond real, furthermore, I was the one doing time; therefore, I needed not to show any open emotions.

"Raheem, what's up?" I said. "Did everything go alright?" I asked.

"Yeah Paul, everything went good," he replied.

"Well, I am going to my hut. I need for you to come down there in about fifteen minutes."

"Okay!" He said. I walked away. On the way to my cell, I didn't talk to anyone else. I was completely in shock. It was indeed hard to fight what Connie just stated to me. This whole situation seems unreal; however, I had to face reality. What she said to me was all too real. I was just facing another experience of friendship, and its clever behaviors. I sat down on the side of my bed looking around at the four walls over, and over. I felt as if I was about to break apart. The passion in my heart for Larry and Connie was unexplained. I placed my large Polo towel up against the cell door. Now can't anyone see in my cell, and nor can I see out. I sat on the edge of my bed once again. This is when I broke down like an emotional female. I needed to do just that, or I would have gotten myself into some trouble, and I needed no more problems. GOD knows I had enough roughness to deal with.

"Only if I could've had bail, I would've paid it. I would've found that mutherfucka, Harvey and killed him. I would've tortured him painfully. I would've made sure he knew the true essence of fucking with Paul Williams," I said to myself. The tears continued to drop as I sat there expressing my anger. I wondered why this had to go down like this. I guess this is the hard way. "After all that we've been through. After all the times' we shared in each other's thoughts." *My heart wasn't ever going to be the same.* I wasn't prepared for the news I just received. It was a connection of three disappointing things all in one. "Who do I blame for their disrespect, and how long will I be in this bitch?" I asked myself many questions. This was indeed my moment on emotion. "How long will it be before I could get revenge on those who betrayed me?" I needed answers to my questions, but again I heard not one word. I placed my hands onto my head and slipped into another deep thought of Larry. This was the beginning of our test of true loyalty.

. . . .

"TRIP TO PITTSBURGH"

1992, I waited by the telephone for Larry to call. Then that's when it rung and I answered.

"Paul?" A voice said. It was Larry.

"Yeah, what's up Larry?" I asked in a low voice tone, while holding the telephone receiver away from my mouth to sip on my strawberry wine cooler.

"I am coming around 3 o'clock, so please be ready little bro."

"Okay," I said as I hung up the telephone gently. Larry has just returned back from the Bombay Island, located west of India. He took a Carnival boat trip for 7 days, and 6 nights. The Bombay Island was nothing more for him but 24 square miles of pure business planning. Larry was what you could consider the mastermind of our small brotherhood. Everyone had their own say so on every situation. Apparently, for some reason, Larry's plans or thoughts would always sound more perfectly thought out, so most of the time every one would agree with Larry's decision. He has now returned from the Luxury Island of Bombay. Larry asked me if I wanted to go on another trip with him out Pittsburgh on business. Bill, Little Harvey and James were out taken care of another job. Normally, it would be Larry and Little Harvey moving out together. I thought that this was just a little time to get away, besides I needed the quality time with my brother. Pittsburgh was located near the Allegheny County and the state of Ohio. Its Population was 369, 879. I was overwhelmed, but more flattered to go. The game plan was to go there, meet this chick name Robin, at a very popular night club called "Static". The club held very tight security. It was placed in the Homewood section of Pittsburgh on 22 & South, directly on the corner of Main St. After our contact with the female she'll then locate her peoples, and well meet up somewhere secluded for business. The drop for us was 10 uncut blue diamonds. The value was priceless. It was nothing but a sweet mission for 250,000.00; besides, I needed the vacation. It was told to Larry, that he needed to take a small amount of cash only and no weapons. All paid trip on the contact. I didn't know who Larry connection was on this mission, but I knew it was someone very powerful. These mutherfucker's, they even supplied us with a car to use. A 1992 Mustang that had features of a more aggressive and aerodynamic style than your average sports car. It was silver and black in color, with chrome cobra wheels. It was a convertible that suited the situation perfectly. Priced at $74,000.00. The trip was a 9hr. drive up. We were going to bullshit for another 24hrs, once the deal was made. We were going to find some out of town females before driving back home. Therefore, if you give or take, we'll be gone from Philadelphia for no more than 1 or 2 days. It was just the trip I needed. At first we thought about flying, but we figured that flying would've taking the excitement away. Furthermore I never been completely too trilled about flying, so we drove. After we drove 9hrs, we both realized that this small Suburban area was full of racist Police Officers. We were stopped several times, but it wasn't really about nothing. Arriving in Pittsburgh was completely satisfying. We knew that the hassles were over. Soon as we found the night club around 12:30 I went into action on this precious sweet thing sitting alone at the bar. As I sat down next to this slim female, I ordered two sexes on a beach. Without asking her if she even wanted a drink, one was for her. Meanwhile, while I was getting' my pimp on, Larry notice the female bartender with a name tag that read of Robin; therefore, he attended that situation with caution so that the business deal could get into motion. As for the female I was chilling with, her name was Linda and she was beautiful. She looked at me with very sexy eyes, and thanked me for the drink, although she made it quite clear that drinking was not her style. I really wondered why the hell is she sitting at a bar in a night club if she didn't drink. Anyway this beauteous female had a sparkle of class in her own form. I liked everything about this woman. Her intellectual stand point was wonderful and went perfectly with her unique body shape, but most of all, I liked the smoothness that followed her conversational flow. She spoke with a soft voice.

"Excuse me, are you always this forward or should I say, are you always this direct with the females you're trying to get to know?" She asked.

"Occasionally, but not always." I said smiling. "So tell me something. What's wrong?" I asked

"What's wrong?" She quickly replied. "Why must something be wrong with me because I am alone? Maybe I am just trying to get a piece of mind.

"Yes, I understand that. I guess what I mean is from the looks of things; someone of something has done some wrong in your life. Only as a man I felt the need to offer you a drink to calm your worries. Furthermore, I felt it was my giving duty to approach the matter with respect and ask if it was anything I could do to get to know you just a bit better. Now if my approach was wrong, then I do apologize, and I'll allow you to continue to yourself, and if not, I must ask. What is your name beautiful?" She just smiled once again, and I knew at that point she was welcoming me. She was going to be the one I was going to spend my little vacation with.

As Linda Devine and I continued to talk, I noticed Larry talking to a few brothers and some bartender chick. It looked like the business deal was about to go down, and it was going good. Whenever Larry was ready, I was also ready; therefore Linda and I exchanged pager numbers. We must definitely meet again. She even had a small Pittsburgh accent that turned me on. She grabbed her small purse and headed towards the door, but before she departed from me she said.

"Oh, by the way, what is your name handsome?"

"Paul. My name is Paul." I never found out why she sat there at the bar that night looking so down, but truthfully I didn't care. At that moment I notice a man looking at Larry from across the room. I watched him strongly as he watched Larry. Who the fuck was this man, I didn't know. Hopefully I could find out before we leave Pittsburgh. Larry looked up and waved his hand for me to come over. We then walked in the direction of the door exit, and headed towards our car. The chick Robin said out loudly.

"Nice Car!" She got into a black Lexus station wagon. As we drove away Larry stated that it was something very funny acting about that bitch Robin. He said that the men were very forward and calm, but Robin appeared to be too talkative, and was showing signs of nervousness. We both agreed that maybe it was her first deal, and she was over doing it. We followed her up to a small house on a hill. Everything was going perfectly. We walked in the house, and met two additional gentlemen. We sat down and talked for half hour or so before the diamonds was brought out. To me they looked like 10 beat-up small rocks. The exchange was about to be made, therefore, we were told to follow the female Robin to another house to make the transaction okayed. Unfortunately, Robin had other plans. She hired these three monkeys to run up on our car before the intersection, and kidnap us by gunpoint for the diamonds. This audacious bitch was going to do her dirty work, and let us go to deal with the repercussions for loosing the priceless blue jewels. Getting stuck up wasn't our style, but we're unarmed and when you're naked and at gunpoint, it's nothing you could do. Suddenly.

"GET ON THE GROUND! GET OUT THE GODDAMN CAR, AND GET THE FUCK ON THE GROUND!" I looked at Larry, and we did what they demanded. We had no weapons. We was out of town, therefore, we was completely fucked. We were blond folded. I got a small peak at the men before I was blond folded, they were dressed like nuns and held fully accurate machinery. They placed the cold weapons on the back of our neck, and placed us in the back of that bitch Robin's wagon. They pilled the tires on the expensive cars as they made a u-turn in the direction of on coming traffic. I asked Larry did he have the diamonds on him. He said no. He said that they were inside the car. I asked where, and he wouldn't tell me. In more ways than one I understood him. It was silence and heavy breathing for minutes. We finally came to a halt. For about 6 minutes of slamming us around in the trunk, my heart thumped wildly. I felt the fear flowing from Larry's body. I thought perhaps that it was our time to die. I heard what appeared to be a garage door open. I knew that the men were going to try to torture us in finding out where directly the diamonds were. I figured, no matter how painful the ordeal turns out to be, I will not fold, besides, I really don't know where the diamonds are anyway. We were tied tightly to a chair, and we heard the men treating our vehicle like trash. Our pockets and clothing were ripped off. Our expensive shoes were shredded to pieces. One of the men asked Larry where the diamonds were. Larry said nothing. It was our code of silence, which we knew and trusted. It was our connection in loyalty until death do us part. The men started shouting louder when they couldn't find the diamonds.

"**WHERE THE FUCK IS THE DIAMONDS YOU PIECES OF SHIT!**" Again, neither Larry nor I said anything. My heart calmed down. If I was going to die, then I wanted to die calmly.

"**OKAY . . . OKAY . . . YOU WANT TO PLAY LIKE THAT. EVERY TIME I ASK YOU A QUESTION AND YOU DON'T TELL ME WHAT I NEED TO KNOW, I AM GOING TO CUT OFF A FINGER.**" My heart jumped silently inside my chest. I was unable to stay calm. I really couldn't sit there un-nervous and listen to my brother get tortured by this bitch and her team of un-experienced kidnappers. I mean, these stupid mutherfuckers knew that we just had the diamonds, so how far could the diamonds be between us and the car. If they would take their time to search the car, or us professionally, maybe they can succeed and forget about all the torturing and just kill us.

"**ONCE AGAIN, WHERE IS THE DIAMONDS**" The one man asked again, and again Larry said nothing. One of the men smacked me across the face with something heavy. I felt the blood flowing down my cheeks as I fell to the ground. I was picked back up swiftly, to prepare for another smack. No less than a second after the smack, the one man who was doing all the talking cut off Larry small pinky. Larry screamed like a bitch in labor. The tears slowly ran down my face as I continued to listen. I now heard the female's voice.

"Cut off another one until one of them starts talking!" Before the man could cut another finger, I heard a loud slam at the garage door. We sat there and listened while the broad and her accomplices begun to panic. The garage door rose up slowly and gun fire started. Gun rounds went off like war-war one. Larry threw his body into mine, and we both fell towards the cold greasy ground. We cuddled close to get out of the line of fire. It went on for about 3 minutes. I heard a man's voice. I then felt his fingers as he took the tight cloth from around my eyes. I slowly turned to look at Larry. The blood from his small finger was flowing heavy. The room looked like we was just in hell, but I have seen worse. I was glad that we weren't killed. As for the men who raged into the room, they were sent to look over Larry, while the deal went down. One of the men was the man I observed looking at Larry in the club. I looked around the room for any survivors. Would you believe that the bitch Robin was still breathing? She held a gunshot wound to the abdomen. She squalled around in pain, and was asking someone to help her. I smiled at the ignorance of the bloody woman. She realized that the tables have turned a complete 360 degrees. I walked over to Larry and the man who held him. I grabbed the man's pistol from his right hand, and walked over to Ms. Robin. I placed the black Magnum thoroughly up against her forehead. She was slowly slipping in and out of consciousness. She was fighting viciously as a victim from her own death. When she slipped back in I pulled the trigger and watched her brains splatter all over the dirty garage floor. I looked at her, and felt nothing.

Nothing could've explained her cleverness. I was very grateful for her death. Meanwhile, Larry walked over to the car. He lifted up the hood and pulled the diamonds from a cooled off place inside the engine. I was like damn. The man makes all the right moves. I realized that no matter what happened to us or the car they would've never found them diamonds. It was a built in compartment that sat on the driver side of the vehicle. Once activated, it would pull whatever it held into the hidden part of the engine. No one knew of this but Larry and the direct connect. Suddenly we heard the police, and needed to go. We thanked the men, and everyone went into different directions. Larry said he didn't want to go to the hospital out there in Pittsburgh, because of the recent killings. He wanted to go to a hospital out in the Ohio area, so that's where we went. No matter what goes on in our lives, pressure will never break us. The mission was completed, and we were rewarded handsomely for our bravery. It was only another situation that has gone sour. This could happen to anyone in the rough world of *Corruption*, and *Double-cross*, At that point in my life, I knew that I could trust Larry with anything at anytime, but sometimes it can also be the one you trust the most to test your heart. Sometimes your friends can be your worse enemies, and your enemies could turn out to be your most trusted friend. Life is unpredictable, but it's also about taken chances. As for my chick Ms. Linda Devine, she was never seen by me again.

. . . .

Several knocks on the cell door snapped me from the thoughts of Larry. I stood up, because I knew exactly who it was.

"Just one second family." I shouted at my cell door. I ran some water on a rag and wiped my face. I needed to straighten up before allowing anyone to enter. Pulling the heavy towel from the doorway, I noticed Raheem standing there waiting patiently against the wall. He looked at me and I invited him into my small place of housing. We shook hands again, as I pulled out a chair, so that he could sit on it. I started talking, telling him about the huge responsibility of the telephone time. What goes on, and what to expect. Even though he was upstate before, the rules were a bit different in the county. He was here in Hamsburg before, but only for one day. He had a quick trial and was transfer up state over night because of his young age.

"Well Raheem it seems to me that you're a well understood person. I like your style. Moreover, I liked the way you have approached me about your situation. I have no problem sharing what we have in our unity as a squad. If you have any problems about that time, I ask that you acknowledge someone, or in the same straighten everything out to the best of your ability." I said.

"So is that my telephone time for now on? Do I use it everyday at the same time?" He asked

"Look here, I am giving that time to you. You can use it everyday, or don't use it at all. The choice is yours. You can give it to anyone you wish to give it to, however, I prefer you give it to someone from South-Philly but like I said, the choice is yours.

"Look here Paul, I really do appreciate the telephone time. I am glad that you can relate to my situation. I thought that I would've gotten myself into some trouble by now behind this telephone shit. I am very thankful that you were thorough enough to see me through this ordeal. If it's anything I could do for you in return you just let me know. I am here for you through thick and thin. My word is my bond, and I don't break my bond for no one." I just looked at him. Only if he knew what I was going through. His bond means nothing to me. His loyalty towards me meant nothing. What do I need him for, nothing? He better be lucky as hell, that I am the man I am, because I give a flying fuck about his problems. However, I must maintain, therefore, I mustn't allow Larry, Connie or Little Harvey to dictate or destroy my personality; fuck them all. Their double cross has nothing to do with the man who sits before me today. I don't know him like that, but sometimes when odd worlds meet, it can be a chance of a life time. It can either be destruction or happiness. I will try his word. I will seek deep into his soul and pull out all the negativity that lies humbly in his heart. The words that sleeps so openly and comfortable upon him.

"Raheem, are we clear to the point of no return? Oh, yeah, one more thing. If you fuck me in anyway, I will make it my personal business to see you myself." He just sat there looking on with eyes of understanding. I then stated that I needed some rest. I told him that I was some difficult times with family and friends. I told him that he could have the rest of my telephone time of that night. I needed not to call anyone. We shook hands before departing once again. I stretched back and laid down on my hard but comfortable bed. I dozed off into another deep dream.

. . . .

"A DREAM OF PASSION"
PART TWO

When I finally do approach my darling, soft and gently I'll hold her in my arms just to daze down at her charming-ness. To look deep into her sparkling eyes, while caressing her thighs tightly. Reminiscing to the sounds of our heard thumping together. I'll then begin to kiss her on her neck, while rubbing my fingertips up and down her back. Over-excited, I'll then grab her bottom lip gently with my teeth and suck on it like a fresh piece of fruit plucked straight from the Bahamas Island. He lips is oh, so sweet and tasteful. Slowly I'll then begin to remove her clothing while romancing her body with my charm and adorable ways, as she begins to undress me as well. The sight of her being 50% percent nude leaves me completely speechless. Right now, I feel as if I am going to explode. I can feel my penis vibrating rapidly through my cotton boxers. I am now hers forever in a day. Passionately, I'll then lay her down comfortable on the king size bed rubbing my harden penis roughly against her thighs. Calling out her name loudly is a whisper, "Oh, Denise my love, you feel so, so good." I'll then make passionate and unforgettable love to her. She is my queen. She is "***My True Desire For Passion***"

I am now kissing on her breast. Licking softly on her nipples until they are dark in color. The dark color symbolizes that they are aroused and full of sexual sensitivity. Now I shall press my penis against her warm vagina. Grinning on her, stroking myself right to left, and left to right. She's now flowing heavier than she has ever flowed through her silk panties. I'll then take my right hand and place it between her thighs. I touch her gently and she moans out with pure pleasure in an aggressive manner. She wants me more. She's so warm, and so wet. As I begin to place the same hand inside her panties, her grip around my body tightens. The love making that she wants more than anything now becomes more predictable. I shall now take my index finger and slid it directly into her warmness. The soft moan she makes arouses me wildly, as I stroke her in and out, out and in until she is unable to handle anymore. She grabs me and holds me tightly. She whispers quietly in my ear.

"Paul please make love to me," She is, "***My True Desire For Passion***".

I jumped up out of my sleep; sweating like the world was against me. My penis was aroused, and I felt like masturbating. I then started thinking about what happened earlier the day and the mood for a fast nut was lost. I wiped my face with a not so hot rag. I was now 2:23a.m., and the institution was sound asleep. My body was tired, so I attended to get more rest. I didn't really know why I kept dreaming of this woman on and off, but maybe it was trying to tell me something. I figured, if I was to dream about her again, I was going to write her a letter simply to find out some things about her. I knew that she was really nothing more than a friend; also she was someone that Larry uses to deal with, and therefore I thought nothing of it. I stretched out wildly and fell back to sleep.

The next morning, I heard something tapping against my cell door. I forced myself to rise up, so that I could get out of bed. My body felt as if I could sleep forever. My muscles were sore. My head was pounding. I stood up and said,

"Yeah! Who is it?" A voice appeared.

"Paul, it's me Raheem. Wake up homie." he said. I walked straight towards the cell door when I heard who it was. Walking towards the door, I wiped the cold out my eyes. I thought that he was waking me up about something that was going on, on the block that I should've known about. Arriving at my cell door, I observed the gentleman who's now a companion of mine. I was upset because of him waking me up, and it was nothing going on bad. He just came to my cell for general purpose. What the hell. I was up, and now ready to stay up. I asked Raheem.

"What is it that you want this early in the morning? I mean, it must be like 7a.m.

"Man, what you talking? It's now 11:25 and it's time for lunch. Goddamn my man you must have had one helluva night. She must be one special chick. You don't even know what time it is." He said as he walked inside my one man cell, with a small noticeable smirk on his sneaky face.

"What do you mean I must have had one helluva night?" I replied. Raheem must have had thought that I was up all night enjoying life with some female photo's or magazines. Little did he understand that them kind of thoughts was far from my head. Connie, Little Harvey, and Larry were the main focus in my thoughts. "I hope you just didn't come in my cell just to assassinate my character by thinking that I was up all night degrading myself on some funky ass smutt photos. Nigga, don't you watch the news. These mutherfuckers are trying their best to hang my black ass. Man I have bigger problems and I thought you knew that. My main thought last night was trying to figure out how to get the hell out of this situation. If you can't understand that I am trying to be free, then I am seriously stating that you stay the fuck away from me."

Raheem Muhammad stood in silence. He figured that he was only trying to make small talk, for a little laughter. He then knew my position and realized that I was not the playing type. As he looked at me, his upper lip quivered, as he spoke.

"Paul, don't take things so serious. I apologize for my early morning interruption, and for my words of disrespect. I assure you that it will never happen again. By the way, are you going to lunch because it's getting late and I am really hungry? Take that walk with me family," he said while looking out the doorway to see if anymore inmates was going towards the door for lunch.

"Common, lets go," I said. I knew that this young fellah was a cocky one. Furthermore, I respected something about him. He had strong confidence in his ways. His approach was appropriate, but besides that, I had no real reason, or reasons to neglect his company. I welcomed his friendship. Anyway Raheem stood at the door leaning against the wall, waiting for me to put my shoes on. I couldn't believe that I have slept so long. I knew I needed that rest; besides, a restful man can always think a bit better, in a situation like mine. As we walked towards the chow hall I quickly shouted,

"Hey big bro. Hole you horses, little brother is here."

"I have been looking for you little brother."

"Man we need to talk." I said. James looked at me and understood instantly that something was wrong. Anyway, I introduced him to Raheem, and the three of us walked towards the chow hall. While walking inside the chow hall, Raheem shouted loudly.

"Hey Paul look over there. Its two homosexuals making out in front of everybody." James looked at me and I just shoved my shoulders at Raheem's ignorance. I couldn't understand his failure to adapt in the rough world of prison. James walked closely towards Raheem and said aggressively.

"Listen here you young chump. Listen to me and listen good nigga. I really don't know you that well, and truthfully I really don't need to know you, but your getting a pass right now because my little brother thinks of you in a good way. What you need to do is find a way to keep your mutherfucking voice down when you're speaking on something that doesn't even concerns you. So mind your own fucking business and focus on your own surroundings. Besides shit like that goes on all the time in this place, so get comfortable with seeing it. Be aware of it, and never ever speak on it again. However, don't get that situation fucked up. They're still men first before anything else, and we don't need no unnecessary wars because of some loose ass trying to prove his manhood, to another man." James turned and picked up his tray of food. He looked at me, and I nodded my head for him to continue. Raheem was okay, but it was some things he needed to work on. After James continued to grind Raheem up about his mistakes, I looked over at the gay men to see how they felt about what they heard Raheem say. Even though they weren't a treat, Raheem still needed to know his place. He must know how to maintain his mouth, before he could belittle someone else. One of the homosexuals dropped a tray of food. I turned back around to see what that was, and I noticed one of them picking up some spilled food; and before I could turn my head away he looked up at me and caught my eye. My mouth opened in disbelief. My heart raced for a second. I couldn't believe who it was I was looking at. It was *Newsy Earl,* and he was definitely someone's bitch. Earl turned his head away quickly, and so did I. I walked away shaking my head. I suddenly realized that this was his reason for not wanting to come back over Hamsburg. I guess in another jail he could be a man but over in Hamsburg he was nothing but a fag, a sweet nigga, who loved to take it up the ass. From the way things looked he was enjoying his lifestyle, so I figured oh well, I had my own problems. Paying *Arleen* no more attention, James and Raheem was getting better acquainted. I sat down as Raheem got up to talk with someone he knew. I broke the news to James about Connie, Little Harvey, and Larry. He was stunned and speechless. He told me to remain strong, and not allow it to distract my current situation. I felt that was impossible to do. However he was right. Again, I mustn't create weakness in my soul because of their betrayal. I have never been faced with such pain. It was even that much harder because I was incarcerated. However, the lifestyle I was involved in, this was part of that territory. I was dealing with people that I loved and because of it, they blood is spilled all over my heart. While eating, James and I talked some more. We then finished and headed back towards our blocks. James said his goodbye's until later at yard time. I left Raheem, and headed down towards my cell. I looked on my cell floor and noticed that I had a pass. I had another visitor. I was hoping that it wasn't Connie, or no one that crossed me. I slowly walked down to the visiting room. A smile came upon my face when I noticed my Attorney, Mr. Donnie. We talked silently about the case. He told me to prepare myself for the unexpected. He asked plenty of questions about my alibi's on these particular days. We talked for a little more then one hour. He stated before I left, that I was going to trial sometime in May. As we departed I felt a little better, but I wanted to get this shit over with as soon as possible. I knew that James was scheduled to go to court in June. I returned back to the block and headed towards the telephone room. I picked up the receiver to call Connie, but I was too hurt to talk to her, so I called my mother instead. She answered, and we talked for about fifteen minutes before we hung up. I told her that I was doing just fine, and she stated that the man who killed my father was schedule to go to court in June. She asked about James and I told her about his court date. I don't know what it was about these months, but a shit load of us was to be tried around the same time. I hung up the telephone receiver, and walked down towards my cell to get some rest. I really wanted to see who that brother was face to face. I was mad at myself, because I felt like I let my father down again. However, I had to stay focus and worry more about what was going to happen to me, but I will kill the man who killed my father. If my father was alive today I could've counted on him to give me some positive advice on how to remain strong. He was a very wise man, and we all listened and respected his authority. I remember our conversational sessions all to well. I will make sure he's at peace.

May 9, 1995, I was scheduled to go to court the next day. My every move appeared to be nervous. Things in the institution were going well. Raheem and I became even closer. He stated that when he was done in court next month, he had to return back up state to finish doing his previous sentence. Raheem was my main man, and if I was going to do any upstate time, then I was going to try very hard to do that time with a soldier. The day quickly came to an end, and I received a message from James saying that he wishes me good luck at trial. I smiled at his brief message, because I needed all the luck in the world. I laid on my bed and looked up at the lights until I silently dozed off.

CHAPTER ELEVEN

TRAIL

"STATEMENT OF THE CASE"

The form of this case is in the nature of the arrest and trial of the defendant *Paul Williams*, hereafter referred to as the accused of the crimes of Aggravated Assault (*one count*), Firearms not to be Carried Without a License (*two counts*) Carrying firearm on Public Streets or Public Property, (*two counts*) Criminal Mischief, (*two counts*) Possessing Instruments of a Crime, (*two counts*) Simple Assault (*three counts*) Recklessly Endangering Another Person (*two counts*) First Degree Murder (*two counts*) Conspiracy to commit murder (*two counts*) in the County of Philadelphia.

Appellant was arrested on August 9, 1994**,** for the charges above which stemmed from two separate shooting incidents, which occurred on ***July 7 1994 & August 3, 1994.*** On August 3, 1994, at around 9:10p.m. Mr. Harvey Bells was at his residence at 3116 South 31 Street, in the ***Tasker Homes*** area in South Philadelphia. Witness stated that some people had gathered outside of his house looking for Mr. Harvey Bells son Little Harvey Bells Jr. However, gunshots rang out, and the community was stunned. Mr. Harvey Bells, house was hit by several bullets. Mr. Bells testified at the evidence hearing on October 20, 1994 that when he heard the gunshots he ran into his house with his family, and then ran out the back door for cover with his family. As they headed in the direction for their car in the parking lot on the side of their house, he heard an additional five to ten more gunshots and was hit almost simultaneously in the left leg by bullets. Once in the kneecap that shattered it into multiple fragments that lay posterior to the tibia. He was also struck once in the hip which shattered that bone as well. One of the bullets was not taken out of his leg do to medical reasons. As he fell to the ground his family rushed him back towards their home for safety. He stated that it was he, his wife and two son's Little Harvey and Aaron. Before the man was completely out his sight, he was able to positively identify his shooter as the defendant. When the police arrived, they found Mr. Bells on the kitchen floor suffering from triple gunshots wounds. When the officers asked Mr. Bells who had shot him, Mr. Bells told the police it was in fact the defendant Mr. Paul Williams. A police officer also testified at the hearing, that when he arrived on the scene, he saw the defendant, whom he knew from the neighborhood and from previous experiences riding away in a white Jeep Cherokee. The police officers gave chase and several gunshots rang from the fleeing truck causing the officers to lose control, therefore the defendant was unable to be apprehended. Mr. Bells also testified that earlier on July 7, 1994 he had a bad confrontation with the defendant. He tried several times to straighten things out with their two families. The defendant was calm, and assured Mr. Bells that the entire incident was over. An unenclosed amount of money was exchanged and the men went their separate ways. The defendant didn't get a chance to testify at the hearing, but he later stated to an investigator that he was home at the time of the shooting, and didn't commit the crime. The defendant had an alibi witness; his girlfriend and soon to be wife Connie Perkins. She would testify that the defendant was indeed at home during the time of the shooting. She characterized her future husband to the investigators as a homebody. A man who loves to spend quality time with family and friends. One who loves to watch television and rarely went out at night. She stated that she could never imagine him as the assaulter, nor a murderous companion. On August 7, 1994, around 7p.m. the defendant was placed on the scene of two double homicides at 9th & Huntington Park. Two people was killed, both in which was Philadelphia Police Officers. The defendant was positively identified as the man who was on the scene of the crime, right before the killings occurred. The witnesses remain anonymous for trail. The defendant would be tried before the Honorable Michael P. Green. Jury selections will be on April 9, 1995, both cases will be heard by the same judge; however the cases will have different juries. Trial date is scheduled for May 10, 1995.

"DAY OF TRIAL"

May 10, 1995, after a long stressful month of jury picking for two different cases. I was exhausted, but now ready for trial.

"Mr. Williams, please stand. Judge Michael P. Green presiding." My heart pumped heavy. I was now standing before the impossible. I have never imagined me being in this situation. I always thought my cleverness would never get caught in the underground world of corruption. I knew that I was going to probably beat the aggravated assault charges because they really had nothing. Besides, I didn't shoot that sonuvabitch Mr. Bells. In fact, I wish that I have shot and killed that double crosser.

As I looked slightly around the courtroom, I realized that the room was very quiet. Set placements were for the cop's family on one side and my family on the other. Before I entered the courtroom, I saw Connie with little Paul, my mother, and several other supporters of me. I looked at the news cameras with eyes of a small puppy, as the clean cut gentleman stated, "This is Jamison Madison, from NBC news with the close up of the case that shocked the nation. Mr. Paul Williams, the man you see going into the courtroom will face his day of faith today. He was charged with the double killings of two police officers in the line of duty last year, at ninth and Hunting Park, located in the lower section of North Philadelphia. The two officers will always be remembered as true heroes. The two officers died helplessly in the hands of the accuser. From what NBC understand, the district attorney will argue that the defendant is guilty of said crimes, while the defendants' attorney will try and prove his innocents beyond a reasonable doubt.

His client is the victim of a racist and corruptive police district. That they would do anything in their power to see his client sit in prison for the rest of his natural life, or die, for the lost of their fellow police officers. It was also said that this man Mr. Paul Williams will be tried for several other charges, including one dramatic aggravated assault charge on a long term neighbor. "This is Jamison Madison, coming live from City Hall in Philadelphia at NBC news. Back to you Scott."

I walked in, sat down, and slowly looked at the district attorney. He looked at me with a small smirk. I smirked back and we were ready for war. The district attorney had to notify me of my rights before the trial judge and jury. After like 15 minutes of questions, the aggravated assault charge was to be tried first. "Trial was ready,"

"COURT IS IN SESSION"

JUDGE: "Mr. Denovicchi, are you ready for trial?"

Lawyer: "Yes your honor."

JUDGE: "Mr. Roger Jones, are you ready for trial?"

District attorney: "Yes I am your honor."

JUDGE: Very well then, Mr. Denovicchi, please bring in your first witness.

Denovicchi: "Your honor, I call Ms. Connie Perkins to the stand."

As Connie opened the courtroom door, my heart was in complete shock because of what she stated to me on a visit a while back. I looked at her and smiled. Even though she crossed me with disrespect, I was still feeling the vibes of love, in which we once shared. We made strong eye contact as she walked by. I questioned myself. "Why did she do something to me so cruel? The world would never know."

Denovicchi:

Question: Ms. Perkins, please state to the court your full name, age, and relations to the defendant.

Answer: My name is C-O-N-N-I-E P-E-R-K-I-N-S, I am nineteen years old, and Paul Williams is my boyfriend.

"Her boyfriend! What the fuck is she on drugs or something. After what she had done towards me she still had the audacity to say that I was her man. Boy, some people have some nerve." I thought. After Connie stated her name and age, she was asked plenty more questions from my lawyer before being crossed examined by the district attorney.

The DA's questions were strong, but Connie has always been a very intellectual woman. She knew all the right words to say and her responses were very accurate. The District Attorney continued to flow with his questions, but it was nothing she couldn't handle. That was check for me on the aggravated assault charge.

JUDGE: "Okay, Ms. Perkins, you may step down. Thank you for your testimony.

Denovicchi: call your next witness."

Denovicchi: "I call upon Mrs. Paulette Williams, the defendant's mother.

Question: Mrs. Williams, will you please state for the record your full name, age, and relation to the defendant.

Answer: Well, my name is Mrs. P-A-U-L-E-T-T-E W-I-L-L-I-A-M-S, I am 42 years old, and the defendant is my son.

I sat there and looked at my mother. I fell deep into a trance. I started memorizing her past, and the things we went through to make it this far.

. . . .

"ANNIVERSARY PARTY"

June 8, 1990, 2:32pm., My mother and father just returned from the grocery store. As they walked in their home, everyone yelled surprise. Some was standing on the top steps, while others were yelling from the kitchen area. My parents were shocked and stunned but full of appreciation. It was their 21st Wedding Anniversary. Larry, James, Billy, Little Harvey, and I have planned a beautiful party for their special-ness, and for their long term relationship. Larry and James has given them both a $2,500.00 necklace, with both of their names printed deep in script writing. Each necklace contains 3 diamonds that circled their names in the rotation of a heart.

Billy, Little Harvey, and I all chipped in and gave them both a large lump of cash. They were overwhelmed and extremely excited. The food was freshly brought from across seas. Everyone they knew and cared for was present for that special occasion. We ordered seven mild bottles of that bubbly stuff, two large Happy Anniversary cakes, shrimp, crab, lobster, and plenty more. We prepared everything to make that special day wonderful. Momma always wanted a trip to Vegas. She has been trying very hard to save up her little pennies to do just that. She worked part time excepting no cash from her boys. Therefore, she did her own thing, but if she needed us, we were always there. Poppa had big plans as well. He always wanted to go to Las Vegas, or maybe Atlantic City, around the healthy casinos, to gamble away his money like a wealthy man.

After a long 2 hours into a helluva party, as the youngest son, it was my destiny to propose a toast. So, I rang a small bell to get everyone's attention. At that time everyone's eyes were locked on me, and they were very quiet. I started grinning like a hyena. Then, "That's right little bro, speak your peace," James said casually. I was nervous, so I spoke softly.

"I would like to propose a toast to the love one's of my life, Mr. and Mrs. Williams, my beloved parents." I placed my wine cooler down on a glass table. I licked my dry lips to make them moist. I then flowed with my words. As I stood there, I saw focus-ness, as everyone just listened on. Momma and Poppa held hands as they smiled at me joyously. "Again," I said, "I would like to propose a toast to the man and woman who gave me such a wonderful childhood. The ones who stayed on top of me, when I lost my head, and needed someone to lean on. The ones who guided me through rough times, and held me and my brothers close when time was at their most drastic points in our lives." I looked directly at them and spoke, "Thank you mother, and thank you father, thank you both for everything. I would like to say that my love for you two will always increase as days grow old. If I could wish for one thing in this world, it would be for me to stay young, and for you two to stay younger. That way I could never leave home and always have you two to hold me when my nights frighten me. May you two love birds enjoy your 21st Wedding Anniversary gifts and the love and joy in this room. Thank you for being who you are. I love you guy's. My mother sat there on my father's lap, as her eyes were misty while listening to her baby son say those things. She looked on with pure happiness. After two more long speeches from Larry and James, they were given two round trip tickets to Las Vegas, and two tickets to Atlantic City. All paid expenses on Billy, Little Harvey, James, Larry, and me.

Even though we wanted our parents to have a wonderful anniversary party, we had to remember that our parents had some serious drinking issues. We watched closely, so that they wouldn't have too much to drink. We have had too many moments that went so perfect, until the ugly-ness turn things around because of their drinking. Casual scenes turned crazy in the matter of minutes. That day was a day we was not having any foolishness because of drinking. After a long day of dancing and partying, it was now time for everyone to say their goodbyes. At 8:30pm the house was clear. My mother and father stood up drinking a little more. Little Harvey and Billy headed towards the door as my father's words started to get louder, as they dragged out.

My parents started rumbling on about things that happened during the party. Billy and Little Harvey was now gone. They knew how ugly things could get with my parents, so before my snapping-out-parents turned on them, they got the hell out of there. Slowly, my tipsy mother started accusing my father of eye watching our long time neighbor and close friend Ms. Hearts. My father returned the argument with,

"You can go to hell Paulette. I don't owe you or any motherfuckin' body an explanation on shit I do in this house. Do you understand that woman?" My mother snapped at his cold words and the fight was now on. Larry, James, and myself was completely happy that everybody was gone before they started blabbering their foul language and expressing behaviors that was completely inappropriate for that occasion. We were now saved from their embarrassment. We figured it was their day, so they can argue if they wanted to.

Things didn't go as we were hoping they go. Like most couples that drink and fight, they either curse themselves to sleep, fall straight asleep, or sometimes make love before sleeping. We were hoping that they fall asleep soon; we needed to go to separate homes. It was now 9:30p.m., and they were still going at it. We really figured that we needed to hang around until they were asleep. While waiting upstairs, we reflected on our younger childhood days and laughed like crazy at our childhood pictures completely paying the argumentative people downstairs no mind whatsoever.

At that moment while being totally relaxed, we heard a loud smash, like something or someone jumped through a window. My mother screamed at the top of her lungs. We quickly jumped to our feet. Each of us pulled out a gun, as we rushed down the steps towards the scene. My mother continued to scream,

"Oh my God, I am so sorry, I am . . ."

"What the hell happened?" Larry shouted at my mother.

"Mom, what did you do?" I asked while I looked past her to see my father. I saw my pops on the floor fighting with his strength to get up. As he fought endlessly with his self, huge chunks of thick blood ran from his arm onto the expensive rug. Apparently, my mother pushed my father backwards as they were arguing. My father being drunk lost his balance and fell hands first into the expensive glass table. The one I just made the speech from earlier that day. The glass shattered and sliced his arm from the palm to the muscular part of the forearm. The blood flowed heavy. My mother sat on the sofa and continued to apologize for her play in the accidental accident. My father continued to move around as if nothing happened. His blood was splashing all over the house. He needed medical treatment and he needed it fast. However, the alcohol had his mind full of aggressive behavior and ignorance. As we tried to calm him down to take him to the hospital, he fought us off one by one. Therefore we had no other choice but to tackle him down and force him to receive the appropriate medical attention needed. The doctor's stated that if he would've continued to fight without the proper attention, he would've died by bleeding to death. The alcohol has made his situation much more complicated. The next day after spending all night in that stinking hospital, we watched the doctors calm him down with medication. Larry, James, mom, and I looked on as they placed 34 butterfly stitches on the in and outside of the large slashed wound. My mother and father talked about their problem and how close someone almost died because of their alcoholic cravings and stupidity.

After they talked they hugged and kissed. They tried hard to put that unfortunate-ness in the past, but my father kept complaining about the agonizing pain he was receiving from the fresh wound. It was a huge lesson that needed to be learned. My mother stood by his side and took care of him until the stitches came out. I guess love is a very powerful thing. When you love someone as much as they love each other, then I guess life can get no greater. After that dramatic experience, Larry, James, and I had a long talk with our parents. We talked about the unawareness of their actions from drinking. We came to a wise conclusion, *no more drinking*, or try hard to come down. My mother agreed and so did my father at that particular time. After like a week later, my father didn't really take heed to the conversation and he started drinking again. Because of it, it caused him his life . . . .

. . . .

I was yanked back into reality from my daze. My mother's vision has never looked so ravishing. I only could imagine what things would be like if my father was alive today simply to see his wife fight so hard for the freedom of her baby son. She testified to the best of her ability, but her luck must face misfortune. The District Attorney has pulled out a considerable large amount of tricks. She was not prepared for his mellow dramatic questions. They came like a runaway train, and she was only a passenger caught in the line of fire. Her responses were sharp, but her sharpness leads to inaccurate time and dates. I was taken into custody on August 9, 1994. She quoted that the police arrested me from her house on August 7, 1994. Her shield was shattered in the blink of an eye. It was all open doors on her. The District Attorney chewed her up like a fresh doggie bone.

I just sat there, looked and listened on. I really couldn't understand most of the language. Besides, I knew that the aggravated assault charge was going to be beat. My whole thought process was focused on the two police officers. I knew that the odds were against me. Here I was a young black male, with no extraordinary education. Sitting in front of the Honorable Judge facing an aggravated assault charge, followed by two cop killings.

"Yeah, my young life was going swell!"

My mother's testimony has come to an end. The look on her face expressed a victory. I just smiled at her as she walked by my chair. My lawyer fumbled with paperwork before speaking to the Judge.

JUDGE: "Mr. Denovicchi please call on your next witness."

Denovicchi: Your Honor, I call upon Mr. Paul Williams.

My heart dropped. The sweat started to run down my face. I felt the warning of cautiousness. I can't explain why I felt fear that day. I have never thought of this position. My legs trembled like I was a weary old man. I took deep breaths to focus on my surroundings. I was not going to hang myself, so I must think wisely. I looked into the District Attorney's eyes as I approached the bench. He stared down on me as if I was a wounded child. His eyes were dark black and cold. He expressed extreme hostility and a pinch of dislike towards me. The reason for his high animosity has no explanation. I must pull back on my animosity towards him, and show no fear, hatred or any emotion. I sipped on a glass of water that was placed in front of me. I cleared my vocal cords and prepared for the pouring of questions.

The District Attorney yelled, pointed, shouted, and threw material as he interrogates my intelligence with professional tactics. I was no idiot, even though I have stumbled over some words. I was feeling my confidence as a winner. He couldn't intimidate my mind, besides I held a heavy heart. As he concluded his questions, the Judge looked on with humbleness. His face expressed no persuasive communication. I was lost and I didn't know where this case was heading.

My Lawyer continued with the questions, then the District Attorney, then my Lawyer again. It went on back and forth for three days. The last day Mr. Harvey Bells was to testify again and like I figured his words flowed through to the jury like electricity. I looked on in complete disappointment. He spoke and spoke and then he contradicted himself. My lawyer rushed and jumped on his faulty allegations, but the District Attorney cleared things up. This man had all his work in order. I admired his aggressiveness and his ability to stay on top of all his errors.

After hearing Mr. Bell's complaint, he was ordered to step down from the stand. The jury went in for deliberation. It was almost an hour before their return. I sat there inpatient. The case that was going so smooth in the beginning has come to its final closure. Everyone was let back into the courtroom. Both victims' families was sitting and awaiting the outcome of the aggravated assault charge. The Bells wanted it all to come to an end, but families of the dead officers' wanted me to suffer by all means necessary, for the double murders of their loved ones.

JUDGE: "Jury, have you reached a verdict?"

JURY: "Yes we have your Honor."

JUDGE: "Mr. Williams, will you please stand?"

JURY: "Your Honor, we the Jury find the defendant Mr. Paul Williams, guilty of all charges. For the brutal crime of first degree aggravated assault and related charges. We the Jur . . . ."

My mind froze. I heard the cheering of the victims and harsh use of profanity from my love ones. The Jury continued to talk, but I heard nothing. I looked at the District Attorney as he was shaking the hands of the Bells family. Mr. Harvey Bells and I made strong eye contact. My grin turned into a smile. I was in hurt amusement at his cowardly acts. However, I showed strong-ness for his *victory*. My mother continued to shout out her words of expression. I couldn't understand my guilty verdict, but I guess that is just the way it is in the eyes of the judicial system.

JUDGE: Mr. Williams, you have been found guilty by the Jury and you have the right to appeal. Sentencing date will be scheduled for July 15, 1995. Take this man away.

I looked at my lawyer and he stated that we will get them on appeals. As I was walking out the courtroom, I looked back and saw Connie looking down at little Paul. I called out her name. She looked up and I said goodbye. I shouted for my mother. I told her that I loved her and that I will never stop fighting. She told me to stay strong. I couldn't believe what has just happened. The news media told the world of my guilty verdict. I listened on while walking down the long hallways. I was on my way back to Hamsburg, awaiting another date for trial. I was embarrassed for not defeating my double crossers'. I lost one and it was one more to go. I had to return back to that courtroom the next day to start trial for the cop killings.

I walked on the block and noticed that James and Raheem were awaiting my return. My face expressions told it all, as well as the discomfort-ness in the way I was walking. Raheem was definitely proving his worthiness as a friend. James was going to trial on June 17, 1995, and Raheem was going on June 28, 1995. I sat them down in my cell to explain the cruelty of my speedy trial. It wasn't much I could say or do. I was going to start trial again the next day and really didn't want to.

James and Raheem exited the cell to allow me to find some peace with myself. I needed a moments alone. I appreciated their company, but I wasn't going to be satisfied until I killed that sonuvabitch Little Harvey. James asked me if Larry was in the courtroom to support me. I just looked at him and shook my head. The tears almost rolled down James face. He couldn't express his weakness in front of Raheem. I thought of James as he left out. I knew James wanted to kill Little Harvey as much as I did. I was now hoping that James defeat his homicide. That way I will have some support in my retaliation. I was definitely going upstate/penitentiary. For how long, I will soon find out.

I just sat there in my cell and realized that I may never see the streets again. I thought of little Paul growing up around a strange father. It was heart-crushing to my soul. How could I be so stupid and irresponsible to leave behind my only child? I was riding that road to success. In the process, I had to take down a few obstacles. Not only did I hurt myself, but I have hurt my son as well. I thought and thought until I fell asleep. It was only 5pm, but my mind was lacking the physical sensitivity of awake-ness. My mind drifted into a world of comfortableness. I needed to hold a woman. I needed some physical attention. I tossed and turned for rest. I was in a tight spot and mentally tired. Everyone that I love or called my friends was gone. I was only down the county and my real time hasn't even begun. I knew that the District Attorney would try and seek the death penalty for the officers. I knew that I was illegally tried at my last trial. I could only imagine the entertainment in the courts tomorrow. I was a sitting duck in the path of a bullet. I understood that I committed these murders and I must face the punishment of guilt. However, I will not give up my rights or innocence until they can prove this fact beyond a reasonable doubt.

At that moment while trying to get some rest, I felt some relief as I understood myself. I was a warrior. I was in a battle by myself and I was against all odds. As my emotions calmly sat aside, I found peace in my heart. I have never prayed to GOD in my life and at that moment I felt the heat, as if I was face to face with Satan. I remember mumbling small words under my breath. I don't recall those words, but I am quite sure that it was a prayer. I don't think that I was asking for help nor was I praying for protection. I believe that I was asking for strength to be me and for the courage to fight my components endlessly.

The dream of a woman has once again come in my vision. The adage once said that your dreams sometimes speak for what you really want. This woman was only a friend, but a friend that I couldn't get off my mind; so I laid there to memorize and dream on.

"A DREAM OF PASSION"
THE CONCLUSION

My hands touch her soft hips. The panties and boxers must now come off. I'll then start kissing her stomach, licking around her belly button, sliding slowly to her pubic hairs. What a sight. I am now face to face with the softest place on earth. My face is now between her. My hands is pressed and placed thoroughly against her vagina so that my two thumbs could gently spread apart her lips. Her lips are so warm and wet. What a position. She tastes like a fresh piece of fruit that has been individually plucked just for the moment. It's so prettily pink. I'll wiggle my tongue like a rattle snakes tail, watching her hands as they tighten with pure pleasure. She moans loudly and is now moving in the motion of making passionate love. She begins to enjoy the moment greatly. I'll then take the index finger of the right hand, while still sucking her clitoris, and slide it into her softness to make the vagina wet enough to put myself inside her. She begins to suck passionately and wildly on the fingers of my right hand. I realized that it is now time to change positions. I watched her long sexy nails on my penis as she stroked and masturbated it. Her lips touch the tip of my stiffness. She moves so slowly and her mouth is so warm. She begins to moan while sucking on me. My eyes close as I feel the overwhelming sensation of delectation. I am deeply in delight of this pleasurable moment. She places her hands onto my buttocks, "Oh my!" I said beneath my breath. Shocking as that was I became enhanced in flattery. At that instant her touch felt good. I was hoping that the moment would never end. My body started tingling all over uncontrollably. I am now ready for an orgasm. My toes tighten together. My eyes, they water in the unadulterated properness of pleasure. The feeling is marvelous. I begin to call out her name softly. "Denise, oh Denise, baby girl, I love . . . I love . . . Oh, baby you make me feel so good." Finally, I whisper almost silently in her ear, "Denise Jamison, I truly love you." I'll lay her on her stomach to place my still hard penis into her vagina, to stroke her slow and strong throughout the night. Holding her hands tightly to suck on her back and neck. We now share orgasms after orgasms. She is now satisfied and I am as well. **She is _My True Desire For Passion_** . . . .

3:12am, I am sweating heavily. I rolled out of bed to get a drink of water. I pause for a moment with a wet rag in my hands. I started thinking of my dream. The dream calmed me down. I knew that I only had another hour in the half or so before I was awaken by the guard for court. I figured I was going to stay awake. While standing there, the night watchmen walked by flashing his flashlight directly into my eyes. He jumped backwards as he saw me standing there. I guess it was the element of surprise that shocked him. He stepped forward and said,

"Hey kid, are you alright?" I just smiled at the old fool. "Why are you standing in the dark son?" he asked.

"Well for one, the courts have just convicted me for some bullshit. Secondly, I am going to court today for a double homicide charge." The old man just looked down at his shoes and said,

"Well, if you are going to court today, I should be around to let you out soon. I wish you luck on your cases. However, you should still try again to get some rest," he said as he walked away.

I turned the light switch on. I looked for my telephone book. I was going to write a letter to that chick Denise. My dream must mean something. How can I avoid her if I continue to dream of her? Connie was the one that I loved and she wasn't even thought about. I tried not to think of trial. I was going to write down my real thoughts on paper. She just had to know my feelings. I couldn't shake what I wanted from her. Besides, I needed her to tell me some good things. My life was in the hands of twelve jurors. I gathered a pen and pad and began to write.

While writing my letter, I heard the guard at my cell door. "Mr. Williams are you ready to take your shower for court?" the old man asked. As I placed down the pen, I asked the guard,

"Say, what time do you have sir?" "It's ummm . . . . 4:45am", the officer said while walking towards another cell to wake up another gentleman. I took a long stretch and stepped out my cell. I was finished my letter, so I walked to the front of the block to mail it off. I heard someone call out my name. I then realized that it was Raheem.

"Say my man, what are you doing up this early in the morning?" I asked.

"I am always up this early," Raheem said. Raheem was following the path of the profit Muhammad. His belief had him up early for prayer. He was making Wudu for prayer. I asked if he would pray for me. He smiled and said, "Hell, I pray for you all the time anyhow."

He asked if I believe in GOD and I said, "Yes." He asked if I believed in Islam. I said nothing and asked, "Why did you ask me that?"

"Because Paul I care about you a lot, as my friend. However, in Islam it states in "THE THREE FUNDAMENTAL PRINCIPLES OF ISLAAM", who was written by the "Noble Shrykh Muhammad idn Saalih Al-'Uthaymeen," that "Whoever is obedient to the messenger and single out Allah with all worship upon tawheed, then it is not permissible for him to have friendship and alliance with those who oppose Allah and his messenger. Even if they most closely related to him. The proof is in the saying of Allah, the most high." "I just looked and listened. I knew that he was taking his religion very serious, but it was now my time to go.

Walking back to my cell, I sat on my bed and thought about what Raheem just stated to me. I was not a religious person. And indeed, our friendship was growing rapidly, but it was nothing that I honored completely. I respected the fact that he was a man on top of his Religion. Most men come to prison and become religious people for different reasons. One is because they follow the rules of their profit. Two is because they need protection. Three is because they have no sense of direction. They need to find ways to stay strong in a rough situation. What is a better way to stay strong then to have faith in GOD? Some men say that they follow the rules of Islam, Christianity, Catholic, or etc . . . etc . . . , but it's only a select few who live by the rules of their profits. I wouldn't mind becoming a religious man, but at this particular moment in my life, I can not think of anything other than revenge. Why would I lie to myself? Moreover, why would I deceive GOD? To say that I am going to be a better man; that I am not going to misrepresent the message of GOD, when in fact, I know that I would. In a religion, you must enter wholeheartedly, not halfheartedly. If it was my will to become a religious person, then my destiny shall prove that speculation. In do time I believe that I'll seek to find the truth. However, now is inappropriate timing. I realize I must learn patience and I know there's a GOD. I also know that I must be obedient in the eyes of my Lord, furthermore I understand that I put myself in this position, therefore I will use myself to get out of it.

After I've taken my shower, dressed, and headed towards the court house. I had a brief meeting with my counsel. He said that the case beatifies itself. He stated who the surprise witness was. My face brought upon a smile. He stated that the District Attorney had two other surprise witnesses that have just been brought to his attention less then an hour ago. See the District Attorney couldn't perform with his witnesses without notifying us of their names, addresses, and characteristics. The second two names have also brought a smile upon my face.

First one was "the two people in the old caddie." Mr. Willie Fats and Mrs. Bernice Screws. They stated that they saw my face on the news and witnessed me at the crime scene. That I was on that road looking for something in a huge puddle of nasty water. That I was standing on the side of the road, expressing a large amount of hostility. They told the police where I was standing and the police found a nine millimeter automatic hand gun at the crime scene.

The second witness was the security guard on the bridge. He stated that I was on the bridge days after the cop killing's and that I threw something into the water. And when he approached me, I became very nervous. I expressed fear of a man trying to cover up something. When he also saw my face on the news, he decided to come forward. The police searched the dirty river for a weapon, but was unable to find anything, due to weather conditions and people swimming to search the bottom for antique treasury.

The last witness was the newsy old neighborly woman of Connie's, Mrs. Mandela Finetain. She stated that I appeared in front of her house days after the shooting arguing with my girlfriend and disrespecting the neighbors with bad language and was expressing emotions of guilt. She stated that I said something horrific to my female companion that traumatized her tremendously. That she saw me days later and decided to call the police. I was finally satisfied that I found out who called the police on me. I guess when you do things in your community that goes against everyone's objectives; you will never know who your worst enemy is. I realized at that moment that I must start respecting people who live among me. My community plays an important part involving salvation. That it braces my backbone to be loved in society. Indeed, I've poured urine on the adults who watched over me as a child. Men and women who tried compulsively to protect many youth from dangerous predators that lurked the streets for minors, simply to manipulate or victimize their minds to become enemies of their own flesh and blood. I remember Mrs. Mandela as a friend of my mothers', but because of my foolish disposition they may never speak again.

I just sat there looking at my attorney. I had not a word to say. Someone tapped on the door. It was a sheriff deputy, who has come from the District Attorney's chambers to notify my lawyer of another witness. I just listen on as he spoke. This witness was another nobody. It was a man by the name of Mr. Ti Komodo. A Korean man who owns a small corner grocery store. He was going to testify that he observed me and my accomplice Billy Green the day of the cop killings. That we came into his store to buy some groceries and no sooner as we stepped foot outside his store, he heard several gunshots and ducked for cover. That he notice a huge print sticking out from my thin shirt. He knew it was a gun and he was sure that we were going to rob his small establishment. However, we both exited the store in peace and paid for everything that we purchased.

My lawyer smiled at the man's statement. Even though the D.A. was presenting himself to be very desperate for my conviction, he wasn't really proving anything. My lawyer stated that, "each and every one of his witnesses hasn't seen anything. Therefore their credibility and testimony was nothing more than hearsay." I was sitting there hoping that he was totally right. He asked me if I was ready to go into the courtroom. I said that I was ready more than anyone. I was glad that I found a lawyer who was enthused to do his job appropriately. He was honest, forward, and paid plenty of attention to everything I had to say. I believe that I've convinced him of my innocence. As I stood up, I looked on into his eyes and wished him luck in winning my trial.

While we were walking down towards the courtroom, I thought that my eyes have deceived me. Standing before me in handcuffs as well, was that lowlife motherfucker Tony. Apparently he was finished his trial and was down there for sentencing. He was found guilty for a chump ass burglary and robbery charge. He was sentenced to two to five with 13 months time served. Even though he was one of my victims, I had some respect for the slimy coward because he didn't snitch on me. Besides, his friends have done me in good. We caught each others eye. He realized that I was the man that captivated the news media's attention. So, he nodded his head at me. Surprising as that was, I nodded my head right back. We battled in a small war that has met no point. It was a battle between the notorious "David and Goliath." But this time, neither man has won. When the smoke cleared, we both remained in the custody of the system.

As I continue to walk into the courtroom, it was like a recap of yesterday's scenery. This time the courtroom was full. I was labeled as a cop killer. I was expecting the worse. I looked at Connie, my mother, little Paul, and plenty of people who was there to support me. I sat down and the court proceedings began.

JUDGE: Mr. Rogers, please call your first witness.

Once again, my lawyer and the D.A. went back and forth; forth and back. Trial went on for 5 days. Once again Connie and my mother would testify on my behalf. This time Connie will state that we were at the movies during the time of the cop killings. It was all an accurate testimony being as though the store manager, who was testifying against me, cameras was used as insufficient evidence, based on unclearness. My mother would testify that she was the one who gave me and Connie the movie tickets so that we could spend some quality time together. She stated that Connie was young and eight months pregnant at that time. Therefore, she needed to be with her boyfriend at all times. We were all on point for this trial.

After everyone has testified including me, the jury went out for deliberation. It was May 19, 1994 and 12 people were out deciding the path of my life. Everyone waited for 3 hours for the jury. That was a sign of goodness. The longer the better, the shorter the worse. I sat there awaiting the jury as my body almost gave away. I felt as if I was about to faint. My lawyer looked down at me and said that everything looks good. I looked up again and the jury was walking out. My fuckin' face turned a pale white. I was scared and I was unsure if I wanted to hear the outcome of it all.

JUDGE: Jury, have you reached a verdict?

Jury: Yes we have your Honor.

JUDGE: Mr. Paul Williams, will you please stand. Jury; please feel free to carry on with the reading of your verdict.

My heart pumped, pumped, and pumped harder. I looked at the door and thought about taking a run for it. However, the police officers who stood there patiently with their guns in holsters changed that thought almost instantly.

JURY: We the jury find the defendant Paul Williams, for the crimes of two counts of first degree murder on police officers, NOT GUILTY! . . . . We th . . . .

My legs gave way. I fell flat to the floor. I was relieved of the death penalty. I continued hearing the jury talking, but everything they stated after that not guilty verdict was irrelevant. The loved ones of the lost officers shouted in disappointment. The news media notified thousands of my innocence. I smiled as I hugged my lawyer tightly. He said that they had nothing and he was right. I looked at Connie and just smiled. She smiled as well. My mother shouted that the Lord was good to me and for me to always have faith in him. My mother was a very religious woman. However, I wonder about my faith. Did I have faith in a religion or my lawyer? I think it was my lawyer at that point. Only if I was found not guilty for that fucking Mr. Bells, I could have dismissed Connie the way that I wanted to and get my vengeance on Little Harvey. There I was, found not guilty for a crime I have committed and found guilty for a crime that I didn't commit. Talk about your screwed up judicial system. However, I was satisfied with that conviction. I was on my way back to Hamsburg. I couldn't wait until I saw James and Raheem's faces when I gave them the good news.

MEANWHILE! While I was at the court house expressing a victorious defeat, James and Raheem were trying to defeat something of their own. Apparently, a member from North Philadelphia has tested the strength of our ability to defend what was ours by jail house regulations. The telephone time was the leading cause of conflicts that lead to prison wars. No soon as North Philadelphia's telephone was broken. They came to the nearest one for a percentage of the time which was South Philadelphia. Everyone notified James, on "A" block, of what was going down. It was around 2:27 and the I-95 traffic had me in a tight spot. As James rushed onto B-block, other members from South Philadelphia were notified from other blocks immediately. As for the correctional officers, they knew somewhat of what was going on, however they stayed where they were needed the most; anywhere but in the area of dangerous, high-tempered nigga's.

It was told that TY a.k.a as Pee-Wee was on the telephone when the leader of their small click ask to use some of their personal time. Pee-Wee told the approaching man to fuck off, and the man became frustrated and embarrassed. He pulled out a large twelve inch jail house shank/ice pick and stuck it into Pee-Wee. The weapon struck him just above the left shoulder. Pee-Wee tried to run for the open door, but he was attacked by another man of that same crew. He was stabbed multiple times, more than fourteen. He was rushed from the institution via helicopter to the nearest hospital. *James, Cappri, Gee, Manny, Vence, Johnny D, Kev, Prime, and Rell.* , and several other accomplices was outraged. Some said that other crews approached YG Members, during the day, mainly from South West/West Philadelphia because they were also having some difficulties with the same men. They wanted to know if their team was welcomed to participate in the ambush against North Philadelphia.

They were honored and welcomed into the planning of that day. North Philly was the largest part of Philadelphia; therefore, our unity meant nothing but a glorious victory. Everyone knew that it was no other way to solve the on hand problem, unless a war irrupts. At 3:00pm it was time for the afternoon yard. Everyone moved silently as if nothing was going down. West Philadelphia had their respect. They called themselves the J.B.M. ". . . **The Junior Black Mafia** . . ." They were well known for their extraordinary tactics, their extortion and killings that shocked Philadelphia for several years, their traditional words of use: "*GET DOWN OR LAY DOWN.*" Their words will go down in history. Their acts would be practiced, duplicated, and produced into the motivation of youngsters. The ones who are in search of the criminality world for many years to come.

They walked pass James and he smiled at their togetherness. Normally the war might have been with them, but this time we were together and chemistry couldn't get any better. The huge group of men from North Philadelphia's organization walked pass. Someone over heard the men bragging about the stabbing of Pee-Wee.

James overheard as well. Moses leaned forward to react on the gentleman's audaciousness. James looked at Moses and just grabbed his arm firmly. He insisted that Moses showed a little patience and obedience in the time of war. The men from North Philadelphia called themselves, ". . . **The Zulu Nation** . . ." Men of respect and honor. These particular men were definitely about their business. They also held in a great amount of reputation for laying down the rules and laws for criminals. Their responsibility and goals was to take down the city by all means necessary.

As time went on, temptation aroused in the atmosphere. Unfortunately, North Philadelphia understood what was about to go down and they were prepared. But fortunately, they didn't know anything about the other half. One of the men from The Zulu click approached James, Raheem, and Rell; a bold fellah who spoke sarcastically. He asked, "What the fuck are you looking at?" replying to Rell. "I am looking at you nigga," as Rell shouted right back at the heavyset fellah. The men got closer. They were now face to face. They exchanged a little more words with hostility. The man threw a wicked right hook at Rell, striking him just above the left eyebrow. The match was lit and the war struck the yard with fights, stabbings, and loud use of languages. Rell was taken completely by surprise. His awareness was un-functional. His brainstems were receiving rapid communications. Although he knew what was going on around him, his body was unable to get up off the ground. His responses was dazed and weakened behind the hard hook of a punch.

Almost instantly, everyone in that yard who was with a certain part of a click drew weapons of all kinds. Catastrophic-ness has shown its face once more. Men ran, pushed, jumped, and shoved to get into or out of harms way. The war was at its peak. People started running towards the doorway for some kind of help from the guards. Unfortunately, it wasn't any. The door was locked and each group was for themselves.

I was told that James and Raheem performed in ways of man to man, true solidarity. The man who stabbed Terrence was overpowered with the aggressiveness of James attitude. They said when the man fell to the ground; James and Raheem placed their steel rides into the man with uncontrolled force. Raheem stated to me later that when the man stopped moving, it was their time to get away. Raheem stated that he also realized that James knife was beginning to bend up. When James realized that his weapon was bending up, he freaked. James snatched his knife from the sedated mans forehead and bent it back into shape. Then he started stabbing the man again. Raheem said that at that moment he looked at James and realized that he wasn't a man, "he was a walking animal."

Several men were injured badly. The war hasn't been completely concluded, but it hasn't escalated either until new members entered the system with hatred. No one has won because no one ever really wins the geographical wars between neighborhoods. However, sometimes a war is appropriate for us. That's why it is important to be very cautious of your surrounded territory. In prison, you must maintain your responsibility accurately and always with a second thought, stay on top of your game.

At that moment I have arrived into the jail. I overheard the guards talking about the previous incident. When I started walking down the hallway, I noticed that the jail was on locked down. I walked onto my block and walked straight to Raheem's cell. He wasn't there. Someone called for me from the cell across the hall. It was Kev. He told me everything that has happened and I stood motionless. James, Raheem, and a few other good men was taken to the hole (Solitary Confinement). They had to serve 14 days for fighting. No weapons were discovered.

I walked to my cell, sat down, and wrote a long letter to James and Raheem, to allowing them to understand that I was going to take the next steps if need be. I also told them about the outcome of my case. I prepared care-bags to send to them and proceeded on about my business until their release.

I started thinking about my mother at trial. How when she suddenly first realized my guilt. The 9mm pistol that was found at the crime scene was my fathers. However, it was also a Birthday gift from my mother, for protection of their house. It held the initials, "M & Y.F. (Me & You Forever.) No one knew of her discovery. She probably knew of my guilt in her heart anyhow, that was just the topping on the cake. I turned on my television and continued to think of my unbelievable victory.

June 30, 1995, everything was considered an ordinary day. James was tried for his murder on the 17th and he was found guilty on all charges on the 21st. His sentencing date was scheduled for July 18, 1995. Raheem has been to trial on the 28th of that month and was found not guilty of all charges. I expressed my happiness for his winnings. However, he was shipped back upstate to finish his previous sentenced. We correspond as much as we could. I knew it was much more I needed to find out about the man before I depended on his loyalty.

I called my mother and we talked about everything. I told her that I was only going to get about 2.5 years for Mr. Bells aggravated assault charge. That was considered nothing. She stated that the man who killed my father was discharged. Apparently the witnesses wouldn't show up at trial, therefore the evidence was shot to shit. I knew once I was home, I could revenge his death. My mother and Larry have taken pictures of the accuser. I told her to hold them until I was released. I was going to plan my attack carefully. I was going to do prison time, so I figured I had plenty of thinking time to think wisely. That man must die. We laughed a little after the disappointing news she stated to me. I was very hurt and expressed my grief, but I couldn't allow her to know of my treacherous thoughts. Not once did she ask me about the 9mm pistol. It was in the past and I knew she wanted to bury it. Even if she would've asked, I know that I would've told her the truth. I knew that she deserved nothing other than the truth. My mother has always expressed greatness in her womanhood. I love her dearly, to death do us part. **July 28, 1995,** two months after I've defeated the two cop murders. It was now my time to be sentenced for the Aggravated Assault on Mr. Harvey Bells. I started thinking of James as I got ready for court. James was sentenced almost a month after he was found guilty on the 21st. The Judge sentenced him to "**Life**" in prison on July 18, 1995, with no chance of parole. My mother said that James threw a chair at the Judge and called him a "house nigga." The police shackled him and dragged him out of the courtroom. I felt every bit of James behavior. It was us two against the world. Larry wasn't at James sentencing either. Raheem was released back into population 3 days after the incident in the yard, for mistaken identity. We talked respectfully before he went back upstate. I know once I am released, I'll be able to do something about James situation. I figured that I could get the witnesses back together again for a new testimony. I can get a better defense attorney and support him financially to the best of my ability. I missed him greatly.

James was sent upstate on the 27th of July. A day before my sentencing I sat in the courtroom and saw my mother with little Paul. She was sitting next to that chick Denise. I looked around for Connie and she wasn't anywhere. My mother and Denise were the only ones there to support me at my sentencing. Everything that I stood for was gone. Everyone who respected me, because they feared me, was now showing their true colors. My life was nothing but a fascinating faze that most people go through throughout their years of coming up.

I have been incarcerated for almost a year now. So far, I have lost more things that meant the world to me than most have lost in 15 years. I stood firm, but I was definitely on my own. I stood up in front of the Judge. My body stood relaxed. He was going to give me my time and I was going to begin the process of thinking and planning for my revenge on everyone. My mother spoke her peace for me. I spoke as well. The Judge sentenced me to **10 to 20** years in prison. I was given that harsh sentence because of my juvenile aggravated assault conviction. The Judge stated that my life was a pattern for trouble and it had to be stopped. I shot a man when I was just 13 years of age and now its here to haunt me. It was a shooting for Larry; I protected him from losing his life and because of it, my sentence was increased. He was really a major problem in my doing time. I wish death upon him. If it must come to the point of me seeking revenge on my own brother, then so be it. I never wanted nor did I ask for the life that I was given. I was in a rough neighborhood, doing drastic things in a hurricane form. I felt so good of what I was doing. Now I feel as if I must be regretful for ever being involved in such behaviors. I was feeling extremely good about the bad things I have accomplished. However, because of my bond with myself, I'll never say that I regret anything. I did what I did to those who oppose themselves in the eyes of the beholder. I stood there looking at the Judge sadly. I turned and walked away. My mother looked on even sadder, but she had to know that it could have been a lot worse.

"GRATERFILD STATE PRISON"

August 11, 1995, I have been riding on the bus for almost an hour. My muscles are stiff from the long ride. We finally arrived at the prison called Graterfild. I heard many things about this penitentiary, but I knew that it was nothing I couldn't handle. After what I've seen and been through, this here place was nothing.

As we unloaded the bus, I thought to myself that I was one year down, nine more to go. I was placed on "F" block and was told I had to stay there until I was properly checked in. After two days I was medically cleared and was allowed to enter population, where I was placed on "D" block. As soon as I arrived into the jail, I sent a message to Raheem to notify him that I have now boarded the ship. I walked down the long block to see if I could recognize anyone, but I knew no one. The blocks were like two of Hamsburgs blocks put together. Men stood around and looked on with disarrangement, as I traveled by. Like many other prisoners, they all expressed images of hurt men, true men of war. Men who showed the characteristics of loneliness, confusion, and fright, but these men spontaneously inhaled spacious oxygen to continue their fight for the freedom of their lives and sanity.

My presence was not very aggressively placed out, nor was I trying to portray an aggressive image. I could tell that I was in a much more intellectual environment of men. Men that stalked and moved without too much vocal use. The weather was warm and men walked around with heavy clothing. It was about seven hundred men to a block. As I stood in front of my cell waiting for my cellmate to arrive from the yard, two doctors, four guards, and three nurses came running from the back of the block. They carried a stretcher and on it laid a man with blood running from his head, onto his face and chest. He was in the shower when someone hit him over the head with a mop ringer. No one said nothing and no one was arrested. I figured that was the reason why the block was so silent. I knew that I had to get a weapon fast.

The yard has now returned. It was as large as a small stadium and as crowded as it could get, with sold-out sets. The entire jail housed about 6,500 inmates. My celli was fairly good but not excellent. He told me of some rules in the big house. I appreciated his intensifying speech, but little did he know my heart was covered in tar. I was a walking explosion with a lit fuse. I was waiting for my emotional ticker to burst at any moment. A man walked up to the cell and asked for me. My celli stood frightened. He was hoping that he didn't receive a cellmate who was a troublemaker, or one that people was looking for.

The man reached out his hand and gave me a note. It was a letter from Raheem. I was told to meet him at the movie theater around five o'clock. We have finally made contact. As for my brother James, he went way out to another jail. He was hoping to fight his case and overturn his conviction. Soon as I got comfortable in my cell, I sat down and wrote James a three page letter. We never thought of our down fall days being so closely together. I met Raheem and we laughed and talked. He gave me everything that I needed (Some food and a weapon). I was now ready to do my time.

CHAPTER TWELVE

"ONE LAST DANCE"

The trees blew wildly throughout the humbled neighborhood. The rough winds hurried through cracks of shallow, abandon buildings, with sounds of a slight whisper, as it whistled slow and fast and then slow again. Larry and Little Harvey were preparing themselves for another transaction in South Philadelphia, near the 76 expressway, in a local bar.

"Larry, are you just about ready?" Little Harvey asked with the over-zealousness of an impatient man. He expressed deep readiness, while placing on his bullet-proof chest and abdomen protector.

"I just told you five minutes ago that I am still waiting for that telephone call from that sorry sonuvabitch Charlie!" Larry said agitatedly. "Besides, why are you walking back and forth as if you can't hold your dick still? I am warning you Harvey!" Larry shouted. "If you fuck up this deal, I will personally stay as far away from you as I possibly can." Larry knew that Little Harvey's use of cocaine was destroying their structure of business. Each time they purchased a brick or two of cocaine, a bird of heron, or maybe just some pills or marijuana, Little Harvey would always find some way to belittle the character of the supplier.

"Yeah, whatever," Harvey responded with a look of ignorance. "Anyway, why are you always waiting on him? I can't believe that the prick hasn't called yet." Little Harvey shouted with disappointment and impatient-ness.

"I'll give him another five minutes or so, and then I'll call him myself," Larry said while tapping his fingers on the side of the Italian, white leather, business type, adjustable chair.

"Larry, you have been sitting there awaiting his call for almost an hour now," Harvey stated. His voice burst through Larry's ears like a horn on a Mack truck. "Why must you wait on him every time we are in need for some re-ups? It's time we started making them bastards wait on us, I am so . . ."

The telephone started ringing. "Ring, ring, ring." Cutting Harvey off instantly. "Talk to me! Larry said when picking up the receiver. He maintained his shy like voice, as if he was never waiting around their telephone call.

"Yeah, it's me Charlie," a voice from the other end of the receiver said. Larry gave Harvey thumbs up.

"Well, it's about time", Larry's words hurtled out.

"Yes, I apologize for the delay, but something terrible has come up," Charlie said. His voice sounding shaky, but calm. "But it has nothing to do with tonight's business deal. I would like to see you as soon as possible. Same place, different time."

"Larry what's happening? Are they ready?" Harvey asked in an overwhelming tension to make the deal. Larry flagged his hand, giving Harvey a sudden gesture to shut the hell up.

"So, I'll meet you at the bar," Larry said.

"Okay," Charlie responded.

"So, meet you in . . . say about thirty minutes tops." Larry said.

"Great time. I'll be there awaiting your arrival," Charlie said, and then he hung up the receiver. Larry on the other hand hung onto the receiver, just to discourage Harvey's impatient ness. He knew that Harvey was too anxious to do the deal. Every since the fall out with Paul and the sudden death of Billy Green, Harvey has been handling personal situations inaccurately. Larry wondered about his long-term friend. He wondered if his overbearing behavior would someday get him killed.

"What did he say?" Harvey asked, with wide eyes and appeared very jumpy, as if he was about to get a hit on a cocaine pipe. Larry knew the days of them doing business successfully together was slightly coming to an end. Larry realized that this may be his last deal making with Harvey.

"We will meet them in twenty-five more minutes at the bar. Harvey, are you sure everything is okay?" Larry asked with suspicion.

"What the fuck do you mean, am I okay? The question is, are you okay?"

"Look lets not bicker about nothing," Larry said. Larry was trying to be open-minded about the go down. Unfortunately, Harvey's arrogance and stubborn brain has not realized the simplicity in the question.

Charlie was a well respected ghetto king pin type, who was well known to take good care of the people he does business with. He was a man of the diamond back family. Men who sat patiently on prey and struck like a snake that hasn't eaten in weeks. Larry knew of his aggression and really didn't want to do business with the old gray hair guy, but he had no choice. It's been many times they fell well behind on their ability to come through and Larry didn't want to fall behind this time. Larry continued to mumble harsh words about Harvey beneath his breath. He was hoping Harvey doesn't destroy or take for lightly Charlie's cool, calm, and collectiveness.

"Larry, why are you till sitting in that chair?" Harvey asked, while putting on the baby-Uzi, shoulder straps. Larry lifts himself from the comfortable chair and also grabbed a baby-Uzi that shot thirty times. He placed the gun in its holster. Looking at Harvey, he let out a whistle that had to squeeze through his tightly locked teeth. Harvey looked at Larry narrow eyed. Larry put on his leather jacket, grabbed the money and car keys and headed towards the front door.

"Damn, Larry! What are you doing? You don't even have on your bulletproof vest," Harvey worried.

"Oh, yeah, I am not going to wear it tonight. Charlie is a good man and I don't think anything will go wrong. That's if you don't start anything," Larry said under his breath. He started walking towards the door.

"Suit yourself, hell, I am ready for whatever," Harvey said pulling out his gun, imitating like he was shooting somebody.

"Yeah, that's what I am afraid of."

"And what is that suppose to mean?" Harvey asked, standing emotional to the question.

"Nothing, nothing at all," Larry said. The two got into a black Legend station wagon, with shiny rims. Slight rain dropped on the slight tinted windows of the vehicle. Larry and Harvey sat quite quietly with the music of R. Kelly, (Bump and Grind CD) as they drove to the bar. Everything but the right things ran through Larry's head. He started to understand the floss in their ability to do business together. Larry was more of a lay back dude, who just wanted his past to be in the past. He inhaled and exhaled deeply. When they arrived at the bar, they noticed Charlie's jeep parked on the side with someone still sitting inside.

"Look Harvey," Larry said while starting to get more worried. "We are going in here calmly. We have been in this kind of situation a thousand times. If anything goes wrong we are going to calmly exit the bar without getting fired up. Is everything coherent?"

"Yeah," Harvey said. "I wish you would relax. Everything is going to be fine." They both opened their door and stepped out. Walking towards the bar the two men was silent and their faces showed seriousness. The bar was very clean due to Charlie's appearance. He was also given an after party after his eighteen thousand dollar pick-up from the men. No one ever tried to rob or steal from Charlie, or it would have gotten real ugly. Not only for the robber, but for their families as well. To Charlie this deal was nothing. He was only trying to satisfy us as customers on every level. Charlie never appeared on the scene of any illegal deal before, but because of the after party, he was there to meet Larry and Harvey face to face. "Who knows, just maybe they will get larger and bring me more business," Charlie thought to himself as the men entered the bar.

"Charlie, hello there young fellah!" Larry said soon as he saw the old gray hair Charlie.

"Hello Larry, it's been a long time," Charlie responded. "Who's your friend?" Charlie asked.

"Who Harvey, oh, he's my main man and a long-term partner," Larry said with a fake smile on his face. "Don't worry Charlie; he is a real cool brother."

"Who me? Ol, I am not worried," Charlie said, sitting on a stool swirling around, sipping on his mild drink. Hell, a friend of yours is a friend of mine."

"Yeah right," Larry stated to himself. Harvey sat down on a near by chair. He observed the conversation closely. Charlie was a well dressed older guy who looked like he had not one worry in the world.

"Is everything alright with you and your lady friend?" Charlie asked, as if he was concerned.

"Yes, everything is just fine and yours?" Larry counter asked.

"Well, I can't complain," Charlie said. He fingered the bartender to bring them all drinks. Harvey looked on wishing that they would skip the small talk and get right to business. Save the sweet talk for somebody who needed sugar in their tea.

"Larry, your friend is quiet. He's the quiet type huh?" Charlie asked, while thanking the bartender for his hospitality.

"Will you be having anything else?" the tall, large face bartender asked.

"No, not at this moment," Charlie replied briefly.

"Look Charlie, I really don't mean to disrupt our conversation, but I am on a real tight schedule. I have something personal to take care of with my family at another location," Larry said, hoping Charlie would take the disruption politely. He looked Charlie deep into his eyes and continued. "So, if we could get on with . . ."

"No need to continue," Charlie said, cutting Larry off. At that moment Harvey got up off the chair he was sitting on and walked over to Charlie and Larry. He was ready for the deal.

"Well, I see your friend raised from the dead," Charlie stated to make small jokes. Harvey stood in silence and didn't laugh at Charlie's way of joking. He ignored the old bastard's negative words of use. Larry looked at Harvey, hoping that he could take sarcastic words from Charlie. Charlie called for the bartender and whispered silent words into his ear. The bartender looked around wildly. He clenched and unclenched his clean shaved jaw muscles. He walked towards the small door on the bar counter and headed outside. Larry and Harvey both observed the bartenders casual movements. Charlie looked at Harvey in the way of dislike. His face expressed a vibrant look. It lit up his face like a night light in a foggy lake. Charlie's eyes were narrow. He looked at Harvey up and down. His face became fiercely while observing Harvey's hip. Charlie wondered why he was carrying a weapon in his presence of doing business. At that point a short fat Asian man, with thick eyebrows and a face that could scare a moose from drinking water from a drinking pool on a hot summer day, walked in and headed towards them all.

"Gents, I would like for you to meet my new friend, and a dear partner of mine. Mr. Hang-yo Yogimeigi," Charlie said. Larry looked at Harvey and Harvey nodded his head in a laughter sort of way. The man was indeed very ugly, but what Larry and Harvey needed to know was that Hang-yo was an assassin who was on the run from three other countries, and two different states. Hang-yo murdered seven men singled handedly in Utah. Afterwards he would travel underground, coming from under his rock only to do business. Hang-yo was a real soul survivor. Death was something he looked forward to.

"Hello sir," Larry said with a barely recognized smile on his face.

"Hello Mr. Yo-hang," Harvey said marking his name. He bowed in front of the Asian man to again mark his customary way of greeting. Hang-yo stood silent. He looked over the marking of the inexperienced men who stood so close to death. Larry felt the dangerousness in the man. His small smirk faded away quickly like a pair of bleached blue jeans. Charlie on the other never once felt a bit happy about how they respected his friend. He watched closely at their eye contact. He wanted to see who was going to blink first. Charlie had Hang-yo around because of the after party; moreover, he wanted to allow the small timers to know that he held men from all over the world. Harvey smiled at Charlie. Charlie's face tightened together as if he wanted to kill Harvey right on the spot. Harvey continued smiling at Charlie.

"Harvey, what the fuck are you doing? Stop that. Have some respect," Larry quickly said, realizing that Charlie was losing his temper.

"What! I was just kidding around. I mean no disrespect for anyone," Harvey sincerely applied.

"Hey no need to apologize," Charlie said briskly. Hang-yo held a black bag containing pure untouched powder of coke. Charlie gave him a nod of his head, telling him to bring it over. Harvey and Larry stood to see what was in the black bag. Charlie opened the bag and placed his hand in. He pulled out a large chunk of powder rapped up in plastic. He placed the rock on the countertop.

"Well, it's about time," Little Harvey said. Charlie was now hurt at Harvey's outburst. Charlie clenched his teeth again and again at Harvey's way of boldness. Larry just shook his head at Harvey in disbelief. Charlie was being humiliated in front of his new business partner. Charlie started focusing on some serious acts of treachery. He really didn't want to do business now because of Harvey having a weapon. Furthermore, Harvey's way of conducting himself was inappropriate and disrespectful in the company of his guest.

"Do you brothers have any money?" Charlie asked. He tried holding in his anger towards Harvey.

"Yes, I have it right here," Larry said. Larry felt the tension of his cold way of asking about the money. He felt the seriousness of Charlie's isolated heart that swept throughout his mouth into words.

"How much is it?" Charlie asked.

"That's eighteen grand of U.S. dollars," Harvey said, rubbing his hands together as he spoke of the money. Charlie looked at Harvey with eyes of a hulk. He was asking Larry the question. Charlie was now fed up with the rudeness of Harvey.

"Eighteen grand you say?" Charlie asked, jumping to his feet. "You guys better have more cash then some damn eighteen grand."

"Charlie, what are you talking about? That's what a kilo goes for these days," Larry said.

"HUH! Not my kilos," Charlie said arrogantly.

"That's bullshit Charlie and you know it!" Harvey said explosively.

"What the fuck you mean that's bullshit kid. Somebody needs to teach you how to conduct yourself in the presence of big shots," Charlie shouted to Harvey. Charlie walked towards Little Harvey. "You can now take your chump change and wipe your mother's funky ass with it. You aren't nothing but a small time monkey that I will never do business with.

"What, wait just a minute please?" Larry shouted, looking at Hang-yo stepping backwards. He now focused on Charlie and Harvey.

"Fuck you, you stubborn bastard!" Harvey shouting with a thunderous tone.

"Fuck me! Fuck me! No, fuck the both of you assholes," Charlie answered harshly. "I want you to take your goddamn money and get the hell out of this bar before I have the bartender mail your mother your bodies."

Larry holding Harvey as he continued to shout. "You want to threaten me you old fucker?" Harvey said, while Larry pushing on his chest towards the door. Larry felt bad vibes from the beginning. Now it was too late to make any kind of deal. Once again Harvey has destroyed the deal behind his impatient behavior. Harvey pushed past Larry like a pro basketball player. He pulled out the mini-Uzi and placed it up against Charlie's head.

"How do you feel now?" Harvey asked in a quivering voice. He also realized that the red button was now for war. A huge war they couldn't handle. Larry realized it as well, but he was in too deep. He pulled out his Uzi and held it down by his waist. Hang-yo has slipped out the door after he noticed the gun being pulled by Harvey. Charlie stood emotionless. He was very shaky and his old weak bladder was about to give way.

"I don't hear you saying a word now," Harvey said, standing in Charlie's face, while particles of saliva shot from between his clenched teeth, onto Charlie's smooth chubby cheeks. Harvey pulled back the hammer on the Uzi, causing one of the bullets to jump into the chamber. The clicking of the stainless steel, semi weapon almost gave Charlie a sudden heart attack. Larry looked around for Hang-yo, but he was no where to be found. Harvey grabbed the powdered stuff with his left hand and placed it back into the black bag. He then tossed it to Larry. He grabbed the money and took two steps back. The bartender was never noticed again. Larry walked out the door looking around nervously. Six seconds later Harvey was right behind him. They both headed towards the car. Charlie burst out the bar doors and started shouting, "You two are dead. I swear it, that you two are dead!"

Larry opened the car door on the passenger side. Harvey started towards the car, when out of no where a voice appeared.

"Hey fellah," the unknown man said with a strange accent. Harvey turned around. Still holding his gun, he was welcomed by a loud flash of light that captivated his brain in a shocking surprise. The bullet hit him dead center in the face; causing his body to jerk back uncontrollably. Larry reached for his gun that he put away to open the car door. The unknown assailant was swiftly aggressive, who wasn't taking a short hand in his profession, by pussyfooting around. He hit Larry several times in the body before Larry was even able to grab the grip to his weapon. Larry fell backwards. Charlie ran back into the bar after the first shots rang out. The cocaine bag flew from Larry's hand onto the hood of the car. The assassin walked over to Larry and put several more bullets into his chest and abdomen area. He clicked his gun at the head of Larry, but the large 357 magnum was empty. He momentarily hesitated, and less then two seconds the speed loader was in. After realizing that both of the men were well on their way to hell, he grabbed the sack of cocaine and large lump of money from Harvey's pocket. He looked around and headed into the dark. As a skillful predator, Hang-yo has once again proven that he couldn't be matched across seas or in America. Charlie stood at the scene in front of the bar where he was arrested and charged as an accomplice, or the accuser in the killing of Harvey Bells and Larry Williams.

February 12, 1996, My time has been flowing with increasing speed. Raheem and I have been living in the same cell for some time now. We have enrolled into school, so that we could follow our plans when we return back into society. I received a letter from Connie stating that she was involved with that lowlife brother, **"Joe Jones, A.K.A. Buggie."** She said that she cared for him a lot and that she was pregnant. Even though she has always stayed in contact with me, her letters were never that uplifting. Her respectful womanhood was being shattered by the day.

My eyes glistened with fluid as I read the letter. I have lost her for good. I haven't seen little Paul in over a year. Connie's actions were unexplained. I realized that I must move on with or without them both. I love my son more then a man could, but I was in a bad position and Connie was stomping on my heart compulsively. She wasn't helping at all.

After what me and Connie were going through, I thought that my days couldn't get any worse. Later on that same day, I was notifying Raheem of my disappointing news. Suddenly! Our attention changed when the ten o'clock news flashed on the television: "*This is Hanna Miller and I am standing in front of a bar in the South Philadelphia area where two men was gunned down behind a drug deal that has reached its final transaction. The one man who was pronounced dead on the scene was Mr. Harvey Bells, a 25 year old resident nicknamed Little Harvey. He was shot twice in the back of the head, where he died instantly. His partner Mr. Laurence Williams, age 24, nicknamed Larry, was shot several times in the chest and abdomen. He was in critical condition at the University of Pennsylvania; however, we just received the news that he has died as well. People in this area are shocked, but they say that they are not surprised behind what has taken place in this bar. They say that it is a get together for all drug dealers. The police do have a man in custody. He is charged with two counts of first degree premeditated murder. They have also recovered three guns from the crime scene. Two Uzi's and a 9mm hand gun. Homicide detectives believed that the 9mm is the murder weapon. Apparently Mr. Harvey Bells was wearing bulletproof protection, but like I stated earlier, he was shot twice in the back of the head. Larry Williams was not wearing any bulletproof protection, but it might just have saved his life if he was. It was a shame that the community must witness such losses of two young men. Back to you in the studio."*

I stood in a daze. Raheem knew who they were. He just looked at me in complete silence. What was I to do? I have once loved these men, but I have grown to hate them. This was the ultimate challenge of my feelings towards the men who betrayed me years ago. At that moment I felt nothing. I asked Raheem if he was still watching the television and he said no. I turned the television off and climbed into bed. I couldn't believe my feelings at that moment. They were cold and expressed nothing. I have four walls. I smiled to myself about Little Harvey's death. I sort of smirked at Larry's death as well. I realized that it was a burden off my back. I felt much lighter. Even though my heart was racing wildly, I felt relaxed. I felt as if I have committed the murders. Raheem asked if I was alright. I said nothing. I was in complete out of space-ness. I was enjoying the moment. I grabbed my pillow tightly and I slept with comfort. **February 13, 1996,** My eyes opened slightly. I jumped off my bed and realized that Raheem wasn't in the cell. I looked at my watch and it was 1:15pm. I have slept like a baby the previous night. I washed my face and hands, brushed my teeth, and prepared my schedule for that day. Even though my brother was just killed, I wasn't bothered all that bad; however, I had a mother who was probably dramatically in shock at that moment. I thought of her constantly. I then realized that I must write her a brief letter and try to comfort her heart. She must try and understand that life has its own picks. We all chose to live in that lifestyle and it wasn't her fault. She mustn't feel guilty for her late son's stupidity and lost. I turned to walk to my bed. I noticed a newspaper on the floor. It held a note on it. It was from Raheem stating that he wanted me to see page 7. He stated that it was about last nights incidents. I hesitated momentarily. I then flicked the pages to the seventh one. However, Charlie's money was bigger then many knew. He had some unknown person to come to court to confess to the murders of the two men.

A huge print stated: **"ACCUSED KILLER HAS NO REGRETS."**

The printing was large and it captivated my attention instantly. I sat down on the floor and read the words carefully. It quoted: **"Some guys just can't say that they are sorry. Even for committing double murder. Take "Michael Davis," 30, for instance. Davis, of Tree Terrace near 29th street, told Homicide Detective Edward Kennedy that he has no regrets for blowing away "Laurence Williams, 24 and Harvey Bells, 25, outside of a bar at 28th and Jackson street in South Philadelphia on Feb. 12, 1996.**

I shot for both of their heads because I knew that they probably had on bulletproof vests." **Davis told Kennedy in a statement read during an interrogation interview.** "I don't really feel sorry," said Davis. "In the last year, I heard how bad these men were. That they were hogs, you know a bully type."

Assistant District Attorney Jermaine Flower said, "Williams and Bells, of Tasker Homes Housing Development near 30th street, were shot to be killed." Municipal Judge Francis L. Tate ordered Davis to stand trial on two counts of murder and weapon charges. Davis said that while he was in the bar, he and two friends "interceded" with a bad drug dispute. That Williams and Bells stated that they were going to straighten the problem out later, said Davis when he left the bar. Williams and Bells were waiting for him and his partners. Bells said "oh aren't you one of the men who had so much to say?" **Williams then punched Davis in the face. Davis said that he then pulled out his gun and before Williams and Bells could reach theirs, Davis said he shot them both.** He said, "that it was no reasoning with the men." **Davis stated that he then tried to take the guns from the men because, "I** was figuring on the retaliation for the boy's out 31st and Tasker." **Defense Lawyer Constance B. Grossburgh couldn't persuade Tate to reduce the charges to voluntary manslaughter. Francis called the double killing, "A slaying of first degree."**

I looked around the cell. I couldn't imagine after all we've been through on the streets with different individuals, they could allow someone to get the drop on them, therefore, I figured they deserved it. I knew if I was home and everything was okay between us, I would've peeped that situation before hand. I am good in that particular area. It's one of my best positions. I guess them bastards needed me more then they may have thought. I couldn't believe the bold statements that man has made to the police. Either he just didn't care about his life or he was just an all around stand up gentlemen, and sadly I kind of admired his ability to put two well trained gunmen down so accurately. It told me a lot about his character. What he stood for and how far he was willing to go to finish his job. I remember times when I would've died for the safety of their lives. Now I was sort of enthused to hear about their deaths. I knew that Billy was somewhere awaiting their arrival to deal with them painfully, as I would've done in the matter of time. In the blink of an eye everyone is dying off. And James was given a lifetime of a living death sentence behind bars.

I was the only one going to have that second chance in life. I figured that me and Raheem were going to get out around the same time. Why not plan a business together. All I really want now is to be happy with my son little Paul. I now have no one to be angry at. I must now plan for my future. I sat down and wrote my mother a message of warmth.

THE CORRUPTION OF BLOOD

February 3, 1996

My Dearest Mother,

As I sit here in this man made hell, I try to cope with the lost of my older brother. I keep asking myself why. Why did he have to be taken from us so soon? I question God when I know it's many more of our brothers and sisters must die before our oppression ends? I know you're asking the question; what does oppression have to do with our lost? You will probably say "nobody made that man kill Larry, but things Larry was involved in." But oppression has everything to do with it. Poverty breeds crime and violence. I wonder how do we live in the richest country in the world and so many of our people are broke? I don't mean to go on about this, it's just that it feels as if apart of me is gone and I don't know how to get it back. I am hurting really bad, but I have to believe that my brother is in a better place because if there's nothing after we're gone, what's our purpose of living? Are we born to struggle for most of our lives, and then die? There has to be something else.

"I love you big brother, I just wish I was out there with you, maybe I could have made a difference when you really needed me the most. Unfortunately, I couldn't be there and I'll take some of the blame for that. I'm writing this letter to mom; yet, I still feel so empty. I can't believe this has happened to our family."

My big brother Larry is gone. This dream is getting too real. I ask for somebody to please wake me up! I wish it was a dream mother. I needed to let that out somehow. You must forgive me, I am just writing my thoughts down because I got to let this out somehow, someway. I thought I could just block it out like I do everything else, but that didn't work. I don't really have no one to talk to, so I am sending my thoughts home to my family and maybe after I'm finished I'll feel a little better.

God Bless You,
Paul

THE CORRUPTION OF BLOOD

February 11, 1996

Dear Son,

That place is a reality check for you. The path you were going in was going to end with nothing. Larry is no longer with us and it's nothing to you or I can do about it. I believe our suffering will stop when our children take better responsibility of the opportunities in front of them. Blaming anything other than yourself for your current situation is wrong. Our so called brothers and sisters you spoke of have decisions to make as well. What happened to our family has nothing to do with oppression. Yes, our community do breeds crime; however, crime breeds off stupidity and ignorance within itself. If we as a people considered the wealth we always waist on cars, clothing, and materialistic things, just maybe we could count on each other for something. But because of greed and inconsiderate people our society is ruined. Regardless if we have a wealthy country or not, selfish behaviors amongst our own has lead life for some people to be very difficult. Unfortunately, we're the ones who fell victim to its cruelty. When you made that statement I wondered why sometimes I used to hear of my kids wealthy-ness from other people. Many months I struggled to satisfy the needs of rent/the possibility of filling up my refrigerator with food. So before you blame oppression for what has taken place, first think about what you have done to change the way oppression has survived in us for hundreds, even thousands of years.

Son, you must think of your future. Don't believe that your brother or father is in a better place, know they are. It's the only thing that keeps me strong. I am hurting as well. I do agree that we live to struggle, but if it wasn't for our struggles then where would we be? If you think jail is hell just imagine what life was like for those who fought and struggled to have you living the way you are. It might not be what you want, but it could have been much worse. The statement you made to your brother, I am sure he is now at peace. I want you to believe what has happened to Larry because it is real. Just figure out what you're going to do to change the way you live. If not for me, then for your son. I wish it was a dream to, but we must move on. Anytime you need to talk I am here for you. The day you left home to go to that place, I've forgiven you. Don't be sorry, be strong. Writing you this letter has made me feel much better, this is why it's important for us to use each other for comfort and no time is greater then the present.

Waiting to hear from you soon.

Love Your Mother

THE CORRUPTION OF BLOOD

March 14, 1996

My Dearest Mother,

I understand that I haven't been writing you as much as I should, but you are always on my mind. I really worry about you sometimes. I often ask myself if you are alright out there. Even though I know you are, I still wonder. Everyday I wish things could be different. Everyday I wish to hold you as your youngest child. I had a lot of hurt in my heart against many people; including my own flesh and blood, (Larry). However, I will allow him to rest in peace. I'll transform my hatred into missing, loving, and forgiving him for all the discomfort-ness he may have brought upon me. Now, I ask you to forgive me. Forgive me for not knowing how to express me emotions and for acting so childishly for many years.

Mother, you've always been a very good provider for my brothers and me; unfortunately, you have suffered for nothing by losing your oldest son Kevin and James to life in prison. You lost out on choices and unwise decisions. I have done nothing to help this matter and I am truly sorry. I know I will maintain my self-sanitary and be strong as I can, but I ask, how strong can a person be when he knows his mother is hurting? I can say now that I will value life a little better. I'll really work hard to take care of my important responsibilities as a man. I will not allow anyone to bring me down again. I promise that to you and to my son.

Before I go, I want you to know that I appreciate your precious time and loving patience. I ask that you take a good look back and rest yourself up a bit. Don't wear yourself down behind other people's foolishness. I love you and I'll always need your support. So for me, please get some rest. Remember that you only can do but so much for some people and you have done all that you could for us all.

God bless you,
Paul

THE CORRUPTION OF BLOOD

March 20, 1996

Dear Son,

Thank you for your letters. I am doing my best to stay strong. Even though you haven't been writing as much, I understand that you must focus and consider nothing other than your ability to survive the best way you can. I love you with all my heart and I pray for your safety everyday, whether you're in prison or home. I really hope your choices is thought of much differently now. Your son needs you and I need you. The differences you and Larry were having was childish and foolish, but it was a matter only you and him could solve. As a parent, I have always been afraid of these streets because our environment hasn't had much to offer, however, the choices were still yours to make.

Baby, deep cries of pain awake me every night. I often dream of a place that is desirably beautiful. A place that's filled with flowers, happiness, and peace. Sometimes, I feel so far away from my family, yet you are all so close to my mind and heart. The strangest things about these dreams are every time I awaken, it's my kids I am thinking of and that young child **Raymond Butler**, who killed your father, which I must also forgive. I often ask God to help my cries of loneliness go away. My days are getting closer and I am afraid.

Being alone, without the affection of love the way it's needed, can almost shatter the enthusiasm or self-esteem one has to offer; however, I will continue to fight. Writing this letter to you son, my eyes are ready to give way with endless cries. I am ashamed. I am ashamed because my kids are very intellectual men, yet, they utilize their intelligence wrong, but my heart will always have a place for each and every one of you. Please feel my thoughts as they entwine with my thin soul. Please, remember the smiles we once shared as a family together. Believe in your good qualities because your vision becomes clearer each day of living. When your nights are in pain, as mine are, feel your pulse throb in your veins and thank God for the satisfaction to understand the preciousness of life. Help make my dreams a reality. Persuade yourself to be a part of me because you're the only one coming home. I am here for you.

Love Your Mother

Placing down my mother's letter, I wiped the falling tears from my face. I understood that my mother was hurting, but she was strong. I also knew no one was home to hug and comfort her in time of needing it. I wanted to call her, but hearing her voice would've made matters worse. I wasn't ready for this part of life; I must now change my ways for the better.

Later that day, I sat down with my friend Raheem and we discussed our on hand matters. We both had plenty of more time to do, therefore, we must focus in on that time because of what my mother has stated to me, I will no longer worry about what has taken place in my past.

Raheem and I both came to the conclusion to understand life educationally. His philosophy was that we get degrees in business that we could work with people on intellectual levels; furthermore, with these degrees we'll have better chances of getting jobs in higher places and we could also build our small business from the ground up. We both went back to school where I later received my G.E.D., my Business Management degree, and even learned how to write creatively. As for Raheem, he already had his secondary diploma; therefore, he successfully graduated from Villanvic University with his bachelor's degree in General Business. We were now sophisticated men. The years were going by like it wasn't nothing. Raheem and I were considered true friends. I wasn't going to allow nothing to happen to him. Our blueprint on business was mapped out. Our business plans was good. It's indeed a new area for me and I was happy. Already my mother was proud of me and I was proud of her for loving me.

I even became Muslim. Raheem stated to me that our God Allah would forgive me for all of my past sins and I was grateful for that. I now have a relationship with God and I have more knowledge on life. Even though little Paul is so far away, he's still my son; therefore, I think of him everyday and soon I'll be home to get him. **March 12, 1998;** many years later. It was 8:27pm. Raheem has just returned to the block. He was going on and on about his brand new tattoo, it was professionally done. It read off ***RAYMOND RAHEEM BUTLER,*** and under the name it said "All Praises due to Allah," written across his chest. I just smirked at him. I never knew Raheem's real name, yet, it sounded so familiar. It was strange that I never knew his real name. I guess that explain why people called him **Ray**. Unfortunately, I was tired; therefore, I went to get some rest. I dozed off while Raheem continued to watch television. Getting up to use the bathroom, the television was off and Raheem was sound asleep. It was 2:34am. I slept like a baby. I looked over at my friend and smiled because his shirt was open and his chest was showing as if he was flirting with a female. Walking towards the toilet I laughed and laughed. I marked his name to myself "Okay, Raymond Butler or Butler Raymond. Raymond Raheem, Raheem Butler." While washing my hands, that last name Butler hit my mind with curiosity. The joking was of no more. I remember my mother saying she must forgive the young child who killed my father. "Could Raheem be the one she was talking about? I wondered. I quickly ran to my mother's mail. I started reading them over and over. The man who killed my father name was Raymond Butler. *It was Raheem!* I threw the letter to the floor. My heart started racing. After all this time, my friend, I couldn't believe it. I went for our stash, (our jail house weapons). I grown to love a man I've hated for many years. We never spoke of our cases because it was one of my rules.

Knife now in hand, I started walking towards him. The tears started to roll with every inch of a step I took. Every breath of oxygen, that flowed into my shivering lungs and heart shattering soul, was a step of me being closer to a man who cleverly smuggled himself into my time challenging world. He's a man of observed honor, loyalty, and good dignity.

Greasy sweat ran down my face endlessly. I felt the warm dampness of the sweat as it made its way down my forehead and into my eyes. I couldn't wipe its flow away. It blurred my vision with the sensation of a slight burn. My neck and chest area was filled with the aroma of nervous aggression. My hand clutched the handle of the knife tightly. The thrives of electricity flowed around my palms with extreme animosity. He looked comfortable at peace; just laying there in silence, sleeping away helplessly. He has not one evil thought. Not one ounce of fear. He was overwhelmingly relaxed as he dreamed on. It was the perfect opportunity to seize this imposter. My heart rhythmically rumbled with loud thunders against my quivering chest, "pound after pound, after pound, after pound." A good man's life was in my hands to face his moment of judgment. I looked down over top of him murderously. It was a vision I hated, but a vision I must oversee. I was now in position. Quickly, I grabbed him roughly around the throat area. His eyes opened with shocking and bone-chilling fear. He observed the sparkling tears flowing down my face. He turned and fought wildly to get me up off of him; unfortunately, my aggressiveness and force made it impossible for him to succeed at releasing my grip. My deep dark eyes connected with his. I read the emotions that sat so openly in his eyes. They asked me why. He fought and struggled no longer, he knew that death has shouted checkmate. Raising the knife as high as I could I froze for a moment. I looked a bit farther past his eyes. His soul was telling me to be at peace. I cried harder. The knife plunged down sticking into the pillow on the side of his face. I couldn't kill my friend. He continued to look on as I cried. Releasing the knife from my hand, I sat on the floor and asked him why. Raheem never said a word. He was wondering what was going on. In reality, I guess I could've answered my own question why, *"Life, poverty, and no real sense of direction"*. My life has changed and for that reason I will kill no more.

I made things clear to Raymond that the old man he killed was my father. He expressed some deep emotion and apologized from his heart. His grief was felt as being true; besides, he was young and foolish with no home or family. Life pushed him to commit crimes. I guess it was his passion for living. At that time of him committing these crimes, he stated that he only wanted to escape reality by getting as high as he could. I forgave Raymond for what he has done. I know God will forgive me for what I've done. The promise to my father is what haunted me the most; simply because I didn't fulfill what I promised. I bet if I was given a second chance to talk with him, I bet he won't want me killing anymore.

As for Raymond, we're taught to **Never Judge a Book by Its Cover**, this is exactly what we do in forming impressions about others. Upon meeting people, we initially notice their race, gender, age, dress, and how physically attractive or unattractive they appear. This tendency to notice such obvious attributes is natural and has a definite impact on our first impression of people. And beyond noticing such superficial appearances, we often begin the character and identity of individuals. Answers to such questions, combined with a conscious or unconscious assessment of a person's verbal or nonverbal behavior, all aid in forming a first impression. Also, past experiences, moods, attitudes, and beliefs at the same time encounter people, aids in the formation of our impression of others. Our overall impression and judgment of another person is influenced more by the first information received about a person than by info that comes later. First impressions are powerful and contribute immensely to the initial info, it the framework through which we interpret later information. Sometimes our expectations about how a person will respond or react in a situation, directly influences a person's actual actions. Expectations may be based on a person's gender, age, racial or ethnic group, social class, role or occupation, personality traits, past behavior, relationships to us, and so on. Once formed, our expectancies effect how we perceive the behavior of others, what we pay attention to or ignore. Expectations also affect our attitude, manner, and treatment of people in such a way that we partly bring about the very behavior we expect (*self-fulfilling prophecies*). When it comes to attraction there are many factors influencing to whom and what we are attracted. Proximity plays a major role in determining our choice of friends, for we are friendlier with those whom are geographically close to us. It seems convenience and comfort-ability increases the frequency with which we interact with others, but on the other hand, if our initial reaction to a person is negative, frequent exposure can increase our negative feelings for them. Also, our moods and emotions greatly influence our attractions to others as well as what's happening in our lives at the time we meet someone, causing us to like or dislike a person simply because they were/weren't present when something negative or positive happened in our lives, associating them with the occurrence.

We also tend to like those who reciprocate our feelings. In other words, we like those who like us. It's said that one of the simplest ways to get others to like you is to genuinely like them. Another factor affecting our attraction to others is physical appearance. When people have one trait or quality that we either admire or dislike, we assure that they have other admirable or negative traits as well (*halo effect*). Attractive people are seen as more exciting, personable, interesting, and socially desirable than unattractive people; *one is as attractive as he/she believes themselves to be.* It is our similarities, not our differences that usually stimulate our capacity to like and love. Getting to know others increases the chances of liking or disliking them. And oh, it's true that birds of a feather do in fact flock together. Behaviors indicating what one should do if they wish to make a better impression on other people and increase their liking to you.

Since first attraction is so powerful, one must always be mindful of how they carry themselves and the type of impression they make on others. People are naturally attracted to those whom they feel they have the most in common. Therefore, when meeting someone for the first time, make an attempt to share and communicate one's common interests. Eye contact, smiling, and displaying a comfortable disposition works well when trying to positively connect with others. Also, there's the issue of reciprocity. It's like what I share with Raymond, years ago regarding the importance of being worthy of that which we seek in others. The willingness to be that which we seek makes us worthy of what we're looking for. If you want someone to value the friendship they share with you, then value what it is you have with them. To me, this concept is a simple one. It's also what I feel that's a sure way to increase people's appreciation for you.

As for what behaviors we should not do in making a favorable impression on others and increasing their liking of us, arrogance and self-centeredness is one sure way to make a bad impression and keep others from liking you. Failing to smile and always displaying a negative attitude, causes others to distant themselves from us. Never taking the time to let people know that they are valued and appreciated isn't a good thing either. Being an un-attentive listener always seems to not be conductive to healthy relationships as well. Associating with individuals with whom one doesn't share similar interests doesn't serve to foster positive connection with others. This book was the best I could do in expressing the understanding of good and bad friendships. I hope you have enjoyed the **Corruption of Blood . . .**

ABOUT THE AUTHOR

I, Jermayne J. Davis, was born to Constance and John Davis; being one of four brothers I grew up in the Tasker Homes Projects in south Philadelphia where I witnessed the underbelly of human nature and learned the harsh facts of life one experiences growing up in the ghetto.

I sustained many painful lessons from my environment, which periodically caused me to inflict understanding upon others, which groomed and prepared me for life's many trials and adventures. I attended Alcorn Elementary School and graduated at Audenried Jr. High; however, I never completed high school, and like many young men my age, I was led by older youth to participate in crime.

By no fault of my loving parents, who gave my brothers, Darryl, Aaron, Terrence, and I moral guidance, love and, when possible, financial support to face the hardships that life would certainly bring; I nevertheless fell victim to my environment. Today, I look back and to my parents, who have been married over forty years, and thank them for all they have done.

Having survived the fate of the juvenile and later the criminal justice system, I decided it was time for a change, so I endeavored to educate myself. I started with learning how to communicate effectively and the ethical and technical aspects of business administration while attending Montgomery County College and Villanova. I also learned the trade of carpentry, HVAC and Masonry. At thirty-two years old, I am actively participating in redeveloping communities through making necessary residential repairs and teaching young men and women how to involve themselves positively in their communities, and someday I envision starting a publishing and distribution company called the Davis Project, LLC. for up-and-coming writers, poets, and authors struggling to get their work known.